The Tide of Deception

The Tide of Deception
Mystery on the Coast of Maine
by
Steven James Hantzis

Alinet, LLC
Alexandria, Virginia USA
2025

Alinet, LLC
P.O. Box 7353
Alexandria, VA 22307

The Tide of Deception is a work of fiction. All incidents and dialogue, and all characters with the exception of some well-known historical figures, are products of the author's imagination and are not to be construed as real. Where real-life historical persons appear, the situations, incidents, and dialogues concerning those persons are entirely fictional and are not intended to depict actual events or to change the entirely fictional nature of the work. In all other respects, any resemblance to persons living or dead is entirely coincidental.

ISBN: 979-8-9986067-1-7

The Tide of Deception
Prologue

Sandy's possessed but channeled. A scientist of above average acumen, Sandy is lovely, wholesome, and a true Mainer. She grapples with a mysterious tide, her daughter, her husband's death, finding love, and befriending a North Korean spy. Oh, and there's Maine.

The Boothbay anomalous tide of October 2008 happened. Yes, it's real, and remains a mystery. Many other plot points and historical references are real. You'll have to read the book to figure out what is what.

The Tide of Deception was fun to write because I let the calendar and Maine lead the way. The storms of January 2024 were real, and their damage is visible today, as it will be for a while. The personalities in the book are fictional . . . mostly . . . and I apply authorial license throughout. Still, I prefer to write the truth. So, the book is lore, part fact and part fiction. Please digest it as such.

I especially want to thank Dr. Patricia Matrai, then a senior research scientist at Bigelow Laboratory for Ocean Sciences. Dr. Matrai indulged my inquiry about the Boothbay tide anomaly when we met in the fall of 2016. A week later, she sent a scientific paper I referenced in the book. Her accompanying email is instructive.

> *I've had some fun researching your question. Nobody seemed to know for sure: suggestions include earthquakes (rare in Maine), sediment slides, uplifting crustal events, faraway storms (none reported that day), until I found two recent publications on meteorological tsunamis (meteotsunami; see below).*
> *I learned something new!*
> *Cheers,*

We visited Maine in 1999, the year we were married. In 2003, we began looking at listings and talking with brokers about buying there. Thirteen years later, in August 2016, we closed on a home on Barters Island in Boothbay. It was a good deal. We were persistent and lucky.

Why Maine?

Romance? A romantic notion of Americanism, conservation, Thoreau-ism? Culture? Maine's working-class aesthetic spiced with notable people from away? Beauty? Yes, indeed. Authors? E. B. White, Harriet Beecher Stowe, Rachel Carson, Rosalie Baker, Richard Ford, Stephen King? Wyeth-worthy ocean shores welcoming easels and oils? Bountiful seafood plied by colorful locals? Chugging lobster boats with stoic sternmen hauling traps? Clammers working the mud flats at low tide? Ice shacks and smelt fishing on frozen rivers? Roadside sellers hawking fiddlehead ferns come spring? Endless blueberries? Yes, all that. But it started thus.

In the mid-1970s, Conrail furloughed me from my job as a railroad brakeman. I packed my Volvo 142, hid some cash under the floor mat, and drove north from Indianapolis. I crossed into Canada at Windsor, then drove east to Quebec City. I had never been on an airplane, so a trip to the strange land of Canada was pure adventure. Most nights, I slept in the car. Some nights I'd camp out under the fall sky in my sleeping bag with an army surplus poncho to ward off the damp.

I turned south at Quebec City and entered Maine at an unguarded crossing near Coburn Gore. It was a different time. The roads in Maine were owned by lumber companies, and I drove miles with no traffic, save the occasional lumbering log-hauler on his way to a mill. My first night back in the States, I slept on the staid shores of Mooselookmeguntic Lake, and while I didn't see a moose, I imagined several. The spooky water was opaque but not threatening. The stars shone proximate on its mirror surface. Above, they lit the heavens with a clarity that absolved my urbanity and apprehension. I carried this impression of Maine for the next forty years.

How Maine?

When I married beautiful Kathleen Flaherty in 1999, I soon gave up trying to outsmart her. I did, however, cling to negotiations. One of our "what direction is this marriage headed?" topics was where we might live in retirement. We were fortunate to have the means to consider a second home. So, in the way verbal accord settles such things, we agreed I could choose the summer home location and Kathy our winter home. I chose Maine, and we started looking. Kathy has yet to tell me where we will live in the winter. Thanks to global warming, we may already be there: Alexandria, Virginia.

So, we have a second home in Maine. We are fortunate. We worked hard, leveraged our educations, and we're lucky. Working-class families, like Kathy's and mine, pass little inheritance to the next generation. Kathy's father came to America from Moycullen, Ireland, in 1949, the oldest of eleven children. He worked as a bellman and bell captain at the Mayflower Hotel in Washington, DC, for forty-five years before retiring on a union pension. Kathy's mother, sweet Mary, worked as a secretary. My father was a machinist for General Motors most of his working life. My mother was a registered nurse who advanced into management. Both of my parents passed away at age fifty-six, both from cancer. Kathy's mother and father lived longer. We are both grateful for what our parents gave to us, but it wasn't windfalls or second homes.

Fortunate us.

We bought a house in Maine and closed in August 2016. Along with the house came a micro economy: a caretaker, snowplow service, lawn service, assorted utilities, and lore. Lore is history, both real and imaginary. Here's the thing about lore. You don't know if it's true, but it's engaging narrative. Lore fills the gap between what you don't know and what might be true. Lore pleases the mind by circling the unknown, dispelling confusion, and promoting patterns. Humans crave patterns, and who doesn't love a good story?

The lore of our house begins with the death of the previous owner, the husband. Lore says he was a plumber by trade and a heating oil vendor in New Hampshire. He died six months after builders completed the house in 2000. His wife lived a few more years; then she passed away. She had unruly Labrador retrievers that she allowed in the house and three contentious adult children. The children inherited the house, then couldn't decide what to do with it. They shared it for a time, then rented it in the summer, and finally sold it. The place had, as they say, good bones. But by the time we took possession, it needed attention. We did a lot of work on the house in the first year. We cleaned with bleach, painted, replaced the roof and main beam, installed a generator, and contracted a new float. We have a float, not a dock. A float moves with the tide which, on the Sheepscot Back River, rises and falls twelve feet every twelve hours and twenty-five minutes. On our float we tie a presentable, Maine appropriate, twenty-five-foot C-Dory cruiser. Our boat, *Catleen*, is an enclosed cabin vessel made in the Pacific Northwest and sold in Alaska. *Catleen* is a distant cousin of local lobster boats and suitable for all weather. According to a friend, a retired Lloyd's of London marine surveyor, *Catleen* fit right in.

From our home on Barters Island, we can boat to interesting coastal features. Our destinations include the decommissioned Maine

Yankee nuclear power plant, oyster farms, and lobster pounds. The open ocean is three miles south via the deep, cold Sheepscot River. One of the easy-to-get-to destinations, only minutes away, is a narrow passage called Oven's Mouth. Through this thousand-yard gut, tidal currents fill and empty a sizable estuary of Back River. At its narrowest, the passage between land reduces to 150 feet, and the navigable channel is even narrower. The current runs six knots with the changing tides. If you're piloting a boat, when traveling with the current, your speed must be faster than the current to maintain control of your vessel. Otherwise, you become buoyant debris at the hydrologic whims of nature.

Wabanaki Native Americans used Oven's Mouth as a shortcut between the Damariscotta and Sheepscot Rivers in pre-colonial times. They paddled birchbark canoes down the Damariscotta, then portaged west through the pines and oaks across what is now the Dolphin Mini Golf attraction. At Oven's Mouth, they paddled to the chilly Sheepscot. This route saved them the longer journey via the choppy mouth of the Damariscotta, across broad Boothbay Harbor, then through Townsend Gut to the Sheepscot. Along their journey these hunter-gathers foraged through varied eco-cultures, enjoying the buffet.

Maine has a long history of getting places by water. Water was conveyance long before roads. Overwater moved the shore's bounty: deer and beaver pelts and luxurious hides of marten, otter, ermine, fisher, and fox. Intricate brown ash basketry and other barterable items made their way to native markets over the free-flowing streams, rivers, and coastal routes. When Europeans arrived, water moved the men and ships, who enforced new rules of trade.

For the Wabanaki, Oven's Mouth was more than just a shortcut. It was a sacred place, a place of spirits that protected and guided them. As they paddled in the narrow channel to the Sheepscot, they sang songs of gratitude to the spirits, the earth, and the water.

On September 9, 1777, as the sun dipped beyond the western shore of the Sheepscot, a clan of Wabanaki hunters pulled their canoes through a muddy flat. Wading in muck to their knees, they reached shore on the northern tip of Barters Island. All were wary of the uncertain sky, turning leaves, and an approaching storm. As they paddled through Oven's Mouth, their laughter and songs echoed off the rocky walls. But when they reached the wider Cross River, they saw something that upset their absorbing rhythm.

A ship approached, her three topsails luffing in the confused wind. Only the small sails fore and aft billowed. Men scrambled on the yardarms, reefing the lower sails. The hunters knew European ships. White men had plied Wabanaki waters for more than a century. But this one was different. The men on the top decks wore red coats, and the pennant flying astern told the Wabanaki this was the British tribe. This ship was bigger and more heavily armed than any they had seen before. The Wabanaki counted twenty-two gunports on her starboard side, with the lower ports battened to thwart the churning chop. The men aboard looked hard and fierce, and the Wabanaki were lucky to be ashore and protected. The spirits were pleased.

The hunters watched the ship pass and wondered where she was going. Was she lost? She was too large for the passage, and there was no settlement or European encampment in her direction. The nearest British town was Wiscasset, five miles to the north on the main channel of the Sheepscot.

Aboard the HMS *Rainbow,* Sir George Collier, captain and acting commodore of the British Royal Navy forces in Halifax, came to the same conclusion. Night approached, and the storm began. Captain Collier was an aggressive, tested commander. But he was now responsible for a British ship of the line floundering in unknown water, amid rocky ledge, submerged hazards, sucking mudflats, and an unforgiving tidal flow. The local fisherman, impressed in Boothbay Harbor as a pilot, claimed to be a royalist. He claimed to know the route to Wiscasset where the mast-ship *Gruel* was loading its nautical contraband for a trip to France. That was Captain Collier's mission. Take or destroy the *Gruel.* Now he suspected his involuntary pilot to be an American militia sympathizer. His compass reading didn't lie. They were sailing east, not north. He would not allow the *Rainbow* to founder. He called the order, "Cut the lashings on the 'best bower' to the starboard foremast channel. We will anchor here. Douse any sails reefed or still set." Thus, the outsized *Rainbow* at 133 feet along her waterline, and drafting twenty feet, set anchor in the narrows of Oven's Mouth.

Amid the endless Maine frontier in 1777, countless white pine trees towered to perfection. The British and the French marveled at their utility for nautical construction. Both nations had depleted their native forests of oak and other suitable timber. Maine's prized specimens rose forty feet or more and measured forty inches in diameter at their flawless trunks. Turned by the hands of journeymen, these 'sticks' became masts, bowsprits, topmasts, yards, and spars at the Halifax Naval Yard or one of six Royal Navy Dockyards in England. They were perfect for masting the brutes of the sea, ships of the line, the vessels that decided battles, blockades, and the fates of nations.

Continental wars blocked British access to Baltic timber in the 1650s. And even with access, Baltic trees were seldom more than twenty-seven inches in diameter. So, King William III appointed a surveyor general for New England. The surveyor's minions tramped the virgin forests and marked ramrod pines greater than twenty-four inches with three axe strikes in the symbol of a broad arrow. These were the king's pines. This possessive insult enraged the American colonists. The British applied severe penalties for stealing these pines, skirmishes erupted, and a black market flourished. In 1772, colonists revolted in Weare, New Hampshire. Early in the morning, after an overnight rally in a local tavern, townspeople blackened their faces. They set upon a dozing sheriff and his deputy and whipped them senseless with switches. The rioters shaved the manes and tails of the lawmen's horses. They even severed the poor beasts' ears, then mounted the sheriff and deputy to ride out of Weare down a gauntlet of the aggrieved. Colonial resentment smoldered as the Pine Tree Riot predated the Boston Tea Party by a year and a half.

By 1777, with the colonies in full revolt and the French backing their rebellion, the British needed masts. These strategic components in the hands of the French would be doubly damaging. The intelligence possessing Captain Collier as he advanced up the treacherous Sheepscot was that a suspected mast shipment was making ready north of Wiscasset, bound for Cherbourg.

In the early hours of September 10, Captain Collier ordered the launch of two of the *Rainbow's* cutters, the smaller boats for transporting the Royal Marines. He ordered a cutting-out raid on the *Gruel,* and a hundred marines and sailors set off from Oven's Mouth under the cover of darkness and rain. Cutting-out was the term for commandeering an enemy vessel, in this case the *Gruel*. The two cutters snuck past the sleeping village of Wiscasset. Then the raiders rowed north on a flood tide where, according to the impressed fisherman now with the raiders, the *Gruel* was loading her contraband.

When dawn broke on the *Rainbow*, Captain Collier saw how close they had come to disaster. The ship could barely swing on her hawser without grounding. Collier launched the remaining cutter, and with deft seamanship, the cutter's crew wrapped the ship out of its predicament and into the main channel of the Sheepscot. By early afternoon, the *Rainbow* anchored off Wiscasset Point, positioned to level the town with cannon fire.

Worried locals breathed easier when Captain Collier sent a party ashore under a flag of truce. Collier's emissary delivered a letter to the local magistrate demanding the surrender of two small cannons and the contraband pines he believed to be loading nearby. Thus, negotiations began with the exchange of letters.

The two cutters arrived at the *Gruel* near sunrise. The Royal Marines surprised the *Gruel's* master, boatswain, and two mates and took them prisoner without a shot or saber slash. After securing the mast-ship, they brought aboard a three-pound cannon and barricaded the boat's deck with planks already aboard the *Gruel.* They were ready to return their prize. But they needed a favorable tide, a slack tide just beginning to ebb to clear the shallows and mudflats of the sinuous Sheepscot.

The *Gruel's* cook, returning to the boat from shore, saw the capture and ran to tell the local militiamen's quartermaster. By nine o'clock, the Lincoln County Regiment of Militia, 150 Sons of Liberty, lined the shore and began pelting the raiders with musket and cannon fire. Trapped by the ebbing tide, the raiders were powerless to wrap the *Gruel* into the river channel. The raiders hunkered down behind their plank armament. Around noon, a second cannon arrived and pulverized the improvised palisade aboard the *Gruel.* The raiders were in a tough spot.

Captain Collier grew concerned around sunset and launched the remaining cutter. But the boat returned, fearing an upriver ambush. They were right.

The raiders were running out of options. The *Gruel* was too large to maneuver down the twisty river. The cutters would have to wrap her off her mooring and tow her to deep water. At ten o'clock, with the moon setting, a raiders' detachment shoved some of the mast and spars into the river and holed the mast-ship. Then they snuck aboard their cutters in the *Gruel's* lee and started downriver. But the Sons of Liberty were waiting. The raiders' flight stalled when they encountered a boom pulled taunt across the river by the militiamen. The raiders were lucky to hack their way through the heavy rope and out of danger with only one man injured by militia fire. At eleven o'clock, the first cutter hove up along the *Rainbow.* Captain Collier recovered all the raiders, their prisoners, and both boats by midnight. But the wind was against them as the militia massed at Wiscasset Point.

Negotiations continued while the *Rainbow* waited for an ebbing flood tide and a favorable wind. Collier bluffed and told the Sons of Liberty they had one hour to evacuate Wiscasset before he opened fire to level the town. It bought him time. Finally, with favorable sailing conditions arriving in the early hours of September 12, Collier relented. He released the prisoners onto a small, commandeered schooner for a promise of safe passage as the *Rainbow* navigated the Sheepscot narrows.

The *Rainbow's* raid on Wiscasset was a measured success. They recovered three main masts and one mizzenmast. The raiders decommissioned the mast-ship and denied the French important contraband. *Rainbow* suffered only one man wounded. Sir George Collier entered history books as a successful, daring naval officer. He won a major victory against the colonialists in the 1779 Battle of Penobscot Bay.

The fisherman, though, that's who interests me. Therein lies the lore.

François Arsenault was the fisherman, but he told the British he was Samuel Jones. He was a linguistic chameleon and spoke the English of the colonists, his mother's tongue. They never suspected he was French. The disdainful British looked down on the colonial dialect and lumped François into the heathen herd.

François was nineteen years old and not yet married. He towered over most other fishermen. His light beard framed his handsome features. He wore rough, sea-worn clothes, and his dark hair flowed from beneath his knit cap pulled low against the Gulf of Maine chill. He was three weeks engaged to Danielle from Monhegan Island.

François was smart. Born and raised on the coast of Maine on the island of Southport, he had learned much in his years fishing with his father. He knew the water, and the vessels that sailed it. But he had never seen a ship the size and menace of the HMS *Rainbow*. He squinted to make out the detachment of Royal Marines approaching in a cutter. The British were ruthless, and François feared impressment or punishment for disobeying their orders. He thought of Danielle on Monhegan's Pebble Beach, propped on a worn wool blanket watching seals cavort on the ledge near shore. Her soft auburn curls danced on her lithe shoulders when she laughed. He would do anything to be with her again.

Six sailors oared the cutter with a coxswain at the stern. It surprised François how fast the boat moved through the chop. Perfectly synced long oars propelled it like a water strider on a pond. Four grim, musket-toting marines stood in the bow of the eight-meter boat, their red coats fluttering in the building nor'easter. Bayonets dangled on their cross belts. François's single-masted fishing skiff could neither outrun them nor defend against them. He had just set sail for Boothbay when the *Rainbow* appeared on the horizon.

The British would take no quarter with a Frenchman. So, when the older marine hailed him, he answered in English, "Yes, I fish the Sheepscot. I have fished as far north as the reversing falls above Wiscasset Point."

The solemn marine declared, "In the name of His Majesty King William III, I order you to come with us. Secure your skiff here and come aboard."

François hesitated, then waved at the approaching front and pleaded, "But, my lord, my boat may swamp in the coming gale. If I lose my boat, I cannot make a living."

The pitiless soldier sneered, his words as cold as the murky depths, "If you do not do as I order, you will have no need to make a living."

A fearful and overwhelmed François played out his anchor, obeyed the order, and began living a lie to save his life.

The Tide of Deception
Chapter 1

Seven generations later, only yards from François's impressment into
the British Navy, Sandy Arsenault began her day with a look in the
mirror. She ran her fingers through her shoulder-length, chaff-blond
hair, tying it back into a loose ponytail. Her green eyes shone with
determination as she studied her reflection. Sandy was a fighter, smart
and organized, just like her ancestors. She radiated the resilience,
courage, and independence that percolated in Mainers like artesian
flow through the granite ledge. These traits served her well, and not
least for the long, dark winters and the fierce storms that lashed the
noble state. Good-looking, tall, and poised, Sandy was often the most
attractive woman in the room. Fit and trim, her wholesome personality
dampened competitive or sexual tension. Those who knew her well
loved her.

As a little girl, growing up on the coast, she listened to the lore
at family gatherings. These get-togethers of thirty or more boisterous
relatives always made her smile and laugh. The men built a raging fire
in a pit on the rocky shore. Then, in a flame-marred kettle, they boiled
lobsters in a stew of salty Atlantic, seaweed, clams, cut potatoes,
whole onions, corn on the cob, and hard-boiled eggs. They drank beer
and coffee brandy and told stories from the dismal past. They told how
François escaped from British servitude, and his subsequent move to
Monhegan. Monhegan was French-controlled territory and had been
since 1689. With the end of the French–Indian War in 1763,
Monhegan became *France paisible*.

François was with the British when they took the *Gruel*. He
withstood the Sons of Liberty's bombardment. When the detachment
from the *Rainbow* snuck from the *Gruel* back to their cutters under fire
in the darkness, François parted company in the chaos. On the river's
bank, the militiamen identified him as a friend. Lucky for him. The
quartermaster recognized François and vouched for him. Fearing the
British might track him and hang him for desertion, François retrieved
his skiff and sailed for Monhegan a day later. He and Danielle married
on Christmas Eve 1777, and over the next thirty-nine years together,
they raised eight healthy, intelligent children with love, hard work, and
good fortune. Not a day passed that François did not thank God for
allowing him to escape the British and marry Danielle. All five of their
sons took wives from Monhegan or Boothbay, and the family grew

from there.

Sandy worked at Bigelow Laboratory in East Boothbay as a senior researcher. She specialized in anomalous wave and tide activity along with biogeochemistry, microbial physiology, and phytoplankton ecology. The latter part of her portfolio had dominated her published research during her ten years at Bigelow. But her other focus, anomalous tide activity, posed an unresolved mystery in the recesses of her analytical mind. A solitary event piqued her, and she sought a logical pattern from a jumbled pile of puzzle bits.

She was only twenty-four, one year into her PhD in Oceanography at the University of Maine, when Boothbay erupted with a series of rogue tides on an October morning in 2008. For over two hours, boats moored in the harbor and tied to floats churned like flimsy rags in a giant washing machine. Now, fifteen years later, she still could not shake the notion that what the scant published research called a meteotsunami might not be that, but something more . . . more directed. More insidious, perhaps sinister. She wasn't a conspiracist, but Sandy recognized the unnatural rapid sequence of tide changes, seven within two hours, could be a potent weapon if human induced.

She banished such notions and called to her daughter, "You better get a move on. I need to gas up before we go to school. And who thought it was a good idea to have Career Day start at eight? Get up. Let's go."

Caroline Arsenault was precocious. Smart as a whip, but an unguided missile. She had Sandy's good looks. In fact, she was the image of her mother when she was seventeen. Her independent phase had started around age four and had yet to resolve. She respected her mother but could weigh like an anchor when passively resisting. And the eye rolls. Sandy worried Caroline might permanently strain her ocular motor muscles. But they were a good team. Caroline's grades were top-notch, and Sandy gave her a long leash. She had to.

Caroline's father, Sandy's husband, Noah, had died ten years before. His was a tragic death, and both women struggled with their emotions to keep the family on an even keel. The trauma had passed. Now Noah was a doleful remembrance. He came and went in dreams but never threatened. Sandy and Caroline were alone, but they were a formidable team. Sandy wondered how lonely she would feel come fall with Caroline off to college. Caroline had no such thoughts.

"What do you think I should wear?" asked Sandy.

From down the hallway, a sleepy voice croaked, "Wear your

lab coat over a bikini.”

Sandy shook her head at no one.

“And red Ferragamos.”

Now it was Sandy, rolling her eyes.

The Tide of Deception
Chapter 2

It is ten miles from Bath to Boothbay by the Sasanoa River and thirty
miles by road. This morning, Brian took the road. In mid-September, a
steady flow of tourists made Route 1 through Wiscasset tedious. The
morning warmed nicely with a promising forecast, and Brian thought
about firing up his runabout, a sixteen-foot Boston Whaler Nauset for
the trip. But he wore a navy-blue sport coat, a starched white shirt,
khakis, and nice shoes. Not typical boat clothing. So, playing it safe,
he drove.

Brian was president of IAM Local S6 at Bath Iron Works,
BIW, a full-time union official. This was his third year in office. He
represented over four thousand skilled tradesmen and women.
Shipfitters, painters, electricians, welders, machinists—they all had
complaints and grievances and disciplinary notices, and they were
never shy. BIW weeded out shy people.

General Dynamics bought BIW in 1995, and the government
contracts kept rolling in. Predictably, US Navy ships kept rolling out.
Or, sailing out . . . or under tow . . . down the dog-legged Kennebec
River, to the Atlantic, and on to assigned missions worldwide. BIW
crafted 425 ships since 1884 making it the largest supplier of US Navy
surface combatants.

BIW had a lot of moving parts, big metal parts. Ship modules,
weapons components, steel plates, skyscraping cranes, and massive
gantries. And paperwork, reams of paperwork. The churn of cost-plus
government contracts, collective bargaining, grievance arbitrations,
and project management snafus. Then there was the gritty federal,
state, and union politics of fraying alliances, cultivating allies, and
compromise. BIW was a busy place.

But this morning would be a cakewalk. Brian would meet a
General Dynamics human resource rep at Boothbay High School.
Together, they would staff a table and encourage young people in their
career choices. BIW, the largest industrial concern in Maine, had a
strong collective bargaining agreement, paid its union employees well,
and offered second-to-none benefits. Many Boothbay students had
relatives working there. So, BIW was an easy sell.

Brian was a Mainer, though not seven generations. His father
had transferred to Maine from the Pentagon when Brian was in grade

school, a retirement move. His father worked in acquisitions and became liaison to BIW as his out-the-door posting, a friendly transfer. Brian's father had land in Camden, an hour up the coast. His final years at BIW allowed him to oversee not only naval contracts but construction of the family's retirement home. Brian had grown up in Bath. The summer between his freshman and sophomore years, he moved to Camden. After high school, he studied econometrics at Bowdoin College in Brunswick. He entered the labor market with a bachelor of arts degree. He didn't want to move to Boston or, God forbid, New York City. He thought of both places as terminal aggregations of humanity, thick with self-absorbed fatalists warring for space. The cities reminded him of B.F. Skinner's rats-in-a-box experiments. He soon saw a skilled trade at BIW as an attractive career path. He enjoyed working with his hands. Young and perhaps randy, Brian saw himself as rugged and outdoorsy. His father made a call and Brian started a machinist apprenticeship that fall.

As an apprentice, Brian learned countless technical skills. He excelled at math and had a visual learning aptitude. The machine tools, the computers, the measurements—these came second nature to Brian. When he earned promotion to journeyman, he and his father reflected on his apprenticeship over beers. In Adirondack chairs on his father's porch on Ogier Point, they watched the pleasure boats come and go in Camden Harbor just beyond Curtis Island Lighthouse.

Brian's father asked, "You seem happy, Son. What struck you the most over these past four years?"

Brian answered, "At first, I was awe-struck by how big everything is. Big components, ship modules, big stock, big cranes . . . big everything. Then I realized that some of the old guys were big in another way."

"How's that," asked his father.

"Big assholes! They wouldn't talk to me!"

Brian's dad snickered.

"I learned perseverance. I mean, high school and college required focus. But an apprenticeship at BIW requires perseverance. There's a big difference."

Brian's dad nodded and smiled and offered his longneck beer for a toast.

And persevere he did.

Brian was elected union steward in his shop the year after turning journeyman. He was smart, and his personality allowed him to

be tough when necessary and conciliatory when called for. He listened
to people, and that was important. He read and knew the collective
bargaining agreement, past practice, and labor law. Two years later,
Brian was elected to the union's executive council. When the longtime
S6 president retired after twenty years, he asked Brian to follow him
into the job. At first, Brian hesitated. Union president meant buck-
stops-here leadership, and that could be a headache. The president took
sides in conflicts between the company and the workers, and that was
tough. But the squabbles and fights within the workforce, within his
own membership . . . those were *real* headaches. Contract negotiations
loomed and, although General Dynamics was a solid employer, like all
mega-corporations in America, they played for keeps. He knew the
rank and file of S6 would vote to strike. That was the natural order at
BIW. Brian remembered his first leadership class at the union's
training center in Maryland. An old-head international union rep told
Brian his take on strikes: "Anybody can get them out . . . but it takes a
real leader to get them back in." Still, the contract would not reopen
for four years, and negotiations would drag out for weeks or months.

Brian sized up his situation, looked around at his support, and
jumped in. He won the election and, as a divorcé still reeling from that
trauma, he was free of family responsibilities and dove headfirst into
the job. He made the rounds, shook hands, showed the flag at district
and international union conferences, and, after three years, he was
competent and comfortable. But this was his first Career Day.

The Boothbay High School auditorium served as a basketball
court and a stage, as well as an auditorium. White cinderblock walls
held up its high structural ceiling. A four-foot blue border accented the
walls. Blue banners declaring basketball and football accomplishments
hung above the entrance. As Brian entered, he saw the basketball
hoops and backboards raised to the ceiling out of the way. His
polished shoes echoed on the hardwood as he crossed to the table with
the BIW bunting. An American flag in a desk mount divided the table.
He greeted Tanya, the General Dynamics rep, with a handshake. They
knew each other from many professional encounters. Tanya was
Brian's age, early forties, and handled all the Title VII workplace
discrimination complaints. She was company all the way but pleasant
to be around. Brian smiled and asked, "Are you ready to shape young
minds?"

Tanya didn't respond but asked, "What's in the box?"
Brian carried a cardboard box under his right arm.

"Hats and pens. I wanted to bring chicken wings, but the kitchen was closed."

Tanya shook her head, "You union guys are nothing if not predictable."

Brian smiled.

Twelve tables formed a semicircle facing the auditorium's entrance. Brian walked to the front of the BIW table to hang the Local S6 standard. Then he arranged a series of baseball hats with the IAM S6 logo. Sandy sat at the table next to him. She smiled. Brian smiled back and saw the wedding ring she wore as a habit, a remembrance, and to ward off male distraction.

Sandy pulled an easel from her tote bag. She had trouble unfolding the metal legs. Finally, she gave up, stacked three chemistry books on her table, and tilted a Bigelow Laboratory placard against them. Then she retrieved a folded cardboard nameplate that read, SANDY ARSENAULT, PHD. BIGELOW LABORATORY, SENIOR RESEARCHER.

Brian and Sandy were elbow to elbow when Brian asked, "Would you like me to help with the easel? I'm Brian." He extended his hand.

Sandy studied him. She saw no presumption in his dark features and clear brown eyes. She was alert to any man who would try to fix her world, but her radar didn't ping.

Brian smiled, "I'm a machinist . . . at BIW . . . I thought maybe I could help."

She said, "Sure. Have a look at it. I think the legs are bent."

Brian took the stand, examined it, applied pressure to the bent leg, expanded the stand, and handed it back to Sandy.

"You're quick. Nicely done. Send the bill to Bigelow."

Brian smiled.

Sandy rearranged the Bigelow placard and sat down just as the first students came through the entrance.

Career Day lasted four hours. During lulls, Sandy and Brian chatted. He found out Sandy was a single mother when her daughter visited her table. He overheard Caroline say something about Sandy being left alone when she goes to college. Sandy retorted that Caroline needed to be accepted first; then she could worry about leaving her mother alone.

Brian asked Sandy about her work and got the template version . . . small things that live in the ocean. Then Sandy asked Brian what he did. She also received a template version . . . collective bargaining and labor relations. Sandy complimented Brian on his swag. Students congregated at the BIW table for the free stuff, and many left wearing the union's baseball hat. Brian smiled. "A trick of the trade."

By noon, Sandy and Brian were friendly. When Career Day was over, they began packing their things. Brian said goodbye to Tanya, who had a one o'clock mediation at BIW. Brian didn't have to be back at the union hall until the six o'clock council meeting.

Sandy folded her easel and returned it to her tote. Brian had nothing but an empty box and the local union standard. As he folded the standard, he looked over at Sandy and asked, "Are you hungry? Would you like to get some lunch?"

Sandy thought this was forward but friendly. Brian seemed like a nice guy. He was attractive, she was forty, he was responsible and not wearing a ring . . . so she replied, "Have you ever been to Baker's Way?"

That night, at dinner, Caroline prodded, "That guy next to you in the auditorium, what's his name?"

"Brian."

"What does he do?"

"He's a union representative at BIW."

"He was kind of cute . . . in that . . . let's-go-chop-down-a-tree kind of way."

Sandy lied. "I didn't notice."

"Well, you should. You're not getting any younger. Did he ask you out?"

Sandy cringed, struggling to hide her annoyance. She said, "Eat your peas."

The Tide of Deception
Chapter 3

Caroline's hunch proved right. Brian had asked Sandy out. The couple
lingered on the deck at Baker's Way for over an hour chatting about
their interests, their backgrounds, and their marital status. When the
meal finished, they cleared their plates back to the kitchen, and as they
tossed their refuse, Brian said he'd like to see Sandy again. Sandy gave
him her number and said to call her in a couple of days, and they could
talk. She would see him again. And here's why.

During the what-are-you-reading segment of their lunch, Brian
mentioned the book *Tides* by Johnathan White. Brian had attended the
author's presentation at the Darling Center, the University of Maine-
affiliated research center on the Damariscotta River. Sandy had read
the book and found it a narrative overview of the astounding dynamics
of tides and the harmonics created by ocean floors worldwide. Not
precise science, but interesting. Yes, she'd read the book, and told
Brian she studied anomalous tide occurrences.

Brian launched into his amateur understanding of the subject,
and Sandy found him knowledgeable, if not honed. He asked her if she
had studied the unusual Boothbay Harbor tides in 2008. She said yes,
but sandbagged Brian on her fixation. She would spend more time
with him.

When he called two days later, he suggested they see *The
Consequences*, a traditional Irish band, playing at the Boothbay Opera
House. She accepted for the sake of . . . research. Then, after sleeping
on her decision, the next morning over coffee, she came clean with
herself. Brian interested her; he was smart, educated, good-looking,
curious . . . employed. But she didn't want to *date*. She'd left that
awkward social vestige behind long ago and far away.

Brian was also skittish. He was busy, almost preoccupied.
Contract negotiations creeped closer, the international union would
convene in September, and a dozen other irons glowed in his fire.
Dating was not first on his to-do list. It wasn't even *on* his list, and he
made one every morning.

Sandy was a knockout. Good-looking, bright, deep . . . the real
deal. Why had she not been . . . what . . . attached, swooped up, carted
off? Maine was sparse, and its 1.3 million people scattered to the ends
of the earth. That meant good-looking, smart, single, accomplished

women were scarce. Sandy was a find. He would go for it. He thought of a date as . . . research. Research into this lovely woman to uncover potential flaws, reasons he should drop the ball and get on with the union game. Who was he kidding? Sandy was hot, and he wanted to know her better. Much better.

The night of the concert, Brian arrived at the Thistle Inn early for dinner. He waited at the bar trying not to appear out of place or nervous. But the eerie flutters came unexpectedly. A confident guy, Brian was respected at BIW and circulated with a natural assurance. He ordered a club soda and watched the barkeep pouring drinks and fending off flirters. This date was more than research. He was excited, anticipatory.

Sandy arrived ten minutes late, looking better than he remembered her. She stood tall in her black, low-heeled boots, jeans, and cashmere rose fisherman sweater. It was a warm night in September, so she had left her denim jacket in the car. The bulky sweater couldn't hide her pleasing form.

Brian turned in her direction on the barstool. Then came the first of several awkward moments. Should he kiss her . . . shake her hand . . . wave to her? They'd never touched before. What was the correct, unpresumptuous first-date greeting? He did nothing. He said, "Hey, you look great."

She smiled.

Brian wore jeans and a white denim shirt. Together, the couple looked the part of traditional Irish music fans. Brian stood slightly taller than Sandy at six feet, his dark features residuals of Italian heritage. His height came thanks to his mother's German stock. He had an athletic build. He ran and went to the gym when time allowed. The problem was the union and the travel on its behalf. Staying in hotels, eating all his meals out, these created obstacles to fitness and health. But he tried his best and swore he would never slip into the condition of so many of his union brothers and sisters, fat and burned out.

Sandy thought Brian was attractive and well-groomed. Many of her male colleagues at Bigelow wore untamed beards, Halloween hair, and clothes that looked like they belonged in a college dorm. Brian was presentable. Even handsome.

They sat in a booth and ordered drinks. Sandy chardonnay and Brian Chianti. They talked about their workdays and ordered entrees. During the wait for dinner, the conversation took up where they'd left off at lunch. Sandy was curious about Brian's divorce, but she didn't approach the subject head-on. She asked, "Was your wife from Maine?"

"No. No. She was from Boston . . . Cambridge . . . actually. We met at Bowdoin."

Sandy remained quiet, employing her gift of telepathic ability to prompt people to talk without saying a word. She had perfected her powers on Caroline. Brian continued, "We were both young. We didn't know what we wanted. She thought of Maine as an adventure, you know, going to school in the wilds of the eastern frontier. We really got along. I met her family, she met mine. We dated exclusively for three years, and we got married the year I graduated, 2005. We stayed married for five years."

Sandy asked, "What happened?"

She—her name is Denise—she didn't really like Maine. I started my apprenticeship. She thought we would be in Boston or some other urban scene. She thought I would have an important office job, advising clients on economic trends, or something, and she would teach school. She had it planned out in her mind. When I decided to take the apprenticeship and live in Bath, her party balloons popped and . . . I worked nights for months at a time. Our friends were mostly my friends. Her family lived on a higher social ladder rung, so . . . things didn't work out.

"Did you have children?"

"No. She got pregnant the year before we divorced. She lost it. She wasn't far along . . . but it put her on an emotional rollercoaster. The trauma probably pushed her to leave for Cambridge. She filed for divorce not long after moving back. We still talk, but not often."

Sandy asked, "Are you seeing anybody now?"

Brian blurted, "You!" And the instant he spoke, he heard the cheekiness.

Sandy didn't react for a second, then chuckled.

Brian smiled.

Sandy probed, "If you're not seeing anyone now . . . other than me . . . how long has it been since you dated?"

Brian said, "This is embarrassing. I haven't *dated* in years . . . at least three years. In fact, I'm not sure I remember *how* to date."

He turned the tables. "How about you?"

"I haven't *dated* since Noah died, ten years ago. I've been on dates, but not dating . . . if that's not too confusing. My heart wasn't in it. It took a long time to . . . to leave Noah behind. He was a great guy, a good husband, and . . . a wonderful father."

Brian shied from wading in deep water. "I'm sorry, I didn't mean to bring up painful memories. Do you want to talk about something else?"

Sandy said, "Here's the thing, Brian. You seem like a good guy. So far, so good, right? Let's just see how we get along, see what we've got in common, and we'll just take it easy. You've got responsibilities at BIW, and I've got Caroline and my job, so neither one of us can launch into a romantic frenzy and pretend nothing else matters. I know that's not what you're asking, but let's just go slow and enjoy what there is to enjoy. And thank you for telling me about Denise."

Brian said, "I *enjoy* you in your sweater. It's a good look for you."

Sandy blushed.

Brian smiled.

Unseen by Brian's warm eyes, a long dormant urge awoke in Sandy.

The Tide of Deception
Chapter 4

Sandy and Brian were both wrong. Somehow, they found time to date
and get to know each other better . . . a lot better. And they liked what
they found. Sandy introduced Brian to Caroline, following a lashing
nor'easter in early November. The storm downed trees that downed
power lines. Sandy's generator wouldn't crank, so she built a wood
fire in her Hearthstone and called Brian. Brian came by and jumped
the generator, which fired and solved the immediate problem. Sandy
needed a new battery. When Sandy introduced Brian, her daughter
played it coy and cordial. On the way to the auto parts store to buy a
battery, the three stopped at Ports for pizza. They drove Brian's Jeep,
which Caroline found not at all embarrassing, unlike her mother's
Subaru.

Brian had never raised a child. But Caroline was not a child in
looks or maturity. She could be childish, especially around her mother,
but in Brian's company, she kept on her best behavior. She thought her
mother needed a boyfriend, and Brian seemed to fit the bill. They
talked about school, college, and Caroline's interest in tennis and
sailing. Caroline wanted to study psychology at the University of
Maine, and her mother nodded while nudging her toward a hard
science. Sandy knew the quickest way to cement Caroline's interest in
what Sandy considered the murky pseudo-science of psychology was
to talk against it. So, she held her tongue and hoped this phase would
pass.

Brian and Sandy spent weekends together, and it became a
matter of routine. As Thanksgiving approached, they talked about
plans and about meeting each other's families. A milestone.

Sandy's mother and father were in their early eighties. Sandy
was the youngest of three and the only daughter. Sandy and Caroline,
along with her parents, planned to go to her uncle's house in the late
afternoon for a family spread.

Brian asked, "How many do you expect?"

Sandy said, "Twenty-five . . . thirty . . . could be more? And a
couple are members of your union."

Brian thought this through. Sandy sensed his hesitation. She
asked, "What's wrong? We're not breaking any rules, are we?"

"No. No. You mean the union, right?"

Sandy nodded.

"No. If you were a member or an officer, I'd be on thin ice. But I'm dating you, not your relatives."

"Oh, so now we're dating, eh?" Sandy chided.

"Umm . . . well. . . ."

"It's okay," she assured him, "we can be dating." And she felt better for saying it.

Brian smiled.

Brian's parents, in their early seventies, held their holiday gathering at Christmas. Brian's younger brother was married with two children, and the family rotated Christmas dinners between Camden and Portsmouth. This year was Camden. The resulting dialogue found Brian committing to Thanksgiving with Sandy's family and Sandy agreeing to go to Christmas dinner with Brian. Caroline might come if she wanted or stay in Boothbay with her friends. She chose friends. Her stated reasoning seemed bulletproof. This would be their last Christmas together before college. But unsaid, Caroline knew that Sandy meeting Brian's parents might be fraught. She didn't want to complicate the situation. She hoped that this Brian–Sandy thing would take off.

Sandy asked Brian, "So . . . what does your brother do?"

Brian's terse response chilled the conversation. "Umm . . . he's with the government."

Sandy looked at Brian with wide eyes and employed her powers to prompt, but they didn't work. She asked, "Okay . . . it's a big government" Then she held her hands in front of her as if to say, *could you give me more?*

Brian said, "He's a contractor with the Navy. He does . . . research. He travels . . . a lot doing research and consulting."

Sandy nodded.

Brian said, "Don't worry, he's a good guy. He's easy to be around, and his wife is a saint. You'll like them. The kids are in their own world. Two boys, twins, fraternal, dizygotic, nine years old. They're usually lost in their electronics."

The mystery of Brian's brother registered, but Brian's endorsement reassured Sandy. Brian had told Sandy about his mother and father earlier in their get-to-know-each-other phase. Brian's dad was quiet and enjoyed sailing and woodworking. Brian's mother was an artist, oils her favorite medium. Demand for her paintings had not reached commercial levels, but she had some interesting works.

Mostly landscapes, ocean scenery, and wildlife. She had a couple of pieces on commission in Camden. She and Brian's dad shared a barn workshop–studio. Brian's parents were happy and in good health.

Sandy's father had worked all his life in construction and fished with his brother, a lobsterman. He was ambulatory, and his mind was sharp, but his body had paid a price. He smoked. Sandy's mother had kept a home, raised the children, attended mass, and organized bake sales and charity events. For the past five years, she'd shown signs of lagging mental acuity. She had yet to be diagnosed with dementia, but the family sensed it. Sandy assured Brian that her parents would be easy to meet, and Brian needed to worry more about her cousins, her male cousins. There were the two who worked at BIW, but the others ranged from lobstermen to clammers to a Congregationalist pastor.

Brian's mind painted a sketchy picture of Sandy's relatives. He saw them as untamed, insular, full of inside jokes, and . . . well . . . that made little sense. Sandy was welcoming and smart. They might be like her. Sandy had an open sense of humor and played along . . . most of the time. But she'd warned him about them. Was that tongue in cheek? Anyway, it didn't matter. Long ago, Brian had overcome shyness and antisocial tendencies when, in his early days as a union representative, he developed a *stage persona*. He was capable, maybe masterly, at acting the part of a pleasant stranger seeking social equilibrium; easy to meet, easy to talk to, and not easily offended. He'd be all right.

Sandy rendered a less threatening mental picture of meeting Brian's family. She did, however, have lingering anxiety over her and Brian's recent intimacy. Niggling disloyalty to Noah, and tart-trampy guilt bayed at the edge of her conscious. But these notions landed less profoundly than the pleasure of sex. She had no regrets. She just had to get used to it. It had been a long time for them both.

Two weeks earlier, they'd gone to a concert at the Chocolate Church in Bath. Caroline had stayed with her friend Elizabeth in Boothbay. Brian owned a two-bedroom house in Woolwich off Maine 128 with a mooring on the Kennebec River. It was a tidy place, small but nicely preserved and well-kept. After the concert, Sandy prompted, "Would you like to show me your place? It's in Woolwich, right?"

Brian didn't hesitate. "Sure. It's a little late, and you won't get back to Southport until . . . eleven thirty . . . or midnight. Will Caroline be okay?"

"She's with Elizabeth tonight. I don't need to go home . . .

tonight.”

Now Brian was stoked.

“Okay,” he said, “But I’ve got to warn you, it might be a little messy. I didn’t expect company. I hope you don’t mind.”

Sandy smiled.

At the house, Brian poured two glasses of wine, white for Sandy and red for him, and when he handed Sandy her glass, she took the wine and kissed him. Then she took a sip. Brian set his glass on the coffee table and pulled Sandy into a fervid embrace. Soon enough, they found their way to his bedroom, and the exploration began. Brian was strong but gentle at the right moments. Her passion and initiative surprised Sandy. Her mindfulness soon faded into a fog of lust and desire. All these years, all these restrictions. It all came tumbling down, and Sandy fell for Brian like the last brick in a wall. They sprawled naked in bed. Both feeling for a new set of rules. Like most things in life, practice makes perfect, so the first encounter was *fine* . . . but would also be . . . *refined*. With the dating-flirting-anticipation milepost now in the rearview mirror, they were . . . whatever the next level might be.

Brian was beyond satisfied. Sandy was the real deal. He forgot all about researching her flaws.

The Tide of Deception
Chapter 5

The frog held a spear. The tattoo sat high on his left arm where his shirt would cover it. Sandy had never seen one before, and she shouldn't have seen this one. She wasn't snooping. But inside of Brian's parents' entranceway, she exchanged pleasantries with his mother and father. As she looked around the well-kept house, she glimpsed Brian's brother through the crack of a guest bedroom door where he was pulling on a T-shirt. A skeleton frog with a spear? Sandy's cousins served in the military. They had tattoos. And many of her non-military cousins had tattoos. But she'd never seen a frog with a spear. A bone frog with a trident spear. Sandy smiled, looked away, and continued meeting Brian's family.

There was, of course, an explanation. Sandy learned it from Brian on their return trip to Southport after a wonderful Christmas dinner, where Sandy scored a unanimous hit. Brian's brother, Jeff, had been a US Navy Seal. But the real story had started a generation before.

Brian's father, Anthony, was not always in Naval Acquisitions. In May 1969, he graduated from the University of Rhode Island with a bachelor of arts in history and a minor in Asian studies. His draft status also graduated from 2-S to 1-A. He was red meat. The United States had 543,000 troops in Vietnam, most of them draftees and most on one-year tours. Anthony did odd jobs that summer expecting to be called up or, just maybe, get a lucky draw in the upcoming draft lottery. On December 1, 1969, General Lewis B. Hershey reached into a large glass bowl and picked one of 366 blue plastic capsules containing birth dates. The first drawn became order-of-call number one. Thus, Uncle Sam would draft men aged eighteen to twenty-six with that birthday in 1970. The drawings continued, and General Hershey retrieved Anthony's birthday on the twelfth draw. Anthony would be drafted. Right after Christmas, he enlisted in the US Navy to beat the draft.

The US Navy is not just a bureaucratic morass with a budget befitting God. They get many things right. After his induction and testing, the service realized they had officer material in Anthony and a budding Asian affairs staffer. After Anthony underwent backgrounding and security clearance certification, the Navy assigned him to the Office of Naval Intelligence, ONI. Anthony worked ONI for twenty years, then moved to acquisitions at the Pentagon, then on to naval liaison at Bath. But why Camden for retirement?

Born and raised in Rhode Island, Anthony loved sailing. The challenging waters of Maine are a sailor's dream—and nightmare. They are waters to measure your skills against. And Camden, Maine, hosted a hotbed of CIA, NSA, DIA, and ONI retirees. Why Camden? That's a secret.

At nineteen, Jeff, Brian's younger brother, then an undergrad at Hunter College in New York City, witnessed the attacks on the Twin Towers and the Pentagon. He rushed to serve for all the right reasons. He dropped out of university, enlisted, and his father helped the Navy put him to good use. He survived the six-months' hell of Basic Underwater Demolition/SEAL training, BUD/S, at the Naval Special Warfare Center in Coronado, California. This earned him the rating of Navy special warfare operator (SO) and the bone frog tattoo. With the rank of petty officer third class, Jeff soon perfected his equestrian skills on dusty mountain crags in Afghanistan's Hindu Kush.

"So, go over the part where your dad bought land in Camden because a friend in the CIA deemed it a good deal," prompted Sandy. She had to raise her voice because Brian's Jeep, with its aggressive off-road tires and lack of interior refinement, was not the quietest vehicle on the road.

"He had a friend. We called him Uncle Dan. Dan told him that Camden was beautiful, lots of IC folks retired there, and a lot of those folks like to sail. Plus, Camden has an annual conference in February that draws in high-level international figures. And they have a local art scene. Dad and Mom love it there. You could tell, right?" answered Brian.

Sandy gestured air quotes, "*IC*?"

Brian answered, "Intelligence Community."

Sandy nodded.

"There's a lot of competition between agency higher-ups, but it's a tight community at the operational level. Dad has a lot of friends from different agencies," Brian assured her.

"So, Brian, is Jeff also IC?" asked Sandy.

"Well . . . he's sort of IC adjacent."

"He never told me who he works for," commented Sandy.

"A contractor."

"Yes, but who?"

"Some international outfit. Smith and Jones Data Research? I don't know . . . honest."

Sandy sensed a brick wall.

Brian asked, "What did you think of Georgia and the kids?"

"Georgia is sweet and pretty and witty, too. I liked her. I bet the students in her third-grade class love her. The boys are the way you described them, lost in their electronics but well-behaved. And your parents, Brian, your parents are saints. And you should have told me they would put out such a spread. I could have made something instead of showing up with wine. That was embarrassing."

"Don't worry. They had it covered. They're hosting pros. You were a hit, I could tell."

Sandy looked unconvinced.

Brian said, "You scored . . . trust me."

Gears meshed in Sandy's head as they turned off Route 1 onto Route 27 to Boothbay. Brian's father had said something that shifted Sandy's curiosity into overdrive. During the after-dinner drinks and one-on-one talk, Brian's father and Sandy sat on the leather sofa in the family room. An unimportant college bowl game played low in the background. Anthony asked Sandy about her work. She initially recited the template version . . . small things that live in the ocean. But Anthony was curious and drew Sandy out. So, she outlined her curriculum vitae, and Anthony followed up with, "Anomalous wave and tide occurrences? Now, that's interesting."

Sandy prodded, "Oh, why is that?"

"Before I retired, I remember an ONI team at BIW. They wanted to determine if unusual tides or currents had disrupted shipbuilding. It was a specialized team out of Suitland. Pretty high-level stuff. I remember CG-two being on the team and an academic from Woods Hole. Sort of unusual."

Sandy nodded. Then she asked, "What is CG-two?"

"Coast Guard Intelligence," replied Anthony.

Sandy nodded again. "Do you remember when they visited?"

"Late 2008 because I retired January 2009."

Sandy asked, "Did you see their report?"

Anthony shook his head. "No. Classified. I wasn't need-to-know."

Sandy nodded.

Anthony went on, "But later, after I retired, I picked up some scuttlebutt."

Sandy asked, "Can you talk about it?"

"Well . . . it's just scuttlebutt."

Sandy nodded.

"So . . . if I tell you, it might advance science? That's a good cause, right?" Anthony smiled. "Besides, I heard this post-retirement, and it's only a rumor. And it didn't come from ONI.

"What I was told was that the services, the Navy in particular, were interested in unusual waves and tides around major shipbuilding sites, naval bases, and commercial ports. They were investigating if these events might have been manmade. You know, nature as a weapon. Like when the Soviets experimented with cloud seeding. There's a long story there, believe me. And we were doing it before the Soviets. We seeded for five years in Vietnam to interdict the Ho Chi Minh Trail. We called it *rain augmentation*. The mission was to soften road surfaces, cause landslides, wash out river crossings, make it impassible for Charlie and NVA regulars. There were some unintended consequences. I imagine those are still classified.

"The Soviets had plans to melt the Arctic ice and increase temperatures in their northern republics. They drew up plans. Grandiose, eh? The Soviets had epic visions, but their economy was precarious. In 1978, the US and the Soviets signed ENMOD. That was a UN convention against modifying weather for military use. I'm pretty sure China signed off, too. Since then, a sequence of tide and wave events have raised red flags in the National Security Council. And one happened right here on the Midcoast.

"I don't know what the ONI team found. I'm sure there's paperwork, but it's classified. It might be an interesting read, right?"

Sandy nodded. "Was the convention limited to weather modification?"

"As I recall, the convention cited 'environmental modification techniques.' I'd have to look it up. But there were no enforcement provisions. It was all political."

Sandy had many questions, more pieces to add to the puzzle. But she had one fact, an unintended Christmas gift that supported her questioning the thin meteotsunami scientific consensus. She was not alone. The United States government also had second thoughts about the mysterious tides of Boothbay.

As Brian's Jeep hummed down Route 27, Sandy wished she had asked Anthony, "How could I see the report? Who was the academic? Who was Anthony's source? And how would such a manmade manipulation be possible?"

The Tide of Deception
Chapter 6

The CIA Reading Room is a wondrous place. But you must know what you are looking for, and Sandy didn't. After two hours of staring at her laptop and collating endless search results, she knew only this: the CIA had its fingers in everything. It had connections everywhere. And she only read declassified documents for public release. She searched "weather modification," "ocean modification," "tidal modification," "Boothbay," and "Woods Hole." Then she searched for her name and realized she had rabbit-holed. It was Sunday morning, and the hours before Caroline awoke should be reflective solitude, spent with coffee and the *New York Times*. Instead, she had scrambled her thoughts with a jigsaw of declassified tedium. She wondered why she was so sworn to solve what was, apparently, a puzzle only to her.

Two things? Related? Noah's death and her preoccupation with the mystery tides? Noah died five years after the tides. But somehow, someway, Sandy conflated the two events, and a web of emotions entwined them. The dry riverbed of her unconscious teemed with two currents. At times, a torrent. She sought an explanation. She had begun seeing a psychiatrist six months after Noah died. She'd even enrolled Caroline. But Sandy came to believe she was smarter than the shrink. She kept her appointments for another three months but excused Caroline, who seemed to adjust better than Sandy. After confronting the fear of raising Caroline alone, making ends meet, managing her grief, and dealing with loneliness, she deemed herself cured.

Noah had died on the water. She used to get so mad at him for stupid shit. Noah didn't deserve it. Such small stuff. Sandy never experienced that visceral anger toward Caroline. And Caroline, in her early teens, pulled some reckless stunts of her own. Sometimes Sandy caught herself still being mad at Noah. A useless and self-defeating emotion. It made her wonder just who or what controlled her mind. She would sleep soundly. Then, at some God-awful hour, she would wake up in a funk of swirling confusion, the result of a repetitive, unresolvable dream. The dream was not about Noah. The dream generated . . . confusion, complicating circumstances, all this mishmash arrayed in an interminable loop. The premise never changed. Sandy had to complete something but couldn't see it through. The most recent *gap* posed Sandy in a hotel lobby, waiting to check in.

But her luggage disappeared. The clerk asked for her phone number, and she could not write it legibly in the ledger. She tried time and time again. Utter frustration. It took her from two until five in the morning to get back to sleep, and then only for an hour. She was an early bird. Sandy awoke most mornings at six and never later than seven, even on weekends. What did it all mean? It usually meant that Sandy needed more sleep. That was the cure. She thought about tracking these gaps. But even though they had disordered her sleep for years, she'd never journaled or plotted them. A hormonal, mental, or emotional pattern, so what? Any discernable cycle meant biology, and biology was to Sandy the unbendable nature of self. Gaps were a nuisance, nothing more. Sandy thrived in her work, raised Caroline without untoward drama, and now was cultivating a new man who seemed to fit nicely into her life. She was functional. By any objective measure, functional. But the connection lingered. Noah and the tides.

The Tide of Deception
Chapter 7

Noah had drowned. That's what the autopsy stated, and there was no reason to think otherwise. They'd found his body washed ashore on Hendricks Head Beach on Southport. Sandy and Noah's powerboat, a twenty-nine-foot Dyer, languished nearby off Cedarbush Island with lobster gear warp tangled around its prop shaft. Nobody knows for sure what happened, but local lore assumed that Noah got into the water to cut the rope away from the prop. He wasn't wearing a personal flotation vest, probably because he had to dive under the boat to make the cut. He was wearing a diver's mask when Boothbay EMS recovered his body. The water was frigid. It was a warm day in early June, but the Sheepscot is a deep, cold river, and Noah had drowned only two miles from the Gulf of Maine. The Coast Guard recorded the water temperature at forty-four degrees Fahrenheit.

Noah was a fit man. He worked out and ran, and nature had blessed him with an athlete's build. He was a confident swimmer and a PADI certified diver. But in forty-four-degree water, it's fat that counts. Noah wasn't fat. There's a reason that seals are fat.

Cold shock had gripped Noah upon entering the water. He'd panicked and hyperventilated, while his heart raced. But a heart attack didn't kill young and healthy Noah. Within five to ten minutes, twenty minutes at most, he couldn't swim. His fine motor control failed soon after entering the water. He dropped whatever knife he hoped to cut the rope with. Minutes later, his gross motor coordination failed, making swimming or climbing onto the boat impossible. His only controlled movement was vertical as he struggled to keep his head above water. Clinical hypothermia was upon him within thirty minutes. Most victims died before this stage. If he survived this far, he would have lost consciousness as his lungs filled with salt water.

A young man with a promising future and a pillar of the community lost to the sea. Boothbay lost men and women to the sea from time to time. Fishermen working offshore. Solo kayakers who capsize an untenable distance from land. All tragic. But Noah's death had resonated in the community, and it resonated like a kettledrum in the lives of Sandy and Caroline. Stupid shit. That's what Sandy thought but never said.

Noah had a VHF radio. Hell, he had his mobile phone. He

should have called someone. He could have called a diver with a proper wetsuit, or a tow service if the engine failed. Sandy knew his thinking. She could hear him reasoning his decision. I can deal with this. I don't want anybody else involved. This is embarrassing. I got tangled in a pot warp, what a rookie move. I can handle this. A dog walker found Noah's body washed ashore in his underwear and a Boothbay Harbor Yacht Club T-shirt. Her 911 call forged the first link in a chain dousing Noah's wish and involving *many* others.

The news spread quickly in tight-knit Boothbay. Overwhelmed by grief, comforting Caroline, arranging Noah's burial, organizing a wake, and receiving the countless casseroles, baked goods, and condolences at her door, Sandy soldiered on. She had no time to indulge the darkness stalking her. That would come later, after the burial, the wake, and the supportive visits of family and friends. These visits were supportive, yes, but each had an element of curiosity. Sandy had to repeat her steps to everyone to reassure them of her soundness. But she wasn't sound, not really. When the attention waned, she fell into the depths with Caroline her only beacon to shore. Sandy knew she had to parent Caroline through her own darkness. She never lost track of that. Caroline was seven. Tender and undeterred, but seven, an age of delicate formation. Sandy shielded her daughter from tragedy and the corruption of innocence. Caroline had lost no one this important. She had been four when her great-grandmother passed away. Caroline's most immediate emotional connection, ripped away by fate, had been the family cat, an orange tom. Chic-Chic had to be put down that winter. The veterinarian came to their house and injected the suffering beast while Noah cradled him in his arms. As the poor animal's pupils dilated to black, all other eyes filled with tears.

Sandy seldom visited Noah's grave. She always took Caroline on his birthday, never on the date of his death. But she visited Hendricks Head Beach when reflection called, and seldom with Caroline. On a sunny, cold New Year's Day, she arrived at a tricolor mosaic—gray sand, blue sea, and a rose sunset—on the Sheepscot's western shore. She stared across the blameless water. A disused lighthouse on Townsend Promontory, unlit but beckoning, rose three hundred yards to the south. Built in 1829, it was said to have caused more fatalities than it prevented. Mariners confused this light with the Burnt Island light in Boothbay Harbor. When they set their course to the east, they crashed into the rocky ledge of Southport. Both lights were fixed and easy to confuse. In 1857, the United States Lighthouse

Service changed the Hendricks lens from fixed to reciprocating. But mariners were still confused. Wrecks littered the Sheepscot, marking the graves of those never seen again. The lighthouse was cursed; Sandy knew the lore. It may well have been the last thing Noah saw.

The tide was ebbing. She felt the surging power of the water as it gained momentum on its journey back to the sea. A tide is a wave, unseen, unappreciated, but inevitable. It moves things, transporting them to places they wish to go and sometimes not. It moves bodies, boats, and thoughts. It moved Sandy's spirit. She longed for a man, far gone, perhaps himself underappreciated, who had taken to his grave a part of her soul.

The Tide of Deception
Chapter 8

A tide is a wave propagated by gravity and guided by the sea floor.
Tides have as many characteristics as there are sea floors. The earth,
the moon, the sun—these are the gravitational motors of a tide.
Sometimes these motors countervail, and at others they combine. The
interplay between these motors creates kinetic energy. The inertia of
Earth's oceans causes a bulge opposite the tidal attractors. Thus, tides
occur simultaneously on the *near side*, the side nearest the moon, and
180 degrees opposite on the *far side*. Think of a sphere with the earth
inside an oval. One end of the oval points to the moon. The other end
of the oval is planetary water resisting the moon's attraction. This
mass of water is inert relative to the moon's attraction and bulges. The
thinned water between inertia and attraction, at roughly ninety degrees
to the moon-bulge axis, is a low tide. Amplitude and frequency are
functions of the above and more.

A physical system with three objects—the sun, the earth, and
the moon—constitutes a three-body problem. In 1687, Isaac Newton
published *Philosophiæ Naturalis Principia Mathematica*. Newton
sought to predict the long-term stability of the earth, moon, and sun
and became the first to tackle the three-body problem. Sir Isaac sought
a general analytic expression, but his exploration left him with more
unknowns than equations describing them. Two bodies, no problem.
Hence Newton's laws of motion: inertia, force-mass, and action-
reaction. But add a third or a fourth or a fifth, and there were simply
too many variables. Newton's exploration relied on Renaissance
astronomers Nicolaus Copernicus, Tycho Brahe, and Johannes Kepler.
The best of company, without a doubt. But to this day,
mathematicians, physicists, philosophers, rank hobbyists like Brian,
and honed academicians like Sandy have yet to crack the three-body
problem. What remains is chaos.

Humans have gotten good at predicting estimated outcomes for
three bodies in motion. Hence, tide tables, satellite orbits, and space
flight. But these are estimates based on near term probabilities. Add an
unexpected protuberance or vary the sea's inertial resistance with
increased salinity or decreased water temperature, and things get
weird. Hell, vary the barometric pressure, and things get weird.
Earthquakes, that'll do it. Hurricanes, you bet. Sediment slides,

uplifting crustal events, faraway storms, they can all massively change a tidal system. So, Sandy's exploration of the mysterious Boothbay tides of 2008, her grappling with the unknowns and pasting together the knowns, was a patchwork with many blanks. But her resolve to find a solution sprung from a deep font. A rushing riverbed that would not be deterred. Unless it was, like now.

She dropped the *Natural Hazards* journal from August 2013 when the smell of burning croissant overpowered the aroma of her coffee. She'd forgotten to adjust the toaster. When she set down the hefty journal, the bent pages flopped over, glancing off her coffee cup and creating a mini tsunami of hot java. The splashing java stained an October 2008 Associated Press clipping entitled "Coastal Maine Tide Change a Mystery." Sandy muttered, "Shit."

It wasn't an enormous loss. The AP clipping contained little useful information other than that a "similar event had occurred on Jan. 9, 1926, in Bass Harbor," seventy miles east. And a quote from the US National Weather Service that the cause of the Boothbay tides, "remains a mystery and may never be known." The other material in her bulging accordion file was unmarred. She pried the burned pastry from the toaster with a kitchen knife and examined it. It was beyond rescue. She tossed it into the trash and started again, this time reducing the toaster's intensity. She brought a kitchen towel to the coffee table to wipe away the mini tsunami and dab her clipping, just as her phone chirped. It was Brian.

"Hey, good-lookin'. What are you doing? Have you solved the crossword yet?" Sandy was a *New York Times* crossword devotee.

"No. I'm cleaning up my first mess of the day."

"Oh, that sounds . . . like a distraction," said Brian. Then he asked, "Are we still on for this party?"

Sandy had yet to confess her obsession, her predilection, her abiding interest in the Boothbay tidal anomaly. Brian had picked up hints from offhand comments Caroline made about "the file" and "crossword puzzles are not the only mystery consuming my mother." But he had yet to grasp Sandy's full immersion. He knew Sandy could be intense, focused, and absorbed. He attributed these moments to her intellectual prowess. Sandy was a notable scientist with an impressive publication resume. Caroline chided her mother when she was relaxing or watching stupid awards shows on television. She'd say, "Your H-index will suffer," or "You're going H-negative," or "My GPA will be higher than your index." Brian was unfamiliar with the term. He didn't want to appear shallow, so he Googled it and learned that it was a measurement of academic output and credibility. The index was the numeric product of a formula more tedious than Brian could recall. It measured the number of scientific publications and how often they were cited in other publications, against the author's career years. Sandy's rating was seventeen, respectable for a hands-on scientist only a decade in the game whose laboratory responsibilities outweighed theoretical musings.

Sandy said, "How bad is the snow in Woolwich? It's fluffy here on Southport, and the wind seems tame."

"About the same here. It's supposed to stop around eleven. Shouldn't be much accumulation," assured Brian.

Sandy looked out her living room picture window at the sliver of the Sheepscot River between Southport Island and Pratts Island. A lone loon was working the choppy water. He was stationary, even though the wind was a steady ten knots out of the east. He dipped his beak and raised it holding a small fish. Then he straightened his neck, beak to the sky, and swallowed the morsel whole. Fascination with the survival imperative overtook her thoughts. He was fed, but was he happy? Was he satisfied? Was he cold? Was he even a he? He might have been a she.

Brian prompted, "Are you still there?"

Sandy's toaster popped.

"Sorry. I had a spiritual moment," mused Sandy.

"What. . . ?"

"I watched a loon catch breakfast. Good for the loon, not so good for the fish. Ain't nature grand?"

Brian tried to pick up the thread, "Ah . . . yeah. Poor fish. So, what about Portsmouth? If you want to go, drive here, then we'll leave from here. Should be about two hours. I've got their presents. All wrapped up, ready to go."

Sandy had told Brian that she would think about attending the twins' tenth birthday party. But now, she was having second thoughts. The weather was threatening, but predicted to clear, and she had a certain foreboding about spending more time with Brian's family. She asked, "Will your parents be there?"

"They should be, as far as I know."

Sandy asked, "And . . . we're driving back this evening, right? I've got an early meeting with my team at the lab tomorrow."

"Right. We'll drive back. We'll probably leave around three.

You should be back on Southport by six. Does Caroline want to come?”

“Ah . . . no. She’s got friend commitments.” She paused. “Okay, Brian, I’ll be at your place at eleven. Anything I should know about this party?”

“Nope. Kids and cake. Probably ice cream. All the good stuff. I’ll see you at eleven.”

When Brian cut the connection, Sandy looked again at the cold, impenetrable river and the swirling snow. The loon had gone. She retrieved her warm, freshly toasted croissant. As she smeared silky Irish butter onto the porous pastry, she thought of the things she had in common with migratory waterfowl.

Screaming. Indoor screaming. Ear-piercing indoor screaming. The highest-pitched screams, which might qualify for use in crowd control, came from little girls, the twins' friends from school. The birthday party was now a nominal game of tag, or hide and seek, or random fall and crawl. The children sprinted through the basement family room, dodging toys and furniture like Seal candidates on Coronado's obstacle course. Jeff tried to coax the party outside, but the basement was warm, the fireplace roaring, and the hot chocolate ever flowing. The scene inside beat the fifteen-degree cloudy outside. Even vintage saucer sleds and a sloping front yard failed to attract. So, the adults sat with their drinks, tried to talk, and picked at crackers and cheese. Jeff and his wife, Georgia, kept busy with resupply and emergency mop-ups. Sandy, Brian, Anthony, and Brian's mother, Stella, pretended to enjoy or tolerate the frolic. Sandy was relieved theirs was only a two-hour commitment. She wanted to talk with Anthony more about wave anomalies and how she might get her hands on sensitive government materials. But the subject seemed fraught and out of place for a kids' party. So, Sandy smiled and bided her time.

She was helping Georgia with the ice cream course when Jeff came into the kitchen to praise them for keeping the party tight. He asked, "How much longer are we responsible for this chaos?"

Georgia said, "We told their parents the party would last until three."

"Any chance they'll take naps?"

"Don't be silly. Kids love this interaction. Yelling, screaming, laughing . . . you should visit my classroom. These kids are on good behavior today," Georgia responded. She asked, "Sandy, could you and Jeff get the cake out of the refrigerator in the garage? It'll take two. It's big. Sandy, you can get the doors."

Sandy nodded, wiped her hands on a kitchen towel, and smiled at Jeff.

Jeff looked a lot like Brian, who looked a lot like his father. He was tall, handsome and had a Mediterranean complexion. He was slimmer than Brian with a full, trimmed, stubble beard, and the same warm eyes. Sandy got her coat, and they walked together to the detached garage with its old refrigerator, the venue for Jeff's beer assortment. Sandy and Jeff had exchanged pleasantries at Christmas dinner, but had not found the time to talk.

Jeff asked, "So, is Brian treating you right?"

Sandy took this as the joke it was. "Sure, he pays for half of our dates."

Jeff laughed. "Okay, don't take this the wrong way, but Brian scored when he found you."

"Oh?"

"Yeah . . . I mean, not that he's been looking. You're the first woman he's brought to meet the family since his divorce. So . . . I guess he thinks you're special."

"Lucky me," replied Sandy.

"Dad tells me you're a scientist at Bigelow. UMaine PhD, right?"

Sandy nodded.

"Way to go. You've got it together," assured Jeff.

"I wouldn't go *that* far," said Sandy.

"A PhD, that's impressive. You put a lot of work into your education. Dad said you studied tides, and he told you about the rogue tide investigation."

Sandy perked up. "Yes. He told me about a commission that investigated an anomaly on the Midcoast in 2008. Do you know anything about that?"

Inside the garage, Jeff stopped and looked at Sandy. "I may."

What kind of response was that? Did he want her to ask more questions? Had he called a halt to the conversation?

Jeff continued, "I assume Brian told you what I do?"

"Not really. He said you are a contractor working for the Navy and consult on matters of data and research. But he left out details."

"Yeah . . . that's what he's supposed to do. There's an element of national security involved in all of this."

"And by *this*, you mean?"

"The family. Keeping things secret."

"Right," said Sandy. "Should I keep this conversation secret?"

"No. Not from the family, but everybody else. What I'd like you to know is that the mystery of the rogue wave in Boothbay, anomalous tide, or . . . whatever . . . that file is still open. I'd like to pick your brain and get your thoughts about how it might have happened. How it might have happened *naturally* . . . or *otherwise*."

Sandy squinted. "Who wants to know?"

Jeff smiled. "Interested parties involved in your nation's security."

"Jeff, who do you work for?"

"Brian told the truth. I'm a contractor. We do research and sell data analysis to the US Navy, among others."

"Yeah . . . but what's the company's name?"

"Does that matter?"

"It does to me."

"The name of the company is Kinnaird International, LLC. And you won't find it on the web, so don't bother," Jeff smiled. "We're Bahamian incorporated, so . . . as the old Hollywood street cop stereotype goes. . . ."

Jeff held up his left hand in a stop position, then circled his right, and said, *"Nothing to see here folks . . . move along . . . move along."*

He smiled at his pantomime, "Sandy, I'd like to share some documents with you to get your thoughts. I'll need your permission to clear you up to *secret*."

"Clear me up to *secret*?"

"Sorry. Right, I need to get you a security clearance to the level of secret. There are three levels: confidential, secret, and top secret. I would like to share material that is classified as secret.

"This means we will document your background, turn over some stones, and check you out. If you don't want to go through this, we can call it off at any time. Unless you're a foreign agent." Jeff smiled.

"But we've got to clear you before you can review the material. We have an expedited process for this scenario, an interim clearance that usually takes thirty days. But we can do it in two weeks, once you've completed the questionnaire, a government SF-eighty-six. There will be an interview. We'll come to you, so no travel required. Oh . . . and we'll be talking to your employers, friends . . . your associates. We'll look at your credit, your bank accounts, court records, law enforcement records, landlords . . . and you'll need to fill out some forms. You can do that online."

"Wow," muttered a disoriented Sandy.

Jeff assured, "Don't worry. We'll be discreet. We'll flash DCSA credentials and make it clear this is a security clearance application, not a criminal investigation."

"Um . . . DCSA?" asked Sandy.

"Defense Counterintelligence and Security Agency," answered Jeff. He went on, "Sorry to hand you this at a kids' party, but . . . I get the sense that you want to review this material. And, perhaps, you can help us sort this . . . um . . . anomaly."

"Jeff, can I think about this?"

"No problem. Call or text on this number." Jeff tore off the flap of a 12-pack of Peroni Nastro Azzurro and wrote a number. As he wrote, he instructed, "These digits are all one greater than the actual phone number." Then, without looking up, he said, "Zero," and pointed to Sandy.

Sandy cocked her head, then puzzled, replied, "Nine?"

"Bingo, you got it. Have you ever used the Signal app?"

Sandy shook her head.

"Download the app . . . you got a six-digit security key for your phone, right?"

Sandy nodded.

"Download the app and use it to call or text. Then destroy the box top after you enter the correct number in your contacts. Okay?"

Sandy wanted to say, *This is a lot of secret-squirrel stuff for a rando.*

Rando was what Caroline called normal people.

Instead, Sandy said, "Right. I'll do all that and get back to you in a day or so. But Jeff, how much of this can I tell Brian?"

"He's in the loop. But once you get into the classified material, that shouldn't be shared. Period. Only you and I will discuss that."

Sandy nodded.

Jeff retrieved an enormous chocolate cake from the refrigerator and motioned Sandy to open the garage door. He kneed the fridge door closed, smiled, and the two made their way back to the party.

Sandy put on a social smile, but she wasn't sure if she had just been gifted by Jeff or impressed by an unseen sovereign.

Just inside the front door, Sandy asked, "Jeff, did you mention the tide investigation to your father? He told me it was scuttlebutt that didn't come from ONI."

Jeff balanced the cake, watching his step to not trip over scattered toys. He shook his head, "Nope."

Jeff didn't tell Sandy that Kinnaird had already run an initial security screening, low-level snooping. Kinnaird had verified her previous and current employment, education, residences, and social media postings, including her social media contacts. But, at Jeff's direction, Kinnaird had held off interviewing friends, neighbors, supervisors, and coworkers. And they'd postponed pulling her phone and E-ZPass logs and surveilling her to develop a pattern-of-life profile. If Sandy agreed to the clearance process, her life would be an open book. And if Jeff knew, Brian might, too. She had TSA PreCheck clearance and CBP Global Entry and NEXUS. Would Kinnaird go deeper than that into her life just to read some dated documents? She didn't think she had anything to hide. Nothing, except . . . her mind traveled back to the year 2000 when she had been a freshman at UMaine. And, yeah, that might be revealing.

A tempest raged across the Midcoast, taking by surprise even salty, storm-vigilant Mainers. And it raged again three days later. Only the wise and weathered few foresaw the multiplication of scale, sequence, and force. The king tide, the fierce south wind, the hammering rain. Together they fused into a trifecta that detonated docks and piers and floats and bridges, roads and cabins and homes. Trees fell throughout the region, taking with them utility lines. Power became a luxury granted only those with residential generators.

For Sandy, the storm was a spiritual experience, vengeance on the scale of the Old Testament, and a preview of nature's bent. Sandy felt in her soul the revelation of that fearful moment. She heard nature's clarion call, "Violating species . . . take warning! I control . . . I vanquish . . . I demand! Ignore at your peril and demise, I will care not. Your doom is but another in my infinite days!"

Kinnaird postponed Sandy's interview. Travel by air, water, or roadway was unwise. A DoD Gulfstream 550 with three VIPs from the Signature Flight terminal at Dulles would not tempt the weather or the post-storm distress.

Tides in Boothbay Harbor reached 14.57 feet mean lower low water (MLLW). The former record was 14.17 feet MLLW set in February 1978. The storms were four feet above normal high tide. But the water rose even higher than the tide. Pushed by an ear-splitting fifty knot southern gale, ocean water surged up the north–south rivers on the Midcoast tide where it met the storm's runoff. Rain poured onto the woodlands, fields, and the sandy loam covering Maine's ubiquitous ledge from Kittery to Eastport. Buckets per hour. Compelled by gravity, swollen streams and creeks emptied their burden into the riverine network. The deluge's route to oceanic equilibrium was the Androscoggin, Kennebec, Sheepscot, and Damariscotta rivers, and the Muscongus and Penobscot Bays. Debris from piers, wharfs, docks, and floats, tree limbs, entire trees, and thick uprooted seaweed coursed on its flow. When the flow met land and structure, the rivers of trash composed sculptures of the devil's charm.

Twenty-four of Maine's sixty-seven lighthouses suffered major damage, and livelihoods fell to the storms. If a moored working boat survived the storm and remained tethered and undamaged, it now had no place to land its fish, lobsters, clams, and waterborne bounty. Uprooted, like tons of seaweed, were the lives of thousands who, in good times, tenuously grasped the margins of prosperity.

The first storm was the worst, with the heaviest rain and winds. But the second storm's tide equaled the first. Any structure that had been merely damaged during the first assault likely fell or washed away in the second. The storm's signature was writ large everywhere, but the unseen damage lurked as well. The compromised pier pilings, the submerged building foundations, the distressed fisheries, the washed-out roadways, and those yet to collapse. The scars were deep, and communities would catalogue them for years to come.

Brian and Sandy were at their respective homes for the first storm. They were both stunned, not that they would have been able to thwart any of the storm's impact. Both had generators and both kicked on. Brian's house had access to a common pier and float. Brian kept his boat on a nearby mooring. The boat had been in storage in January, but the pier's float had broken free and washed away down the bulging Kennebec to the Gulf of Maine. Brian's house was undamaged.

Sandy's float rode the tide to unintended heights, and as the tide slackened, then ebbed, the float became stuck atop the north piling. She was shocked to see the float draped over the piling at an unimaginable angle. She called Brian, upset. Caroline counseled patience, but Sandy foresaw only disaster. Her gut wrenched at *the karma of cascading catastrophes*. She'd lived it before when escalating setbacks had swept her and people she loved into a vortex of predicaments. It's what had killed Noah. The displaced float was presage. What came next would be worse. One calamity begets another. Her cousins in the military called this sequence a shit show. What if her float broke free of the now twisted walkway? The tide and flow might launch it to God-knows-where and damage someone else's structure. Would she be responsible? A couple of hours later, as the tide receded, the weight of the contorted float dropped it back into position between the two pilings. But the north piling, which was old and partially rotten, had split at the top.

Brian came as soon as he could. He had to make certain the IAM Local S6 Emergency Response Committee mustered and got organized. They did. The committee had seasoned leadership, and the men and women volunteers were as rugged and resourceful as they come. They set up a command post in the union hall, distributed first-aid kits, and started cooking soups and chowders that they could deliver in thermos containers to members in distress. The volunteers with capable four-wheel drive vehicles began inventorying their gear. They enumerated chainsaws, chains, pry bars, towlines, and jerricans of gasoline and diesel fuel.

With everything as it should be, Brian drove to Southport. He had checked the web and knew to arrive at ebb tide because the high tide had sent water over the roadway just beyond Southport Bridge at Robinson's Wharf. The overflow was too deep and turbulent for his Jeep. When he arrived, he embraced a jittery Sandy. The float worried her. It was back in position between the pilings. But the chain that secured it to the north end had slipped between the piling and the float when the float fell into place. Another high tide was four hours away, and the river was rising. It was three-thirty in the afternoon and soon would be dark. Brian put on an LED headlamp and walked to the float to have a look. The chain was out of position, which meant the float was unattached to anything that would prevent it from launching from the pilings.

Shackles coupled the chain to eyelets on the float, securing it to the piling. Brian tried to break free the bolt on one shackle so he could move the chain back around the piling into the proper position. It had been in salt water too long and had seized like a weld. He tried a blowtorch on the nut of the shackle and got nowhere. He walked to his Jeep and retrieved a battery-powered metal saw. With Sandy holding a light, he lay flat on his belly on the soaking wet float and reached into the cold murky river to secure the chain and shackle. Seaweed and tree limbs permeated the chain, making it heavy as hell. He struggled to get the shackle above water, where he sawed away at the galvanized metal. It took two cuts to separate a chunk of the shackle and free it from the eyelet so he could move the chain around the piling. Now he needed another shackle. Sandy sent Caroline to Grover's Hardware and Brian told Caroline to drive the Jeep because it had better clearance over water. Caroline thought this was a great idea. Sandy warned her to drive slowly. Meanwhile, Brian secured the chain with an industrial strength zip tie from BIW's endless supply. Then he secured the float with two lines to Sandy's pier, which was covered with a weave of seaweed and storm detritus. When Caroline returned, Brian replaced the sawed-off shackle with the new item and secured the chain in the correct position. Now, they only hoped that the next tide and the one after that might be less than the storm tide, and that the float would remain attached.

A wet and sweaty Brian followed Sandy and Caroline to their house, unsure of what came next. He said, "That's as good a fix as we can do for now. We've got the chain where it belongs, and the extra lines attached to the float will keep it from drifting off if it breaks free. I guess what we do now is wait and hope.

"Um . . . I should go home and change."

Sandy said, "No. Stay here, unless you need to be home or go to the union."

She looked at Caroline, who nodded approval.

"Get out of those clothes, take a shower. You can wear my robe until everything is dry. We're all adults here."

Caroline grinned.

The shower felt wonderful. Brian warmed, recharged, toweled off, then donned Sandy's plush turquoise fleece robe. He stepped out of the bathroom, into the hallway, where Sandy waited with a pair of athletic socks. She said, "I'm sorry. I don't have slippers your size."

Brian smiled. "Don't expect five stars on Yelp. How's the float?"

"From what I can tell, it's where it's supposed to be. Thank you, Brian. Thanks for coming to our rescue." Sandy leaned forward and kissed him.

"Shucks, ma'am . . . that's just what we do up here on the eastern frontier," Brian said, affecting a good-old-boy persona.

Sandy shook her head and smiled. "Come on down. I've heated some chili from the freezer, and Caroline is making macaroni. I hope you take your chili over macaroni. You're not a rice guy, are you?"

"Macaroni sounds great. Am I okay parading in front of Caroline like this?" He motioned both hands up and down his robed figure.

"She doesn't care. She knows."

"Knows what?" Brian asked.

Sandy looked at him as if to say, *did you have to ask that question?*

"Oh, yeah . . . okay. We're all adults, right?" said Brian.

At the dinner table, Caroline stifled a smirk. And Brian registered her amusement, but he played it straight like he always ate dinner in a woman's robe. When they finished eating, Brian heard the dryer signal cycle finish, and Sandy retrieved his clothes. She handed them to him, folded in a neat stack and said, "You're welcome to change, unless you like the robe better?"

Brian smiled, said thank you, and excused himself to go to Sandy's bedroom.

Caroline gathered the dirty dishes, placed them in the washer, and told Sandy she had an English paper due. Caroline dried her hands, then climbed the stairs to her room. When Brian returned, the couple went to the living room where Sandy had a banked fire in the Hearthstone in case the generator fizzled. They sat on the sofa facing the fire.

Sandy thought, this is as good a time as any. Her confession began, "So, Brian, your brother has something that interests me."

Brian cocked his head.

Sandy continued. "You know, I studied anomalous tides in my PhD program?"

Brian nodded.

"Well, I've been curious about one occurrence in particular, an anomaly that happened here in Boothbay in 2008. I've mentioned it, right?"

Brian nodded.

"Well, your father and I talked about it at Christmas. He told me that his agency sent a team to BIW to investigate the event, thinking there might be something . . . nefarious going on. Maybe another country carrying out some sort of environmental attack. Sounds crazy, right?"

Brian wasn't sure how to respond. He just looked puzzled.

"Anyway, Jeff brought up the Boothbay tide at the twins' party and said his employer had an open file on the occurrence. He asked if I wanted to review the documentation and weigh in with my thoughts."

Brian said, "Wait. Jeff wants to involve you in his work?"

Sandy nodded.

"What did he say? asked Brian.

"He said I would need to be *cleared up to secret* to review the file. That means I will have to undergo a background check."

Brian said, "Okay. So far, so good. Did you agree?"

Sandy nodded. "The thing is, Brian, I have something that might come out in the clearance investigation. I thought I should tell you, now, to avoid any surprises. I was younger, and it involves Noah."

Brian's eyes widened.

Sandy smiled.

Sandy took a deep breath and exhaled slowly. The fire crackled as embers spit from the oak. She began, "When I was a freshman at UMaine, we didn't have much money. We had a lot of friends and family support, but not much money. I told you, Dad worked construction and helped his brother lobstering, but he never made a lot of money. That fall, when I started school, the construction company furloughed him. Mom didn't work, so . . . it was new. Somebody going to college was new to the family. I was the first. I received a small grant from the state. I worked in the bookstore ten to fifteen hours a week, made a little money, and attended class. But it wasn't enough. I couldn't lean on my family any more than they could afford, and they didn't realize how expensive things were going to be.

"During my first semester, I took an art appreciation class. That's where I met Noah. He became a graphic artist. I don't think I ever told you that. Noah was from Portland, and he had friends at the Maine College of Art. Noah was a free spirit in those days. He suggested I model at the college. He said they paid a hundred dollars a session. I drove to Portland . . . they looked me over . . . and hired me.

"So, I would drive to Portland after classes on Thursday, pose Friday, Saturday, and sometimes Sunday, and drive back to UMaine for class. A lot of times, Noah came with me, and we'd stay with his friends. That's how we became close. We dated for the next four years and got married the year after he graduated.

"What you need to know, Brian, and I'm sure Jeff will find out . . . I posed nude. The college had students and instructors who wanted to study the female form, and I was that form. I don't know if there is art in circulation today that, um . . . captured me.

"The job was legit, and the college filed W-two wage and tax forms. So, I'm sure a security clearance check will uncover it."

She glanced down the sofa at Brian, noting the disbelief on his scrunched face. A second later Brian blurted, "*That's* what's got you worried? You posing nude? I thought you were going to tell me you and Noah robbed a bank. Or got busted smuggling liquor into Canada! I mean, nude modeling? That's not really that big of a deal. It was just modeling, right?"

Sandy's eyes dropped to the floor. "Brian, this is embarrassing.

I don't want this to be public information. My family never found out, and I don't want them to find out. It would. . . ."

Brian interrupted, "Okay. I get it. It goes no further. Your secret is safe. But where can I buy some of this art? A velvet Sandy nude would be priceless."

Brian laughed, but Sandy didn't share his humor. She drew back and made a fist, like her brothers had taught her.

Brian sobered and said, "Jeff may never find out. The W-2twos may have you classified as 'modeling service' or something non-incriminating. Hell . . . it's not a crime, anyway. How long did you work there?"

"I quit the second semester of my sophomore year," said Sandy.

"Why?"

"Honestly . . . I didn't like some of Noah's friends, people we stayed with."

Brian didn't pry.

Sandy went on, "I started an RA job my junior year, and that helped pay the bills. Plus, I'd saved a stash from the modeling."

Then Sandy spoke in earnest, "Brian . . . you cannot tell Caroline. Never. Please."

Brian nodded.

Sandy's tone lightened, "I mean . . . maybe when I'm eighty, you can tell her then."

Brian burst into laughter just as Caroline came down the stairs. She asked, "What's so funny?"

The Tide of Deception
Chapter 12

The Gulfstream touched down at Brunswick Executive Airport five days later. Three surveillance teams drove up separately in unmarked cars from Ashburn, Virginia, Kinnaird's low-profile headquarters. They arrived a day before the jet. Each team was a man and a woman, posing as a married couple with matching wedding bands. Theirs was not a simple assignment. Sandy was not a trained operative, and she had no countersurveillance skills. But Boothbay was a small community, especially without tourists in January. The locals would notice and talk about anyone or anything that seemed out of place. Eyes-on surveillance goes best in crowded environments and urban settings, where tails can blend into crowds and disappear. The only crowds in Boothbay in January were Saturday morning at the refuse center.

The three deplaned, carrying grips and aluminum cases to the waiting Suburban. As they squared away in the Suburban with Jeff at the wheel, Jeff looked over at the interrogator. "Is this wise? A black Suburban in Boothbay in January with DoD plates? We'd be less noticeable in a crew cab with a snowblade."

The interrogator, a trim, middle-aged African American with a military bearing and crew cut, replied, "They may not even notice. FEMA and other Feds will be all over this area assessing storm damage. The locals will assume we're part of the FEMA operation."

Jeff didn't buy it.

The interrogation cohort stayed at the Hampton Inn in Bath. There wasn't much in the way of lodging in Boothbay in January. The surveillance teams stayed at separate, year-round B&Bs scattered in towns near Boothbay. The teams and interrogation cohort made sure never to be seen together. They stayed in contact via encrypted mobiles that looked like ordinary iPhones.

The interrogator asked Jeff, "Where do you want to set up the interview?"

"Probably at the hotel. I'm not sure. We can always use the secure conference room at BIW, but that might be intimidating."

"She's mobile, right?" asked the interrogator.

Jeff nodded. "I've thought about doing it at her house. We could sweep first and ask for privacy. I don't want her daughter or my brother nearby. I'll think about it. I'll call her this afternoon and set the meeting. Tomorrow should work. It's MLK Day. She has the day off, but Caroline may be out of school. So, her house is probably out."

"How long will you need?"

The interrogator shrugged. "Depends."

The interrogator looked over his shoulder into the back seat. "What do you think, Angi?"

The polygraph technician was a pert forty-something white woman with a business bob. She stared wistfully out the Suburban's tinted side window at the control tower and tarmac beyond. Jeff had neglected to tell Sandy about the polygraph.

Angi said, "I flew out of here about a million times when I was in the service, P-Three Orion patrols all up and down the coast from Canada to Washington. Congress BRACed this place in 2011, and the Navy dispersed the units.

"Brunswick was a tight base. I enjoyed my posting. Back then, we called Boothbay . . . Booze-bay. It's a beautiful town with a postcard harbor. We had a couple of favorite bars and restaurants. Lots of fried haddock and lobster rolls and the bluefin tuna in the summer . . . boy, that was good. Local fishermen land all that seafood on the east side of the harbor. So, everything is fresh . . . right off the boat."

The interrogator smiled. "How long will the flutter take?"

"We're doing lifestyle only, right? No counterintelligence?"

Jeff nodded.

"And we're expediting, right?"

"Roger," said Jeff.

"So . . . probably an hour if she's cooperative," said Angi.

"Do you have a location preference?" asked the interrogator.

Angi thought for a second, "The hotel or the secure conference room. Her home might skew the machine. Too many distractions and associations."

Jeff said, "She knows me. So, for this assignment, you're Mr. Jones and you're Ms. Cartwright . . . okay?"

Both car mates nodded.

The interrogation team checked into the hotel. Jeff had texted the day before to let Sandy know they were flying to Maine. When Sandy received his text, she texted Brian. Brian texted his brother that he wanted them to talk before Jeff talked to Sandy and before any interview. Jeff told the team he was going to see his brother in Woolwich, just a few minutes away, and drove to Brian's house. It was Sunday afternoon, but not all was peace and quiet.

Brian was the older brother. His was the status of birthright that elevated the sibling relationship, if ever so tenuous and often challenged. Brian and his brother were accomplished, smart, and opinionated. Both were single-minded about their jobs and responsibilities. Jeff had the veneer of national security, but Brian was older and not without rank in the family pecking order.

Brian greeted Jeff at his front door. "A black Suburban with tinted windows? You couldn't book something more . . . *Look at me, I'm a Fed?*

"Yeah. I told the team we'd look better in a crew cab with a snow blade."

Brian laughed. "Come on in."

Jeff took off his shoes at the door and walked through to Brian's living room. He went to the picture window, stared at the Kennebec, and said, "Hey, you're missing something."

"Yep, the storm got it. Our float is somewhere in the Gulf Stream by now."

"Any other damage?" asked Jeff.

"Nope, not here. Sandy needs to replace the pilings for her float. God knows when that'll happen. The marine construction business will boom from now on. Local contractors can't find the help to do the work, and there's more work than ever. The Feds and the state can pour Fort Knox into the post-storm rebuild, but it won't happen fast. There's nobody to do the work," said Brian.

Jeff shook his head. "We didn't get hit as badly in Portsmouth. Nothing to report."

"That's good news. Can I get you any coffee? Anything to drink?" asked Brian.

Jeff shook his head. "I'm fine, thanks."

"Do you want a sandwich?"

"No, I'm fine. They fed us on the jet."

Brian nodded.

Jeff sat on the sofa, and Brian sat in a high-back chair near the fireplace. Jeff said, "So, I guess you're concerned about Sandy and this document review?"

Brian nodded.

"Well, it boils down to this. Sandy's a qualified expert on the subject. We're going to show her classified material and get her take. It's about as simple as that, Brother."

Brian knew from experience that nothing involving Jeff's work was ever simple or as plain as it seemed. He asked, "Jeff, Sandy is an expert, and she has a certain bent about this tide event. She's mentioned it before, more than once. And Caroline has described it as a preoccupation. Sandy is unconvinced by the published analysis, and I feel she thinks there's more to the story. But, why Sandy? I'm sure you guys can pull in a dozen academics to weigh in who already have security clearance."

"Well . . . Sandy is an expert. And she's *organic*. She lives here . . . where it happened. That adds a certain . . . cachet . . . um, credibility . . . right?"

"Why does she need credibility . . . beyond her professional status?"

"Um . . . it's mostly about her professional opinion. The other thing, her cachet . . . that's how it is today. Every product, intelligence, politics, union, they all have an optical dimension. You must put a face to everything. Sandy's got the presence, that's all."

"Why does she need presence? Will she be public? Will you use her for. . . ."

Jeff interrupted, "No . . . nobody's going to use her, Brian. We'd just like her opinion and analysis."

"Jeff, you've pulled this before. And you don't call all the shots. You guys play high-stakes, and you've got a boss, just like everybody. But . . . Sandy means a lot to me. She's the real deal, and she's got Caroline to raise and support. You can't put her in any danger, Jeff. You can't put her at risk. I've supported your program so far. Solving this tide puzzle means a lot to her. I'm not sure where that comes from. Part of it's professional, but part of it seems personal. Either way, I know it means a lot. But . . . if I sense you're roping her into something and putting her at risk, I'll tell her to back out. Understand?"

"No . . . no . . . it's not like that, Brian. She'll be fine. And, congratulations, I don't know how you found her or how she's even interested in you, but . . . she's a keeper, Brother."

Brian nodded.

With the heart of their discussion over, the brothers drifted into talk about Jeff's kids and Georgia's work. Then they talked about Jeff's travels and Brian's upcoming strike vote. Eventually, they weighed in on their parents' health and mental faculties. Finally, Jeff drove off in the black Suburban back to the hotel where he called

Sandy and set the "interview" for the following day, MLK Day. Jeff picked up Sandy the next morning on Southport.

Jeff knocked on Sandy's door wearing an N-95 mask. Sandy opened the door, said good morning, and handed Jeff a baggie with the used implements of a Covid test. She said, "I'm negative."

Jeff took the baggie, removed his mask, and said, "Congratulations. Sorry for the inconvenience. Standard protocol for these things. Shall we?"

The Suburban was quieter than Brian's Jeep, and the two conversed in normal tones as they turned onto Route 1 north of Wiscasset. Brian, of course, was right. Jeff had his orders, and he was not showing his cards to Sandy or Brian. She sensed it. Something was off. Jeff was too engaging, too open, too smiley. He was hiding something.

"So, Sandy . . . I didn't mention it before because I didn't know. I mean, we've changed our protocols for expedited clearances. Um . . . you'll need to take a polygraph when we get to the hotel; it's part of the process now. It's not a big deal. The technician will ask some questions about . . . lifestyle . . . well, first she'll ask some baseline questions, yes or no stuff, to calibrate the machine. It shouldn't take long.

"After the polygraph, the interviewer will go over the SF-eighty-six. It may be repetitive, but just answer like you did on the form. He's a good guy, and he won't try to intimidate you. We just need to check some boxes for the review team, the folks at HQ who will make your application. We should be done by lunchtime. Is there any place you want to eat in Bath . . . or Wiscasset . . . on the way back?"

Jeff smiled.

Sandy stayed calm. A polygraph? That was an entirely unexpected dimension. Could she refuse to answer if questions were . . . invasive? She still had a certain right to privacy, didn't she? Was this clearance process worth it?

She asked, "Jeff, you didn't mention a polygraph? Is this special for my clearance?"

"Well, only in the sense that yours is an expedited scenario. And, honestly, we've changed our components. I mean . . . I think it's because of the recent snafus in the Air Force . . . the Air Guard kid out of Otis."

Sandy processed the excuse. "So, can I refuse to answer if questions are too personal? Something I consider . . . invasive?"

"Well, you can refuse, but it will count against your clearance. I think you'll be fine, answer truthfully. I flutter every year to maintain my clearance. It's not a big deal."

"So, you call it a *flutter?*"

"Yeah, that's the jargon."

Sandy rode all the way through Wiscasset without talking. Jeff rambled about how lucky Brian had been to find Sandy. He talked about Georgia's classroom dramas. He asked about Sandy's float and pilings. He asked if Caroline was excited about going to college. Sandy gave guarded, unengaging answers, trying not to chill the conversation or appear standoffish.

At the hotel, they entered a conference room where Jeff introduced the interrogator and polygraph technician. The polygraph was behind a partition in a corner of the room. This would come first.

It looked to Sandy like a miniature electric chair, not that she'd ever seen one. Across a blue, low-back upholstered chair were draped two corrugated rubber tubes. Over its wooden arm hung a blood pressure cuff. A jumble of cables and sensors rested on an adjoining table next to a laptop.

Angi sat at the laptop and opened a program. She said, "Okay . . . this is your standard Stoelting's CPSpro."

Angi flashed a comforting smile.

Angi explained, "The polygraph collects physiological data using electric sensors. You're a scientist, so I'm sure this is obvious."

Angi rose from the laptop and motioned Sandy to take a seat. She snugged the two elastic corrugated bands around Sandy's chest, one above her breasts and one below. She fitted the blood pressure cuff around Sandy's upper left arm and inflated it. She asked, "Is that comfortable . . . not too tight?"

Sandy nodded.

Angi attached two adhesive electrode plates to Sandy's fingers for recording perspiration. To expedite the process, Angi skipped using finger plethysmographs to monitor blood volume in the fingertips and motion sensors to monitor gross anatomy movements.

The two corrugated pneumography bands strapped tightly around Sandy's chest accentuated her breasts under her blue wool sweater. Sandy looked down at her chest, and Angi caught the glance.

Angi said, "Don't worry about the men. They won't be involved. This should take less than an hour. Okay? Ready?"

Sandy nodded.

Angi said, "Sit comfortably and answer yes or no, for now."

Sandy nodded.

Angi, "Is your name Sandra Louise Arsenault?"

Sandy nodded, "Yes."

"Do you live on Southport Island in Boothbay, Maine?"

"Yes."

"Is your name Secret Squirrel?"

Sandy chuckled, "No."

"Is your daughter named Caroline?"

"Yes."

"Are you sixty-two years old?"

"No." Tinged with indignity.

"Is your daughter seventeen years old?"

"Yes."

The questioning swerved into areas covered in the SF-86. Sandy would answer two or three questions from the government form, and Angi directed the questioning back to the baseline inquiries for the next twenty minutes.

Then Angi transitioned into areas concerning Sandy's sex life, drug use, arrest record, and criminal associations. Sandy had a large extended family, so, yes, she had relatives who had broken the law.

Angi asked, "Have you ever had sex with someone of your own sex?"

This bothered Sandy. She was heterosexual and always had been. But this seemed intrusive. She asked Angi if they could pause for clarification. Angi looked up from her laptop.

Sandy asked, "Why is this important? There's nothing criminal about same-sex relations."

Angi said, "This is part of the protocol. A same-sex relationship, or orientation, could make a person a blackmail target in some areas of this country, or . . . in some other areas of the world. It's not about the sex . . . or the judgment . . . it's about leverage. Leverage and truth.

"Are you ready to continue?"

Sandy nodded.

Angi repeated the question, "Have you ever had sex with someone of your own sex?"

Sandy answered, "No."

"Do you fantasize about having sex with someone of your own sex?"

"No."

"Was your late husband's name Noah?"

"Yes."

"Do you have a mortgage on your house on Southport?"

"Yes."

Angi asked a series of questions about bank accounts, retirement plans, credit cards, and savings. Then the questions turned to drugs and alcohol.

"Have you ever used illegal drugs?"

Sandy smoked pot with Noah in college before Caroline was born. But in Maine, pot was legal, and most towns had a recreational storefront.

"Yes. But can I explain?"

Angi held up her hand, then asked. "Did you use pot before the legalization?"

"Yes."

"Have you used it since legalization?"

"No."

"Have you ever had a dependency on drugs of any kind?""

"No."

"Do you drink alcohol?"

"Yes."

"On average, do you drink over two drinks a day?"

"No."

"Have you ever been addicted to alcohol?"

"No."

"Have you ever seen a psychiatrist or psychologist or any other mental health professional for personal issues?"

"Yes."

"Did these visits last over six months?"

"No."

"Were you prescribed drugs during this treatment?"

"No."

"Do you have a family pet?"

"No."

Angi was right, the polygraph took less than an hour. When they finished, Angi helped Sandy out of the cuff and the tubes, and disconnected the sensors.

Sandy asked, "Did I pass?"

Angi rarely explained the process and ratings to her subject, but she liked Sandy and could tell Sandy had an analytical mindset. She said, "I'll need to review the data. And, we don't say *pass or fail*. There are five categories for your responses: NDI for no deception indicated, DI for deception indicated, NO for no opinion, NSR for no significant response, and SR for significant response. Basically, you don't want a response or deception. I'll let the clearance team know your results.

"Do you need a break before we start the interview?"

Sandy said, "Maybe five minutes."

Angi said, "The bathrooms are in the hallway. But let's do this first."

Angi reached for an instrument about the size of an iPad. She said, "Place your four fingertips on the screen, right hand first."

Sandy complied.

"Now put your right thumb on."

Sandy did as asked.

"Now, let's do the left."

Sandy nodded and repeated the procedure for her lefthand.

Angi said, "Great. Thanks. No muss, no fuss. Better than ink and paper, right?" And she smiled her pleasant, disarming smile again.

"Now, one more thing," said Angi. And she reached for another device, this one a squarish box a little larger than a pack of cigarettes.

Angi said, "This is a portable iris enrollment recognition scanner, it's a little dated but it'll get the job done. I need you to look into the lens."

Sandy thought, *Well, I gave them my fingerprints. . . .*

She again did as asked.

Angi said, "That's great. Thanks. I think we're done here."

Sandy nodded, rose from her chair, then left the conference room. Angi called the interrogator.

The interrogator arrived and set two chairs across from one another at a conference table. His back would be to the window, and Sandy would squint to see him on this sunny morning in January.

When Sandy came back, Angi had left. The interrogator rose from behind his spread of papers to introduce himself.

"Ms. Arsenault, I'm David Jones."

Sandy's hands were still damp from exiting the bathroom when she reached to shake his. His shake felt like cuddling a brick. He was tall and impenetrable. Sandy didn't feel threatened, more like she was in the presence of a robot.

Mr. Jones motioned for her to have a seat.

"What we have here, Ms. Arsenault, is a printout of your SF-eighty-six. We'll be going over that, plus I have some other questions. I will record our conversation."

He pulled from his sports coat an iPhone, placed it on the table between them, and set the record function. There was another recording underway, too. The camera hidden in the ceiling's corner was so small it looked like just another pockmark in the fissured tiles. Jeff and Angi watched the interview in Jeff's hotel room as it recorded on a laptop.

"Shall we begin?" he asked without a hint of impropriety.

Sandy nodded.

The United States government's Standard Form 86 is 136 pages. It's not all questions, but it's mostly questions. It is tedious, requires documentation, and reaches back into the dawn of a person's time on earth and the humble beginnings of their careers. It took Sandy nine hours to complete over three consecutive days. She could only hold her focus for about three hours.

The interrogator slogged away at questions Sandy knew from the form. She repeated her written answers as best she could remember. About an hour into this tedium, the questions veered toward the hypothetical.

"Ms. Arsenault, would you help a foreign government with information or otherwise, should you disagree strongly with your own government?"

Sandy said, "No."

"What if your government was in the wrong, and the foreign government offered you money?"

"No."

"Why not?"

Sandy had to think. "I trust my government, and I would assume they are doing the right thing."

"What if they were doing the wrong thing? What if your government were locking up Chinese citizens without judicial review?"

"But they aren't. I don't know what to say except I would not help a foreign government for money . . . or anything. I trust the US government."

The interrogator veered back into SF-86 territory.

Twenty minutes later, he asked, "Ms. Arsenault, if you had valuable information, information that might impact our national security, and a foreign government abducted your daughter, would you hand over that information to save your daughter?"

A blush warmed her cheeks. She said, "Wait a minute. What in the world do you want me to say? I'd do anything for my daughter, but . . . this is ridiculous. I don't have an answer. This will never happen, so. . . ."

The interrogator calmly asked, "Is that your answer?"

By now, Sandy had finished playing the game and didn't care if she ever read secret government documents. She said firmly, "Yes."

The interrogator got what he wanted. He had triggered Sandy into an emotional response to gauge the depth of her commitment and containment under stress. She had boundaries.

The interview went another half hour and concluded with the interrogator thanking Sandy for her cooperation and time. He made a show of *notifying* Jeff and Angi that the interview was over. They, of course, knew because they had been watching live.

Drained and not that friendly, Sandy declined Jeff's suggestion that they have lunch in Wiscasset.

"She *is* good-looking. Attractive but not flirtatious. She's not threatening. Shouldn't rouse other women to competition. Very *girl next door*. Wholesome. She's present and poised. Not easily provoked. Smart. Perhaps stubborn? Independent? What do you think? Will she come along?"

Jeff concurred. "She's the package we need. We have what she wants. We should be able to bring her along. I'll work on it over the next couple of weeks while her clearance goes through. We may need to offer something to her employer to free her up. We can cross that bridge when we get to it."

"All right. Congratulate your cohort on their work. I've yet to see anything conclusive from the surveillance teams, but I don't expect any torpedoes.

"When do you touch down?"

"We should land IAD in twenty-five minutes."

"Jeff, come by the office. I need to talk to you about something else."

"Yes, ma'am. Will do."

Joan Samuels was a tall, fastidious white woman in her early sixties. She wore her hair to her shoulders, straight and unabashedly silver-gray. She dressed like a Nordstrom showroom mannequin, impeccably dark tones over ecru. She never failed to look like she just returned from closed-door testimony before the Senate Select Committee on Intelligence. A fixture on Capitol Hill for the past three decades, Joan's career had begun with her appointment as CIA deputy director for analysis under Bill Clinton during his second term.

Her husband, Joseph, was a retired Department of State ambassadorial appointee whose culminating posting had been Brazil. They lived in Northern Virginia's horse country on a modest estate where they stabled Irish draught-thoroughbred mixes, hosted fox hunts, and rode occasionally. Joseph lived on the farm, and Joan spent the workweek at their apartment in Ashburn. This they leased through Lockheed Martin with no public registry.

As Jeff and Angi watched Sandy's interrogation, they simultaneously uploaded the video to a secure cloud for Joan. She watched it all on an imposing curved monitor in her wood-paneled office. Sandy was clueless. That she was a subject in the shadowy world of government contractors outside of the Beltway in Northern Virginia would have spooked her. The thing was, Kinnaird had a file entry on Sandy before she and Brian had met at the Boothbay High School Career Day.

Joan and Joseph had founded Kinnaird International following the September 2001 attacks. They sold data analysis, personal profiles, psychological profiles, threat assessments, and strategic planning to the IC writ large. Jeff worked closely with the Navy, but Kinnaird was an equal opportunity for-profit vendor. The CIA was particularly interested in Kinnaird's products. The National Security Act and Updated Executive Order 12333 prohibits the CIA from exercising police or subpoena powers in America or otherwise engaging in law enforcement or internal security functions. The only exception is for the security protective officers who guard CIA facilities. But nothing prevents the agency from buying on the open market intelligence or consultation services deemed helpful to accomplishing their mission. For this and other sensitive activities, the CIA has a capacious, undisclosed black budget. Hence, the closed-door oversight meetings on Capitol Hill.

Personal profiles and pattern-of-life assessments steered much of Kinnaird's resources. These products, in the hands of government agencies, proved pivotal in the recruitment of foreign sources, contacts, and moles. Their targets were big fish working for peer-level countries, countries that played for keeps. One specialty scenario for Kinnaird was the foreign target who spent time in America or other NATO-block nations. The IC faced restrictions on domestic surveillance, and America's NATO allies were sensitive to friendly snooping on their turf. But a private company had leeway and could bend the rules, laws, and norms to fit the mission. If an operation went south, and Kinnaird was caught breaching allies' protocols or breaking into a target's apartment in Oslo, they had no direct connection to the United States government. In that regard, Kinnaird was a private investigator or bounty hunter to the government's police.

Why not the FBI? They spy domestically. They run counterintelligence operations. They arrest and prosecute through the Department of Justice. For an answer, ask the ghost of J. Edgar Hoover. The FBI, arguably America's first intelligence agency, didn't like to share. Hoover and his G-men had taken the field fourteen years before America got around to enabling the Office of Strategic Services in 1942. The CIA hadn't come along until 1947. From the standpoint of J. Edgar, any powers granted late-to-the-party spy outfits encroached on his fiefdom. The CIA and FBI, both charged with protecting America's secrets, have been cross, standoffish, distrustful, and territorial from day one.

Kinnaird shied from kinetic projects. But they employed experienced kinetic specialists, like Jeff, who were called upon for sensitive assignments. These assignments never generated paper, text, or email trails and involved only word-of-mouth communications. Specialists like Jeff rarely communicated via phone on these assignments. When they did, they used NSA-level satellite-encrypted units and spoke in code. It was one such assignment that Joan needed to discuss with Jeff.

Sandy's name, or rather, her article, was in the Kinnaird open file entitled "Anomalous Non-Attributed Tide and Wave Events, Document ONI/CG2-2008.10.28-UR." Sandy had authored a rebuttal to a paper published in 2013 by Vilibić, I., Horvath, K., and Strelec Mahović titled "Atmospheric Processes Responsible for Generation of the 2008 Boothbay Meteotsunami." She had found issue with the following, among other assertions and findings:

> *A cold front moved over the area at the time of the event, with embedded convective clouds detected by satellite and radar data and the internal gravity waves (IGWs) detected by radar and reproduced by the model at the rear of the frontal precipitation band. According to the model, the IGWs that passed over Boothbay Harbor generated strong ground air-pressure oscillations, reaching 2.5 hPa/3 min. The IGWs were ducted toward the coast without significant dissipation, propagating in a stable near-surface layer capped by an instability at approximately 3.5 km height and satisfying all conditions for their maintenance over larger areas. The intensity, speed and direction of the IGWs were favourable for generation of a meteotsunami wave along the Gulf of Maine shelf.*

Sandy did not concur that "internal gravity waves" acted in a way set forth by the authors, nor could IGWs be reliably quantified. Her reasoning was studied and credible. She questioned the triadic resonant instability, which she calculated generated two secondary wave beams, and she disputed the IGW's streaming instability relative to mean flow. Thus, Sandy's name and her rebuttal seeped into the classified file which, in 2013, belonged to ONI and Coast Guard Intelligence. Kinnaird received the open file in 2017 along with dozens of others that were placed on various agencies' back burners.

After Christmas dinner, Jeff submitted Sandy's name for cursory backgrounding. This was standard operating procedure. All Kinnaird employees and management staff followed strict guidelines regarding new or unexpected contacts with themselves or close family. That's when Sandy's name popped. And that's when the outlines of a project involving Sandy took root in Kinnaird's product planning team.

Jeff neither promoted the project nor encouraged its advancement. He knew how his brother felt about Sandy. Brian was an open book, obviously spellbound and in the grip of his attraction. But, just as Brian noted, Jeff had a boss. A successful project on the scale Kinnaird envisioned would generate millions in fees. Sentimentality was never a factor in product planning. Sandy was now part of the product.

"You did what? You took a lie detector test? With Brian's brother? Who is he anyway? And why do you need security clearance? Now they'll know everything about you. *The government* is not your friend! How can you be so smart . . . and so . . . blind? At the same time! Hmm?"

Caroline's pointed critique struck deeper than Sandy expected. But Sandy would never let Caroline see chink in her armor. She deflected.

"What are you talking about? *The government* already knows! They know about you . . . and about me. Every time you go on TikTok, Facebook, Instagram, you tell them everything. If you answer those insidious surveys . . . *How old were you when you first kissed a boy* . . . or . . . *What's your favorite color* . . . the entire world knows, and it's public knowledge forever.

"Caroline, understand this . . . are you listening?"

Caroline's perpetual eye roll showed she was listening and was tortured by it.

"Caroline, the government has certain documents I want to review. This is the only way for me to get my hands on them. They might be important to understanding a subject that I'm interested in."

"You mean the tide, right? The tide from 2008. Sixteen years ago. When I was one? Why is this important enough that you involve yourself with the government? Hmm?"

Sandy didn't have a ready response. She said, "It's science . . . that's what I do."

Caroline, exasperated and triggered, was ever the foil for her mother.

"So . . . what's Brian think about this?"

"He understands."

Caroline probed, "He understands you are obsessed with a sixteen-year-old tide mystery that everyone else has forgotten about?"

"It's not obsession. It's science. That's all. I wanted to tell you what I've done . . . tell you about the security clearance . . . because government representatives may talk with coworkers, friends . . . teachers. It's part of the clearance protocol. Someone may tell you that someone was asking about your mother. I wanted you to hear it from me. When they finish, they will grant me an interim clearance for secret materials related to the 2008 tide."

"If you pass," Caroline qualified.

"Yes," answered Sandy.

"And if you don't? They still have your information. Plus, they'll think you're suspicious. What happens after that? Hmm. . . ?"

Sandy flashed back to the question about a foreign power abducting Caroline, now a tempting proposition. She put it out of her mind. She said, "I'm not suspicious. Not now, never have been."

Caroline shook her head. Then she asked, "Can I go now?"

Sandy said, "Sure. I wanted to keep you up to date. We don't hide things from each other, right? No secrets?"

Caroline reluctantly nodded. Then said, "So . . . should I call you Secret Sandy? Or, how about . . . Agent Two-o-seven? Or. . . ."

Sandy waved her off. Caroline rose from the dinner table, reached for a handful of corn chips, then climbed the stairs to her room. When Caroline's door closed, she assumed her daughter was texting friends about the monster who was raising her.

Sandy and Caroline had no secrets. They didn't have that luxury. They were a tight team navigating life's swift currents and depending on each other for love and support. Not that they didn't maintain confidences. Confidences with friends, confidences about unimportant things. And, confidences, in Sandy's case, about her emotional quandaries. Sandy did not think Caroline should see her mother vulnerable. And Sandy was right. Caroline, for all her maturity, depended still on her mother for stability and decisive intervention.

Early in the new year, Sandy had told Caroline about her feelings for Brian. She described their relationship as "budding and progressing nicely."

To this, Caroline responded, "So, you're still making out? You haven't had sex? What's it been . . . five months?"

Sandy shook her head, composed herself, then answered, "We *are* intimate . . . and that's all you get."

Caroline chuckled. She loved besting her mother, it was such grand entertainment.

The Tide of Deception
Chapter 16

The article on Sandy's laptop seemed to rule out an unsubstantiated
premise that an earthquake had caused the Boothbay tides of 2008. She
hit the print button for a copy to add to her file. The earthquake
postulation often appeared in less credible papers. But seismic
evidence for this and anecdotal support fell short of convincing. On
October 28, 2008, the date of the Boothbay tides, United States and
European agencies had accurate seismic monitors, onshore and off.
Although Maine was not an active seismic zone, earthquakes happened
occasionally. In Maine on October 24 and 25, 2008, for instance. Both
quakes registered scarcely above microquakes, meaning they were too
minor for people to notice. In Livermore, forty-eight miles away, the
quake registered magnitude 2.6. Exeter, eighty-two miles away,
registered magnitude 2.2. Neither quake occurred near the coast. In
1926, during the anomalous tide in Bass Harbor, witnesses reported
rumbles. To Sandy, this implied a natural causation, an offshore
earthquake, and ruled out the 1926 event being comparable to
Boothbay in 2008. The article appeared in the *New York Times*, on
January 10, 1926. The headline read, *Tidal Waves Sweep Harbor in
Maine*.

> *At 12:02, the water suddenly began to drain out of the
> harbor as by some powerful suction from the sea bottom. When
> the basin had been drained almost dry, the water came rushing
> back again in a curling wave whose crest was estimated to be
> eight to twelve feet high.*
>
> *The tidal wave was preceded by two distinct rumbles,
> which led to the belief that an earthquake under the sea may
> have caused the phenomenon, although no tremors were felt.*
>
> *Immediately after the rumbles, the water began to flow
> out of the harbor. It was about half tide at the time the rapid
> outflow left the bottom exposed at points where a few seconds
> before the water had been ten feet deep.*
>
> *The upper part of the Bay was filled with cakes of ice
> which fell on the bottom of the harbor as the water receded.*
>
> *Several minutes later, the first tidal wave crashed
> ashore. It was followed by two other waves, each smaller than*

Her focus slipped as she read the article. She was tired. She drifted into perplexity. Last night was a gap night. She woke at two and didn't fall back asleep until five, then only for an hour. The clearance interview preoccupied her, but a deeper anxiety stirred. A niggling unease, a persistent association. Noah's death and the tide. Both rode the stream of her consciousness where they merged astride parallel psychic drivers. Why?

Sandy was not a trained mental health professional. She had taken only one related class at UMaine, Introduction to Modern Psychology, 101. She might only guess at what was going on. The topic remained unbroached with her psychiatrist. Indeed, her psychic drivers had yet to reach full career during her visits in the months following Noah's death. A numbness had fallen on Sandy after his death. She remained functional but always drained, disengaged. She lost her sense of humor. Her zest. Her detachment masked her emerging compulsion. In retrospect, Sandy didn't believe this association, this complexity might be something Dr. Lines could help unravel even had she broached it. She thought of him as a nice, well-meaning person, but she knew she was smarter than him. The hard science of oceanography proceeded from data and repeatable experimentation. Psychology and its practitioners she believed to operate on premise and opinion.

While she was in treatment, she had gone through the motions. She'd talked about her feelings and her profound sadness but kept to herself that which might point to resolution. She kept this association to herself for years and years without telling another soul. And now, as she reflected on the article about Bass Harbor, she slipped into self-examination. She thought, *perhaps it's the water, that's the obvious explanation. Maybe it's that simple. Water killed Noah. Tides are water in motion. Water here, water there.* The answer was obvious. She was overthinking things.

The association between Noah and the tides, she decided, was because of brain malfunction. Her brain had generated a biological network of synapsis forged in error or misalignment. She was familiar enough with brain function and electrochemical interactions to know that the brain was not a perfect organ. It made mistakes. It forged false memories and dissolved real ones. A brain manifested things that were not present. It manifested nuance and intention from thin air. Sandy concluded hers was a biological malfunction, but one she could manage and mitigate. The malfunction lived in her consciousness, generated by her over-tasked and faulty gray matter. The notion lurked like Noah's ghost, haunting but ephemeral. There, but not. Sandy could control her thoughts, her focus, and, to an extent, her emotions. She had the patience of Job for Caroline. She was able, most of the time, to humor and mentor those on her team who fell short of her expectations. Her discipline, however, waned when she was weary or overwhelmed by events. Like now.

It had been a week since her security clearance interview. In that week, the sting of the interviewer's provocations and the lie detector's intrusion had faded, superseded by anticipation of seeing new documents. Sandy couldn't wait to get her hands on material that few other scientists had reviewed or commented on. She didn't know the origins of the documents in Kinnaird's file, but she assumed they would have a national security bent. Sandy concluded that her fresh set of eyes would be like shining a lamp into a dark cellar. Even if she couldn't add anything to Jeff's analysis, she was certain that she would add to her own box of puzzle pieces about the events of October 2008.

They had argued the day Noah drowned. It was a Saturday morning, and Sandy got up earlier than normal, around five o'clock, and sequestered herself with her tide file. She made coffee and was reading a paper that concluded that underwater quakes must have triggered the Boothbay tides. But the authors of the paper provided scant seismic or other evidence for their claim. She was jotting notes for a rebuttal when Noah shuffled into the kitchen, where Sandy had spread her papers on the table. She said, "Good morning," without looking up.

Noah poured a cup of coffee, and said, "This would be a great day to go fishing, don't you think? Bucky told me the stripers are running at Ram Island. If we leave now, we can hit 'em on a going tide. How 'bout it?"

Sandy looked up from the article and her notepad. She said, "I'm into this review, and I need to stay here and make notes while the data is fresh in my mind."

His delivery sharper than intended, Noah said, "You're always working. You're always involved in research for that mystery tide or something else. I wish you would wake up. It's Saturday! This is the weekend. I'll rack Caroline, make her a peanut butter and jelly sandwich, and she can sleep on the boat. Get your nose out of the books and on to the boat. Let's go catch dinner." He clapped his hands twice.

Sandy was much better at argumentation than Noah. She said, "What you do, Noah, your graphic art, is important. It's a good income, and it's something you like to do, and you're good at it. I get that. But the things that *I* must do to stay on top of my professional credibility are things that require more than my entertainment on the weekends."

And with that comment, Sandy provoked Noah, who heard it as belittlement of his profession and him as a man. He reacted badly. He reacted defensively. He reacted loudly. Then he huffed to the boat by himself without another word. Boating in Maine should never be a solo experience. There are too many things to go wrong, too many things that can upset a peaceful day on the water. Sandy knew she'd hurt Noah's feelings with her comparison of their livelihoods. It was a stupid argument. The couple loved each other. They had a wonderful daughter and a glorious life together. But the error of a single moment drove them to their corners. It was not a mature moment for either of them.

Sandy's guilt stole away in a crevasse of her consciousness, emerging unprompted like a hissing ferret. On good days, she willed the beast back into its den. But she would never forget that morning and their squabble. Instead, she busied her mind on a subject that would wrap her thoughts around a mystery that might be indeterminable, perhaps unsolvable. Noah's death and her obsession with the 2008 tide were redirection or self-deflection from the guilt of Noah's misfortune and her insensitivity. Had she permitted Dr. Lines enough time, they might have figured it out. And had they identified the complex, Dr. Lines might have said, "Noah decided to go to the boat. Noah decided to go fishing alone. Noah decided to enter the water. You . . . Sandy Arsenault, made none of those decisions. Your guilt is remembrance. You still miss him, and you will miss him for a very long time. The longing, the emptiness you will live with and adjust your life. You are strong and smart, and you will adjust and do all that you need to do. But Sandy, listen and brand this to your soul . . . you did not kill Noah."

Kinetic missions involve physical force or the distinct possibility of it. An assassination is a kinetic mission. Car bombing an assassination target is an example of "going loud," on a kinetic mission. Gunshots also qualify as going loud. Kinnaird shied from kinetic missions for many reasons, primarily criminal exposure. Every country frowns upon killing someone, blowing up their car, or firebombing their apartment to send a message. Kinnaird was much more comfortable in a surveillance role, developing lifestyle profiles or uncovering psychological predilections and sexual peccadilloes. This they accomplished through good old private investigative gumshoe detecting, invasion of privacy, snooping, querying data vendors, and digital incision. The bounty hunter side of the market qualified as high risk, high reward.

A kinetic transaction begins when the Department of Defense or other US government agency confirms a high-value target on an elimination list. Then, with a wink and a nod and never in writing, this contact sets in motion a private sector solution to a government problem. These targets are bad people, and the government has resources to deal with them. Preferred methods might include special forces like Jeff, or drones, or black op IC assets like CIA's Ground Branch. But plausible deniability has a fair market value. These HVTs typically resided overseas in non-allied countries. But things can get murky, as Joan Samuels discussed with Jeff.

Good-looking, well-fed, and a tall white guy, Jeff might not be the best fit for a country like, say, North Korea. While he had some foreign language skills, Urdu and Arabic, those neither gave him entry nor helped him blend into North Korea. But, if the target landed on American soil, circumstances improved. The same would apply to America's NATO allies. But allies were reactive to American covert kinetic action on their soil.

Joan laid out the scenario like this.

The target was Russian by birth and pivotal in the North Korean top secret environmental modification program. The public was not aware of the target's connection to the Reconnaissance General Bureau (RGB) and its Department of Environmental Security. In public, the target presented as a scientist and lecturer who published peer-reviewed papers on climate change. She was in her forties, striking, and a devout syncretic Chondogyo. Kinnaird's mission, as developed by the product planning team, was to turn the target and enlist her as a deep penetration mole. The fallback was defection to a NATO country, preferably the United States. Failing either of these outcomes, the target was to be eliminated.

A rather lavish scenario, but Kinnaird often delved into scrambled plots and the intrigue generated by convulsing politics and competing nations. Hardened to these vagaries and randomness, the product planning team proceeded point by point and named this product Brizo.

Vera Berg was a scientist, born on Sakhalin Island and raised in Vladivostok on Golden Horn Bay in the Sea of Japan. The same age as Sandy and divorced with a teenage son, Berg enjoyed well-earned academic notoriety. In Vladivostok, she had studied at the Far Eastern National University, earning her bachelor's and master's degrees from the Institute of the World Ocean. The Far Eastern Branch of the Russian Academy of Sciences published her research. Instead of studying for an advanced degree in Russia, she'd traveled to America. There, she earned her PhD and conducted postdoctoral research at the University of Washington in Seattle.

Vera was the daughter of a Russian and an ethnic Korean. She stood tall and trim and wore her brunette hair straight, parted in the middle, tucked under her pronounced jawline. She had deep-set hazel eyes and moved with rectitude and poise. Her skin was pallid and flawless. She came across as confident and smart, but standoffish. She could have landed a lucrative professional career in the States or any Western country. Many blue-chip businesses, energy companies, shipping conglomerates, and aqua farming operations needed oceanographers. She would have been a welcome addition to the US National Oceanic and Atmospheric Administration. But after seven years in America, she returned to the Russian Far East where North Korea had activated her.

But *why* and *how*? These questions Kinnaird needed to answer pre-approach. They had already decided on the *where* and *who*.

Vera specialized in geological oceanography, the study of the structure, creation, evolution, and history of the sea floor. She knew tides. At the Korea Institute of Ocean Science and Technology in Busan, South Korea, she conducted research and transferred all relevant data and findings to the North Korean RGB. The RGB used the data to program computer models, build tank mockups, and manufacture prototypes for creating or directing natural phenomena against enemy installations. The North's Department of Environmental Security had a mandate as bold as any Soviet Cold War wish list. They sought to weaponize typhoons, tidal waves, monsoons, tornados, and earthquakes. They were especially interested in cloud seeding and drought mitigation since climate change had not been kind to the Hermit Kingdom. North Korea had long struggled to produce enough food for its twenty-six million citizens. Estimates vary, but according to the United Nations, from 2019 to 2022, 41 percent of the population was undernourished. Over one-fifth of its children suffered impaired growth because of malnutrition. In 2023, the military leadership, a privileged class in Pyongyang and the political base of the regime, received no food rations for their families for months. The twin scourges of droughts and floods ravaged the country for decades. The North Korean political leadership envisioned the day when they could stop the rain in a flood and make it rain in a drought. And even grander, they envisioned wielding withering environmental weapons against the South and their American protectors. A news wary public assumed North Korea tested nuclear weapons to launch them on rockets at perceived enemies. True enough, but the energy of a nuke also has application for weaponizing environmental phenomena. A nuke positioned on the right fault line, near a precarious shelf, in the right seabed . . . then boom! As the theory goes, now you have a tidal wave or a rogue tide. This vast kinetic energy, if aimed and focused on an enemy, results in minimal fallout to hinder your advancing ground troops. And ground troops were plentiful in the North, over two million active and reserve. The Korean People's Army constituted the fourth largest on the planet. So, yes, the North Korean political leadership might have been crazy, but crazy can do a lot of damage if left to its own paranoia and obsession.

Vera was not crazy, quite the opposite. Her commitment to help the North sprung from deep maternal influence. Childhood conditioning had forged her allegiance, a bond requiring little self-examination. It was baked in. Vera's mother, Sun-ja, the primal force in her upbringing, adhered staunchly to Chondogyo.

Chongjin, North Korea, the home of Vera's ancestors, is one hundred miles southwest of Vladivostok, Russia. In the years following World War II, thousands of Koreans flowed to Russia's Kamchatka Peninsula as migrant workers. Many, like Sun-ja's father, worked in the state-owned fisheries on Sakhalin. And many, like him, stayed behind and refused repatriation orders. It's estimated that half a million Koryoin, ethnic Koreans, now call post-Soviet Russia home. Vera was born in Russia, and since her father was a Russian citizen, she too became a citizen. Her father was someone she never knew. He died aboard the *Dalniy Vostok*, a massive factory fishing and freezing trawler, in 1985, a year after Vera was born. His was an industrial accident aboard a ship known for unsafe practices. An untethered crane cable struck him, pitching him overboard with two other workers. The *Dalniy Vostok* would go to the bottom of the Sea of Okhotsk in 2015. An investigation found the vessel, "loaded to the eyeballs" with an unmanageable 1,150 tons of pollock, had struck an ice shelf. The impact pierced the engine room, which filled with rushing water in seconds. The *Dalniy Vostok* went down in fifteen minutes, the icy sea swallowing fifty-four illegal, underpaid foreign workers. She sank so fast that the doomed captain never sent an SOS.

With the death of her husband, Sun-ja moved with her daughter from Sakhalin Island to Vladivostok. Vladivostok had Korean schools and long-established Korean neighborhoods. Vera's mother was without a skilled profession. She found work as a seamstress in a dingy, dust-plagued factory that allowed her to bring her daughter with her to work. These were the waning days of Soviet childcare. Ethnic Koreans looked after Vera and instructed their young wards in Marxism. Vera attended one of the three Korean primary schools in Vladivostok. By 1991, with the disintegration of the Soviet Union, Vera had shown herself to be an exceptional student.

As the Soviet Union crumbled, one institution survived. As had always been the case for the Russian people, a state security establishment shadowed their lives and spied on foreigners. The KGB changed during the transition from communist rule, but its raison d'être did not.

Dating back to the 1940s, the Soviet secret police, the NKGB in those days, ran an operation called Maki-Mirage. Broadly speaking, this operation sought to infiltrate ethnic minorities back to their home countries to serve as spies and monitors. They sent 1,200 Koreans back during Japanese occupation. After World War II, the operation lived on in the stone-encased bureaucracy of Soviet intelligence. By the 1980s, the operation's name had changed, but the operational need remained. A KGB officer, claiming to be a *friend* of Sun-ja's husband, a classmate in Vladivostok, recruited Sun-ja. His was an attractive proposition. Sun-ja would receive a stipend and the KGB would see to Vera's advanced education. Otherwise, the KGB implied Sun-ja would face forced repatriation, leaving Vera, a Russian citizen, alone in Vladivostok.

Sun-ja repatriated to Chongjin bringing Vera. There they lived and worked for the next two years. Vera studied and her mother worked. Vera did not know what her mother did. She was told that the move to Korea was so Vera could learn her heritage and venerate her ancestors. Meanwhile, Sun-ja reported dutifully to the KGB and received a stipend deposited in a Vladivostok bank.

Sun-ja worked as a secretary at the Kimchaek Iron & Steel complex, the largest steel production center in North Korea. Sun-ja was literate and bilingual, and the KGB placed her inside the headquarters building.

On a chilly morning in November 1993, Vera and all her classmates from the North Korea Chongjin School, marched to the banks of the Suseong Stream. Thousands gathered there, and Vera saw her mother in a group of office employees. Three managers from the steel mill, dressed in suits and ties and prodded at the barrel of military rifles, formed a line on the banks of the stream. Vera strained to hear the pronouncements from a government official. Then, upon command, the soldiers took aim, and shot all three managers. Then they marched away. Vera later learned that their crime was using the company's secure, transnational telephone for personal calls. Speaking to foreigners was against the law, and punishable by death. Justice was served, North Korean style.

Vera and Sun-ja returned to Vladivostok two months later at the end of Sun-ja's posting. The thing was, the North Korea GSD, General Staff Department of the Korean People's Army, predecessor of the RGB, suspected Sun-ja from day one. She was on their list, under surveillance, then taken into custody for ten days when Vera was eleven years old. Vera remembered that time because she stayed with her aunt and worried about her mother's safety. Her aunt would say nothing about what was happening. The GSD interrogated and abused Sun-ja. When mother and daughter reunited, Sun-ja had changed. Where life had danced in her eyes before, now despair lolled. Unknown to her young daughter, Sun-ja had agreed to return to Russia and spy for North Korea. The GSD had given her an option: turn or die. Her death would have orphaned Vera, Sun-ja's only link to her deified ancestors. Nor was this a conflict for Sun-ja. She had little allegiance to Russia and had always thought of herself as Korean. She had accepted the KGB's recruitment as a spy primarily because of the income and the agency's pledge to finance her daughter's education. From the day the GSD released her from custody until she returned to Russia, she gave her Russian handler only GSD-approved misinformation.

When they returned to Russia, Sun-ja worked as a secretary in the offices of the Vladivostok Sea Trade Port. In the late 1950s, the Soviets had closed Vladivostok Port to foreign traffic when it became the home base of their Pacific Naval Fleet. In 1991, the port reopened to foreign commercial traffic. Sun-ja had access to fleet approach data listing all ships and cargo, off-loading and loading, along with railroad arrival and departure schedules.

Meat-packing industries, ship repair operations, and fish processing plants surrounded the port. Sun-ja spent her lunch breaks and hours after work walking the perimeter of the port through a pall of diesel fumes, gritty coal smoke, and industrial pollutants. She recorded ships coming and going and reported on the activity in factories and shops.

Vera was thirteen when she and Sun-ja returned to Russia. Her fondest memories of time with Sun-ja were rare Sunday afternoons when mother and daughter would dress smartly, pack a lunch, and board a ferry in Golden Horn Bay. Chondogyo venerates Cheon. It means Sky or Heaven or, more divinely, Oneness. Thus, bird life represented to Sun-ja a most reverend form. She thought of birds as earthly citizens of heaven. Standing at the rail on the ferry's open deck, Sun-ja would point out seabirds. She could identify them all. Mother and daughter laughed and attributed make-believe conversations to barking spotted seals lounging at low tide on the Tokarevskaya Koshka sandbar. When the ferry docked, Sun-ja would treat Vera to ice cream or a visit to a confectioner. Their time together burned into Vera's soul, and she prized it as life itself.

But Sun-ja was not well, and the foul air of the port didn't help. With her return from Chongjin, she began a long decline. When Vera was sixteen, her mother died of an acute respiratory infection. It was then that the GSD approached Vera.

Vera was alone. She was a stellar student with another year to complete her upper secondary school certification. She knew of the Russian promise to see her through college and graduate studies. Her mother, in her last days, told her about her involvement with the KGB and GSD. In fact, Sun-ja, upon her return to Russia, remained a KGB informant while she was spying for the GSD. Hers was a complicated life whose stress diminished her immune response and promoted her illness. Sun-ja offered Vera this terminal wisdom: "You, my lovely daughter, are Korean, as were your ancestors. Korea is your destiny."

Vera knew little about espionage when her mother died. She knew only that she should keep her mouth shut and make no commitments. This worked until she contacted the *friend* of her father, the man who had recruited Sun-ja. Vera needed to discuss with him her approaching attendance at Far Eastern National University.

She sat first in the booth. Then he forced her over and sat next to her. Vera winced at his foul body and the alcohol on his breath. Then he propositioned her for sex and moved his hand under the table, onto her thigh and up to her crotch. School children in North Korea learn Gjogsul. Vera learned in Chongjin. While not a master, she knew enough to defend herself. From rote memory, she made a three-knuckle fist and struck as hard as she could the soft tissue below his Adam's apple. He toppled out of the booth onto the restaurant's floor, choking and gasping for breath. And with her martial declination, the KGB reneged. Her mother was dead, and so was the KGB's commitment to Vera's education and well-being.

The Russian KGB was corrupt and shortsighted. It was now a criminal enterprise incapable of foresight or fidelity. The Koreans, however, played the long game.

"Jeff said he wants to talk to me about my clearance. Did he say anything to you?" Sandy prodded Brian.

"I haven't talked to him since your interview. What'd he say? Exactly?"

He said, "The clearance is progressing, and he didn't foresee any snags. He didn't mention my modeling. And he said we need to talk about *specifics*. He wants to do that in person, next week, on Southport.

"And Brian, I asked if you should be there. He said, 'No. There is no reason for you to be involved.' His 'no' was more of a command than a suggestion."

"Sandy, I'm going to tell you something because I care for you. I mean . . . you mean a lot to me. Hell . . . I'll just say it . . . I'm in love with you . . . I love you."

Sandy's eyes widened. She smiled, and she nodded.

"Here's the deal. Jeff's work is . . . baffling. He operates in a different world than you and me. In his world, things get a little . . . knotty . . . spooky . . . thorny. He's not a liar, but sometimes he simply can't tell you the story. His work requires him to . . . um . . . manipulate situations to his advantage. He does this for the right cause. He's playing on the right team . . . national security, and all that, but . . . just watch yourself. Don't get sucked into something you can't pull back from. That's my take."

"So, your brother may try to rope me into something . . . what . . . something illegal?"

"No. Not illegal, just more than you might expect.

"You want to review the documents and data in the file, right?" Sandy nodded.

"Then just make sure that's where you're headed."

"You mean the security clearance?"

"Well, the security clearance may be the tip of the iceberg. Jeff is probably under orders, need-to-know protocol, and all that. He probably can't talk about the nine-tenths of the iceberg under the surface. He works for an outfit that supports the government's IC heavy hitters. The tide file may be important, but that could be a way to get you involved in something . . . bigger . . . something . . . not public . . . clandestine.

"Jeff's my brother, and I wish him well. He's good at what he does. He always has been. He made O-three in just over three years in the Seals."

Sandy's eyes quizzed Brian.

"O-three is like a lieutenant, an officer in charge of a platoon. That was fast, even in Afghanistan. Kinnaird scooped him up and pays him well. But what he does is . . . tricky. You don't want to become part of the trick. Right?"

Brian delivered his advice with a hint of annoyance and sibling competition. His concern for Sandy was paramount, she could tell. But Brian didn't trust Jeff. Sandy registered Brian's nuance. She said, "Okay, you're scaring me. All I want is to review the file he says they have on a subject I am interested in. I'll give him my take on their data, then we're done."

Brian nodded.

"Brian, exactly what is it that Jeff does?"

"If you were anybody else, I'd stonewall you. But you're not. You're damn near family and you and Caroline mean a lot to me. And to be honest, I don't know the details of what Jeff does. A lot of it . . . everything . . . is secret and classified and involves the government."

Sandy glowed at Brian's pronouncement of *love* and her being *near family*.

"So . . . he's CIA?"

"Nope. Private sector, but in the IC orbit. Kinnaird is sort of like . . . IC for hire."

"So . . . does he have the file, the anomalous tide file?" asked Sandy.

"Oh, I'm sure he does. I've never asked, but dad told me he's cleared all the way to SCI."

Another puzzled pout.

Brian explained, "Um . . . that's *sensitive compartmented information,* national security level stuff."

"So, you're telling me to be careful and that you love me and that I'm nearly family? Should I write this down?" Sandy chided.

Brian, sheepish but undeterred, "I'm just trying to help."

"Well, Brian, we could not have picked a more romantic venue for our first declaration of love. So . . . I love you, too."

Brian smiled.

Brian and Sandy sat on a folded sleeping bag on the top row of wooden bleachers at the Topsham Fair Grounds. They drank coffee from Brian's dented metal thermos. They were in cheap seats because Brian had underestimated public interest in equine skijoring. Horses racing on the snow, pulling ski jumpers, had a faithful following in Midcoast Maine.

The day was fair and chilly. They dressed for the weather, bundled in layers. They sat on the home stretch of a snow-covered half mile oval racetrack. Four shoulder-high, packed snow jumps rose both right and left off the track's center line. Three mogul bumps completed the course. Breakaway gates—red for right, and blue for left—marked the skier's route. A skijoring team is a rider, a horse, and a skier. The horse pulls the skier tethered by a fifty-foot rope secured to the rear of the saddle. The quickest time wins. The horses are fast. They run flat out, nostrils flaring, their steamy breath exhausting like an ancient locomotive. Fitted with special shoes that prevent the snow from packing, they are speed demons. Galloping hoofs fling chunks of snow and ice as the skier crisscrosses behind, lining up alternating jumps. Skijoring is exciting. And, thanks to Norwegians, it was almost an Olympic sport, as Sandy later learned.

In Topsham, they raced in four classes: Pro, Novice, Junior, and Mini Horse. With the announcement of class winners, each team took a parade lap at a canter, with the skier shouldering an American flag.

On the way back to Brian's house, Sandy asked about the union's contract negotiations. She knew Brian had a lot on his mind with electing a bargaining committee, scheduling training, and probing the company to show their hand. The contract expired on July 31. He said, "We'll face some headwinds. The company always leads with concessionary proposals. They'll want to contract our work and maybe try to increase health care copays or cut benefits. They'll propose a flat wage scale and want us to work outside of our JDs. It's all murky right now. I don't think local management has their marching orders.

"JDs? Job descriptions?" asked Sandy.

Brian nodded. "I'm trying to schedule training for mid-April. Hey, come with me."

Sandy cocked her head.

"Our training center is on Chesapeake Bay at the mouth of the Patuxent River in Southern Maryland. It's a great getaway. It used to be a resort. I'll be busy during the day, and probably some evenings.

I'll be in class and planning groups. There's golf and tennis and swimming and hiking. The food is wonderful, and endless. You'd love it. Plenty of Wi-Fi. You can take the shuttle to IAMAW Headquarters or to DC. Everything will be free, except for your flight. We'll fly into BWI, and they'll pick us up. It's about an hour to the center. Maryland will be beautiful, spring in full bloom, and the stripers will be running. Stripers are called rockfish on the Chesapeake. We can get you on a charter boat. Those local captains haul fish like a trawler. Big ones." Brian released the steering wheel and held his arms wide.

Sandy was curious, "In April?"

Brian nodded.

"When you get a firm date, we can talk then,"

For an instant, Sandy flashed back to Noah's insistence that they go fishing for stripers the day he died. Then she bounced back into the moment from transitory remembrance.

Brian said, "We could be on strike during the convention in September in Toronto. That would be a double headache. Oh, and you're welcome to come along for the convention, too. That'll take a couple of weeks. I'm on the international union's nominating committee. Either way, if you want to come along for training or the convention, you don't have to stay for my full schedule. You can come and go as you like. Oh, hey, bring Caroline. She'd love Toronto. Major fashion statements on every corner."

Sandy warmed inside when Brian offered to include Caroline. She asked, "So you think there will be a strike?"

"I think BIW will want to bargain. I don't think they want a strike. They've got government contracts up the wazoo. Plenty of work. We're already behind. Our biggest problem is finding qualified employees. I don't think they'll want a strike. General Dynamics made forty-two billion last year. The union will audit their books if they plead poverty. They ain't hurting."

Sandy marveled at Brian's casual description of his responsibilities. His was a world unknown to her. She admired his steadfastness and confidence in the face of challenges she could only estimate. His concern for her and Caroline was sincere. Of that she was certain, and he had plenty of other things to worry about. It was a big deal for him to tell her he loved her, much more than a relationship milepost. The same was true for her. But her world was on paper or in a lab or on a research vessel. Brian's world was in-your-face reality. His world turned on people's livelihoods and their families' well-being. Thousands of them. It was a world of immediate consequence. A world of vulnerable souls at the whims of an employer who was, itself, at the whims of politics and the economy. The union was there to even the score. And Brian was in charge. The way he approached his responsibilities and navigated politics intrigued Sandy. On that level, Brian was a mystery. A good-looking mystery. She gazed across the Jeep at him, questions lurking behind a smile. She felt attracted, excited, and aroused. Her feelings were physical, long-lost, but returned in the moment. She liked it. It made her smile and her eyes dance.

She teased him. "Brian, when we get to your house, we'll need further clarification of our earlier exchange."

Brian said, "What?"

"Brian, I think we need to define *love* in a more . . . *concrete* fashion. Hmm?"

Brian grinned.

"Your clearance is on track. I expect VRO will be back with approval next week."

Sandy asked, "VRO?"

"Yeah, that's DoD's Vetting Risk Operations. They'll pass along your approval to DISS."

Sandy offered an exasperated sigh.

"Oh, DISS is Defense Information System for Security. Sorry, lost in the weeds."

"Jeff, why is the Department of Defense involved?"

"DoD issues the clearance. Kinnaird, my employer, is a cleared contractor." Jeff gestured air quotes. "Kinnaird sponsored your application. The government issues clearance. We . . . Kinnaird . . . operate with certain internal quality control procedures and security protocols as a matter of corporate policy. But we don't issue clearance. You don't need to worry about Kinnaird protocols. Not now.

"Sorry, back in the weeds."

Sandy stifled a Caroline eye roll.

Jeff picked up on Sandy's hesitancy. He backpedaled before broaching the real reason for his visit. "Any word on your float? You need new pilings, right?"

Sandy recognized the soft approach. She played along. "We're on a list. It will take months. The marine construction crews in Boothbay are in high demand. Lots of work."

Jeff nodded, and a moment of silence passed.

The two sat in Sandy's living room, facing one another on parallel sofas with a coffee table between them. It was nine o'clock in the morning. Sandy planned to go to Bigelow for an afternoon team report since Jeff told her their meeting should only take an hour.

Jeff launched into his real reason for the visit. "Sandy, have you heard of Vera Berg? She's a Russian oceanographer, PhD, studied at the University of Washington?"

Sandy took a moment. Why would Jeff be interested in Berg? Berg was outside his wheelhouse. She answered guardedly, "She's well-known. I've read her work on ocean floor geology. She's at the Korea Institute of Ocean Science and Technology. Why do you ask?"

"You're right. She's a senior scientist at the institute in Busan.

She's ethnically Korean. She's coming to the States. She has a six-month fellowship at the University of New Hampshire, lecturing in their Earth Sciences Department. She'll focus on ocean basin modeling."

"Jeff, how did you come about this information?"

"Um . . . we learn things . . . in advance. They haven't announced her fellowship yet. She will speak at the Camden Conference on Global Climate Change, and that's when they will announce her appointment.

"The Camden Conference? Three weeks away?"

"Yep. She'll be there."

Now Sandy's wheels turned. Vera Berg was a star in the tidal anomaly firmament. Sandy was easy to read, and Jeff saw she had taken the bait.

Jeff asked, "Would you like to meet her? I think we can arrange it."

Sandy flashed on the adage, *If it's too good to be true, it probably isn't*. She said, "Jeff, how is it you can *arrange* this meeting? With all respect, you're not a scientist. You are not involved in oceanography."

Sandy may have taken the bait, but she would not be duped.

Jeff said, "We . . . Kinnaird . . . have connections. I thought you might like to meet her. You and she are the same generation of scientists. Your interest overlap, and she might help in understanding tide oddities or anomalies or whatever."

Sandy remained skeptical.

Jeff went on, "Her name popped when our research folks updated the tide file. I had them go through the file for publication updates, response papers, PAI, and new open-source material . . . anything that might help your review."

Sandy assessed the explanation. It was plausible. But still . . .

She asked, "PAI?"

"Publicly available information."

Sandy nodded.

After a moment, she relented, "Jeff, I'd love to meet her. What do you have in mind?"

"I'll work on it. She's headed this way for the conference, so that might work best. I'll check into it. Could you come to the conference if that's the plan?"

Sandy thought about this. The conference was a three-day

affair, Friday through Sunday. There was a registration fee. She'd need to ask for time off work, ask for reimbursement, and offer a convincing work-related reason for her interest in the conference.

The Camden Conference was not a scientific gathering. Sandy knew it for its internationalist bent and broad topics. It featured notable speakers and focused on global politics. The conference played to the retired IC of Midcoast Maine, primarily the Camden crowd. It was a fascinating spectacle of ideas and personalities, but it wasn't a scientific necessity.

Sandy said, "I'll get back to you, Jeff. We don't consider the Camden Conference part of our extracurricular activities."

Jeff said, "Just let me know. I might help with that, too. And don't ask to attend until they announce her presentation to the public. Don't tell anybody she's booked. I'll text a link when the information goes public."

"Anybody? Even Brian?"

"No. Not even Brian."

Sandy was beyond curious . . . perhaps perplexed, quizzical, even bedeviled. Kinnaird commanded myriad tendrils, connections, and resources. It operated with entitlement. There was a world of magical strings and potent levers. What the hell was Jeff into? And . . . what the hell was *she* doing? Brian's caution looped in her thoughts. Jeff wanted her to lie to Brian by omission. That didn't feel right. Jeff was walling her off from her world. Still, Berg was renowned, a leading mind in her field. A collegial relationship for the coming months could prove productive. What harm could come from meeting her?

The Tide of Deception
Chapter 20

Vera wheeled the rain off her umbrella, retrieved her mail in the lobby, and took the elevator to her apartment. She put her key in her lock and checked the paint fleck she had placed between the door and the jam. It was still there. She entered her apartment and set her mail on the coffee table, removed her raincoat and hung it on a hook inside the coat closet door. The clock above the sink read 7:00 p.m. She placed her takeaway order from Myeongryun Jinsa Ribs on her kitchen counter. She was hungry but equally interested in a letter she had just received.

Vera's modest two-bedroom apartment on the twelfth floor of a modern high-rise in the Yeongdo District of Busan was housing North Koreans could only dream of. She had reliable electricity, day and night, and she turned on a floor lamp beside her leather sofa. Vera was not rich, but she was a successful professional in the world's thirteenth ranked economy. She lived comfortably. By comparison, North Korea's centrally planned economy ranked 215th. She had lived in Busan for eleven years. Early in her stay, Western amenities had disturbed her, as did the decadent sexualization of women and, even worse, their willing acceptance. But slowly, she had adapted. An attractive woman, she drew attention. So, she dressed conservatively, even dowdily. But her attempt to downplay her sexual presence hid only so much. She deflected male advances weekly. She turned away her would-be suitors and dutifully reported her contacts to the RGB. These come-ons and rejections made her feel in command. She liked that feeling, and over the years, she liberalized her wardrobe. And the come-ons kept coming. It was but a gratifying game, and her life outside the institute languished. She ran religiously and attended a weekly Gjogsul class. On Sundays, in nice weather, she gathered her binoculars and enjoyed a reflective hike on the Igidae Coastal Trail. She spent hours spotting wildlife and birds, and, occasionally, she smiled. But her abbreviated life held no men, few friends, the institute, and constant oversight by the RGB.

Over the years, elements of South Korean culture molded her life. She no longer scoffed at office gossip about boyfriends, husbands, other women, children, and pets. South Koreans kept pets! They had food enough that they could feed animals they did not plan to eat!

Now she lightly joined in the gossip and small talk. And, truth be told, she enjoyed sharing opinions on the soap operas and cable dramas that comprised much of the institute's chatter. When her department celebrated the week's end on Friday afternoon, Vera often joined them. They went to a small place near the institute, and Vera would have one drink. As soon as her coworkers became loud, and their laughter became louder, she'd make an excuse to leave. She was not a party girl.

Eclectic might charitably describe Vera's fellow scientists. They perceived Vera as smart, self-contained, antisocial, and somebody you could bring a scientific problem to and get a reliable answer. She fit within suitable, scientist appropriate, social parameters. But still they rumored. Early in her tenure, her coworkers rumored about her cloistered life. She's always gotten by on her looks. That's why she doesn't have a personality. Or, she has an undisclosed career as a model and used to be an actress under a stage name. That's who she was in Busan, rumored about, but acceptable. A good-looking, intelligent loner. She was Russian, so that tempered talk about her working for the North. Vera knew people talked, and she didn't want to draw suspicion. So, she adjusted her activities and interactions to fit their comfort zone.

RGB handlers warned her about infatuation with the West. And any warning coming from the RGB was a death threat. She spoke carefully with them in their rare face-to-face meetings. She assumed they watched her for signs of compromise. She wondered how closely the RGB would monitor her when she traveled to the States.

Vera was in demand. Several US institutes and universities had invited her to be a lecturer or visiting professor. After informing the RGB of these invitations, they ordered her to accept the offer from the University of New Hampshire. From her post in the Earth Sciences Department, she could use university resources to detail the northeastern ocean floor. The seabeds near Bath Iron Works, Portsmouth Naval Shipyard, and the Naval Submarine Base New London, Connecticut, held military potential.

These seabeds and installations were critically important to US defense production, training, and deployment. BIW built and upgraded the venerable Arleigh Burke-class destroyers, the backbone of the US Navy's surface fleet. BIW had also built three of the world's most advanced surface warships, the Zumwalt-class destroyers. Portsmouth Naval Shipyard overhauled and modernized the US Navy's nuclear-powered attack submarines specializing in the Los Angeles and Virginia-class vessels. And Naval Submarine Base New London is the premier underwater warfare center on the East Coast. Here the Navy trains officers and submarine crews. Just two miles down the Thames River, only a mile from the open Atlantic, sprawls General Dynamics' Electric Boat works. Electric Boat builds the most advanced subs in the American fleet. These subs house the missiles, nuclear and non, that would obliterate North Korea if they attacked the South. Or brazenly attacked America.

Vera's former husband and teenage son complicated her trip to the States. Vera and Thomas had met in Seattle at the university where they were both studying for advanced degrees. There they dated and married and remained married for five years. Vera gave birth to their son, Richard, in the second year. When she and Thomas divorced, Richard stayed with his father, and months later, Vera returned to Vladivostok.

Her marriage had both pleased and plagued her. Doubt and uncertainty cohabitated with love and attachment during her years with Thomas. She loved Thomas. He was an energetic American of Korean descent, and Vera believed their marriage honored her mother's wishes and Vera's destiny. Thus, her Korean son and husband. In these years of happiness and concealed concern, her studies preoccupied her, while the social life of Seattle opened her eyes. The lights rose around her as the drab sameness of Vladivostok and North Korea faded. Her world expanded and richened, and she subsumed previous obligations. Then, without warning, the dread of her undisclosed commitment to the RGB would overtake her thoughts. For days, she would wall herself off and explain her mood away as a critical juncture in her studies or research. She rode an emotional roller coaster but kept it to herself, and she never told Thomas.

The RGB upheld their end of the bargain, paying for her housing and education through a trust established in her name as executor of her mother's estate. The RGB lurked in her future, but she was young, in love, and distracted by new experiences. Even the brightest adults, the scholastically accomplished, faulted to youthful impulse. She didn't know she would work in Busan and have a comfortable life among fellow countrymen. She did not know how the RGB planned to use her. She assumed they would leverage her education, but this she only guessed at. The uncertain times played against Thomas, an immediate tangible anchor in her young life. She accepted his proposal for marriage and found rare happiness.

Vera and her son had a long-distance relationship. Vera called and Skyped with him on his birthday and major American holidays. She was proud of how good-looking and accomplished Richard had grown. He was smart, with an engineering bent like his father. Richard was tall, like Vera, and pitched on his high school baseball team. Vera didn't know what Richard meant by *being scouted*, but it pleased him. From what Vera sussed, Richard lived a predictably American childhood.

Thomas had remarried, and Richard's stepmother fit warmly into his life. He now had two stepsiblings. His new family was too large and too well established for Vera to compete. And she didn't try. She monitored her son and occasionally imparted wisdom or advice, but she never invaded his family's structure or contradicted his parents. Her trip to the States meant Vera would see her son, their first meeting in fourteen years.

With her divorce and her return to Russia, there were days and weeks when she sunk into depression. The broken bond of motherhood tormented her. And deeper still, she carried the burden of letting down Sun-ja and breaching Chondogyo. The RGB had ordered Vera to Russia. She had no choice. But guilt followed her like the ferret haunting Sandy.

Richard believed his parents had divorced because his mother had to return to Vladivostok for family responsibilities. A partial truth. She had obligations. That much was true, but they tilted more spiritual than temporal. When she returned to Vladivostok, the RGB had activated her, trained her, and facilitated her position at the institute in Busan. Richard thought of his mother as an accomplished woman, a celebrity scientist on the cusp of a triumphant return to the States. His thoughts jumbled and ambivalent, Richard resisted meeting in person. Their chats were composed and friendly, but meeting his mother, after all this time apart posed an emotional hurdle. Emotional maturity is not typically associated with teenage boys.

The letter sitting on Vera's coffee table was from Thomas, confirming their family's plans for the coming months and suggesting when and where Vera and Richard might spend time together. This she would not show the RGB.

Jeff texted Sandy a link to the University of New Hampshire's Earth Sciences Newsroom. The university's Media Relations Department had crafted an economical, no-frills announcement of Dr. Vera Berg's visiting professorship to follow her presentation at the Camden Conference. The media release described Berg as:

> *. . . a leading authority in oceanography with extensive published works on seabed and geological influences. Dr. Berg will be part of an enhanced presence in the world of ocean research and key to the launch of our Center of Excellence.*

The UNH release quoted from a US National Oceanic and Atmospheric Administration announcement of a $10 million partnership with UNH.

> *NOAA and the University of New Hampshire are expanding a 24-year ocean and Great Lakes mapping partnership through the creation of a new Center of Excellence for Operational Ocean and Great Lakes Mapping.*

> *NOAA and UNH have a long history of collaborating to advance the latest technologies and tools to map our ocean, coasts and Great Lakes—a cornerstone of the blue economy. Our continued partnership on the Center of Excellence will help build a workforce ready to tackle the mapping challenges of the future and further our understanding of our changing ocean and coasts.*

The release included photographs of a NOAA uncrewed surface vessel during survey operations, an autonomous underwater vehicle being deployed, and a digital terrain map of the entrance to Portsmouth Harbor.

Sandy read the release and shook her head. Jeff was right. But how in the world had he found out before the information went public? She would need to draft a memo to Bigelow management, requesting time off and asking for reimbursement to attend the conference. She did a quick calculation. It was a two-hour drive to the University of New Hampshire. She assumed Berg would live nearby. So, in theory, she and Berg could have a collegial relationship, work together in person, and share insight. They might commute using Amtrak's Downeaster. This just might be doable. Sandy looked forward to meeting her. But she was getting ahead of herself.

She opened her laptop and began a memo to Bigelow's president and chief operating officer. Just then, Caroline came down the stairs in her flannel pajamas. Sandy looked up and said, "I'm surprised to see you this early. It's only . . . eight o'clock. What's the rush?"

Caroline had this Monday off school thanks to a teacher's professional development day.

Caroline croaked, "I told Elizabeth that I would help her with her science project."

"Oh, what's that?"

"The Maine State Science Fair. They judge at Bowdoin College in April."

Sandy wondered if this conversation would be a tooth-pulling affair. She asked, "What is her project?"

"I think it's got to do with water temperature and seaweed. Like . . . can seaweed grow in warmer water? Elizabeth wants to predict the effects of ocean temperature rise. I don't think she's settled on a project. We're going to brainstorm.

"Hey, you're a scientist, any thoughts? Last year's winners received a four-year, full tuition scholarship to UMaine, a research stipend, and admissions to the Honors College."

Sandy wondered how they planned to stage this experiment. But she was more curious about something else. She asked, "Who else is on Elizabeth's team?"

Caroline balked, then relented. Boothbay was too small to keep anything from her mother, plus there loomed Caroline's pledge to be open with her mother. She said, "Jimmy might be there."

This confirmed Sandy's suspicion. She'd registered telltale signs of Jimmy's entrance into Caroline's life since the holidays. Hushed phone conversations, drop by visits . . . small things any mother would notice.

Sandy asked, "Are you and Jimmy dating?"

"Mom . . . stop it. No. If we were *dating*, I'd let you know. We just . . . hang out . . . sometimes."

Caroline's emphasis on *dating* implied involvement more than making out. She added, "By the way, how long did it take for you to tell me you and Brian were *dating?* Hmm? Five months?"

Sandy didn't take the bait.

Sandy knew Jimmy and his family. Jimmy was a good kid. He

kept his grades above average, dressed presentably, and was polite in her presence. But he was a teenage boy, a walking vial of hormones. And Caroline was, too. She was smarter and more mature than Jimmy, but just as hormonal. The biology scared Sandy.

Jimmy's father fished as a lobsterman, and his mother worked in the school cafeteria. They were respectable folks, members of the Congregationalist church, who cheerfully volunteered for community events. Sandy got the inside scoop from her cousin, Todd, the Congregationalist pastor.

Jimmy remained in school, even with his father's occupation. In Sandy's estimation, this spoke well of their family. Far too many Midcoast boys, once they reached sixteen, dropped out to work as sternmen on lobster boats. They could make $60,000 a year or more, buy a pickup truck, and have cash for hunting and fishing gear. Sandy didn't want to nose into Caroline's affairs unnecessarily. She didn't want to push her away. Jimmy was probably as good a high school boyfriend as any. But Sandy worried about her daughter overextending, God forbid getting pregnant, and losing sight of her college commitment. Hers was Mothering 101.

Caroline fed the toaster two slices of wheat bread. She went to the refrigerator and poured a glass of orange juice. When the toaster popped, she lathered the bread with butter, added strawberry jam, then carried her plate to sit next to her mother. She noticed Sandy had started an email and asked, "Who are you writing?"

Sandy said, "I'm requesting permission to attend the Camden Conference and be reimbursed."

Caroline nodded, "What's happening there?"

"There's a scientist who will be presenting on oceanography I'd like to meet."

"Who's that?"

"Her name is Vera Berg. She's Russian but she works in South Korea."

"How do you plan to meet her?"

Sandy was stumped. "Well . . . I plan to go to the conference and . . . I believe we will have a meeting set up in advance."

"Who's going to do that?"

"Uh . . . Jeff."

"Brian's brother? The guy who hooked you up to a lie detector?" Caroline laughed, then blurted, "Secret Sandy strikes again!"

"Our University of New Hampshire benefactor will host a small reception for Dr. Berg following her presentation at the conference. He's booked the penthouse suite at the Norumbega Inn in Camden. I'm told it is very nice, and there will be only a dozen people. Very intimate. Dr. Arsenault can meet Dr. Berg there. Our profile of Berg suggests she's standoffish. Will Ms. Arsenault have the prerequisite social skills to mollify interactive inertia?"

Jeff listened carefully to Joan Samuels. He pictured the scenario in his mind and, knowing Sandy, he answered, "Dr. Arsenault has the skills. She can be personable, and she doesn't come across like she's after something. She doesn't present as transactional."

Jeff thought, *It's her smile and her fresh, trusting eyes.*

Jeff went on, "I'm sure Berg is on guard for provocative advances. The RGB has trained her for that, and she's had years of practice. We could leapfrog ahead and simply make contact directly. But, having Sandy bird-dog for us will benefit the mission in the long run. Berg will be wary. I'm sure the RGB has coached her, told her she might face recruitment. But Sandy is an innocent. She has no motive beyond her interest in science and the Boothbay tide anomaly. She's credentialed. Sandy is who she says she is. Both women are the same age, with teenagers. They are both noted scientists . . . there are a lot of commonalities. Sandy is local, not an interloper. Berg will probably sense all this. When the RGB runs Sandy, she'll come back clean. The reassurance may put Berg at ease.

"A lot will depend on Berg's mental state. We just don't know. This will be a dramatic time in her life. Renewing the bond with her son. Integrating at UNH. Setting up an RGB conduit for her data drops. These are not small endeavors. She's going to be jumpy and anxious. Sandy may be able to put her at ease. Once she's out of Korea, beyond the immediate reach of the RGB, and once she reconnects with her son, she may be receptive to our approach. Basically, we need Sandy to be her new best friend.

"We should give this buddy-buddy approach a six-week window for results. After that, we go direct and let the chips fall."

Chips falling for Vera Berg meant turning on the RGB, defection, or elimination. Kinnaird's contract for Project Brizo delineated these three outcomes. Turning Vera paid the best, defection second best, and elimination, slightly less than defection. All three payouts were seven figures. Sandy's cut would be exactly zero.

"Jeff, I don't know these people. Why am I on this list? President of the university, head of the Earth Sciences Department, conference board members . . . why am I on this list? Are you going to be there? These are high-flyers. I'm a nobody. I won't fit in." Sandy was unconvincing that she thought of herself as a nobody.

"Sandy," Jeff said, taking a breath, "you're a PhD oceanographer, a senior scientist at a respected laboratory, smarter than anybody in that room except maybe Berg, so don't fret. Be yourself. You're charming, witty, engaging, good-looking, you can handle a little elbow rubbing. It'll be fun."

Sandy stared back, employing her powers to draw out others.

"Yeah. No. I will not be there. You're on your own. Keep me out of this, please," Jeff's somberness stilled the conversation.

"A Mr. Davidson will be there. He's the UNH alumni writing the check for this affair. Meet him first. He knows about you. He'll facilitate you meeting Dr. Berg. The rest of the people at the party, that's up to you. Meet them if you like, but Berg is your priority."

Sandy didn't like Jeff's tone . . . commanding, hierarchical, perhaps militaristic?

"I think you'll hit it off with her. You've got a lot in common," Jeff assured her.

"Jeff, is this Mr. Davidson a friend of yours?"

"Nope. Never met him. Don't mention me. He's a friend of our director, and don't mention her, either."

"How can I? I don't know who she is."

Jeff smiled and nodded.

Sandy eye rolled.

They sat across from each other in a booth at Jodie's Cafe and Bakery in Wiscasset. They had a view out the window of Red's Eats, the locally reviled lobster shed that generated a line of sweltering traffic-stalling tourists in season. February was not in season.

Jeff said, "I want to tell you about Berg. Personal stuff, okay?"

Sandy nodded. She was beyond the point of asking where Jeff got his information.

"She's Korean with Russian citizenship. She grew up in Russia's Far East. Her father died when she was a baby, and her

Korean mother raised her. The mother–daughter bond, very important
to her psychology. Berg studied in the Far East and then came to
America for her PhD, University of Washington.”

Sandy nodded.

“Berg has a sixteen-year-old son. He lives in Seattle with his
father who remarried. Berg was married for five years when she lived
in the States. The divorce was uncontested. We speculate the divorce
was related to her untimely return to Russia, cause unknown.”

“Jeff, wait a minute. Why are you telling me this? I don’t care
about her personal life . . . I mean, that’s not the most important thing
to me. I want to . . . pick her brain and get her take on . . . science . . . I
want to collaborate.”

“Well, this might make things go smoother if you understand
what makes her tick. For instance, this trip to the States will be the first
time in fourteen years she’s reunited with her son. We assume that will
happen on the West Coast.”

“We?” Sandy asked.

“Right. Kinnaird. We.”

Sandy wasn’t sure if she was part of *We*. She wasn’t sure she
wanted to be.

Jeff picked up on Sandy’s renewed hesitancy. He said, “Let’s
go on; this will only take a second.”

Sandy nodded and stifled another eye roll.

“She’s fluent in English, Russian, and Korean. She’s a runner.
She takes martial arts classes in Busan, and she’s assumed to be at a
high level of proficiency. No known boyfriends or sexual attachments.
She’s assumed to be heterosexual, with no contrary indications.”

Sandy was now certain that Berg was more than a lucky
happenstance wandering into her life to help Sandy understand the
Boothbay tide. To Kinnaird and Jeff, Berg was a subject, someone
they studied. So where did that leave Sandy?

Jeff asked, “Any questions?”

Sandy had so many questions, she didn’t know where to begin.
She gazed straight ahead, a shell-shocked, thousand-yard stare, her lips
slightly parted.

Jeff said, “Okay. Now, before I forget, we’ve booked you a
room at the Norumbega. It’s not as fancy as the penthouse where the
reception will be, but it should be nice.”

Sandy was puzzled. “Why did you do that? Camden’s only a
forty-minute drive.”

Jeff smiled, "Were you planning to change in your car? That Subaru is going to be cramped."

"Change?"

"We assumed you would like to change into something more social for the reception. You wouldn't wear evening wear to Berg's presentation. Right?"

"Jeff, what the heck have you gotten me into? This is Maine, blue jeans and a hoodie are all that's required. Maybe a baseball cap, preferably Sox or Pats."

Jeff pulled an envelope from his inside jacket pocket and offered it to Sandy. Reaching for it, she asked, "What's this?"

"Incidental expenses."

Sandy nosed open the envelope and saw ten $100 bills. She exclaimed, "Jeff! What the hell?"

Jeff said, "Put the bills in your jacket. Sign and date the envelope and give it back." Then he handed her a pen.

Sandy, riled, said, "I'm not signing anything! And I'm not taking your money! I am not on your payroll!"

Jeff took a deep breath, "Sandy, you are right. You are not on our payroll. You are not an employee. This may be new to you, but this is how business is done. We have a business need for you to meet Dr. Berg and enlist her, indirectly, in your exploration of the anomalous tide file. If we, Kinnaird, successfully close that file, reach a ninety percent probable conclusion, we will be paid an amazing amount of money. That is what we do. We solve problems for the federal government. You are receiving the same consideration and treatment as any consultant or partner working with Kinnaird. By the way, you can request reimbursement for your mileage or any business meals you initiate during the conference. All meals with Berg and mileage or transportation and lodging required to consult with her are also reimbursable."

Sandy had to lift her jaw from the red gingham tablecloth.

Jeff said, "Take the money and sign the envelope. I need to get back to Portsmouth. Text or call if you have any more questions. Otherwise, enjoy the conference and the reception, and we'll talk early next week.

"Oh . . . congratulations, your clearance went through. We can start working on your access to the file next week, as well."

Sandy still balked.

Jeff said, "Sandy. We operate above board. We don't just hand out cash. We file with the IRS, and we need your receipt. Just your initials and a date. What you do with the cash is up to you, but I suggest a new pair of jeans and a fresh hoodie might be in order."

Dr. Berg's presentation and the reception to follow were on Saturday. It was Tuesday, and Sandy had taken Jeff's suggestion to heart. She had nice dresses but nothing classically cocktail, nothing that qualified as *evening wear*. There was no call for such a dress because there weren't that many high-end cocktail receptions in Boothbay. She called Brian.

"Hey, can you get away this afternoon? Want to drive to Portland?"

"Umm . . . sure. What are we doing there?"

"Shopping."

"For what?"

"A dress."

"Okay? Wouldn't Caroline be a better shopping partner for a dress?"

"Probably, but she's got school, and she's working on a science project after that."

"You sound urgent."

"Not urgent . . . just a little rushed. I need something for the reception in Camden on Saturday evening. I need to fit in."

Sandy briefed Brian on the reception and her stay in Camden. He thought of her as a fish slightly out of water, but he had no doubt she would fit in.

"Okay, when do you want to leave? We can go to Fore Street for dinner."

Sandy said, "I'll pick you up at three. How's that?"

"Okay. Come by the union and we'll leave from here."

Sandy met Brian a little after three. As he slid into her Subaru, he said, "Okay, let's get you a dress."

Brian had not been dress shopping since forever. He tried to remember if he and Denise had gone shopping together . . . for dresses. Surely, they must have. But nothing came to mind.

Sandy said, "I need to look here in Bath. There's a little shop downtown. Let's just pop in and check. They might have something there. It could save us a trip. I checked at Logan in Boothbay and. . . ." Sandy shrugged her shoulders and shook her head.

"Right. Okay, I'm along for the ride," said Brian. "I'm your moral support."

Thus began the search for Sandy's perfect cocktail dress. Five more boutiques and four hours later, it ended at Macy's in the South Portland Maine Mall. After shop number three, Brian felt like someone had smeared dental Lidocaine over his entire body. He was numb.

Sandy was a lovely, shapely woman, and everything she tried on looked good to him. Sandy didn't go for the twenty-something frills and high hemlines. Although Brian thought she would easily rock those numbers. She landed on a knee-length, compression-embellished, ruched sheath in navy. Brian memorized the description in case Caroline asked so he might appear attentive. Although, by this point in their adventure, he was barely ambulatory. The salesperson tried to sell Sandy a pair of heels to match. But Sandy, a frugal Yankee by birth and disposition, waved off temptation. She *had* navy heels, a bit scuffed and not up-to-the-minute styling, but they would work fine.

It was nearly eight o'clock when the couple arrived at Fore Street in downtown Portland. The restaurant, as usual, was packed. When Brian asked for a table, the hostess told him the restaurant was booked, but they could eat in the bar. And that's what they did.

In a not too noisy booth, they ordered drinks and then dinner. Brian was bushed. His brain was mush.

Sandy said, "You look tired."

"Right. Yeah. Overstimulated."

"Well, we're finished. We won't have to do this again."

When their drinks arrived, Brian rallied and reengaged in conversation.

"So, are you excited to meet Dr. Berg?"

Sandy was reflective. "I want to meet her. I hope we can work together. She's a major force in our field. She began publishing as an undergraduate, and most of her work holds up well. Yeah, I guess I'm excited."

Brian sensed her hesitancy. He prompted, "But. . . ?"

"It's just that your brother has me a bit spooked."

"What's he done?" Brian asked accusingly.

"I'm not supposed to talk about . . . details. It's that . . . he, or they, know a whole lot about Dr. Berg. Her personal life, things like that."

Brian said, "That's what they do, Sandy. They investigate people. And these days, there's not much they can't find out."

Brian held up his beer.

Sandy held up her wineglass and asked, "What are we toasting?"

"Your clearance!"

Their glasses clinked.

"Where are you going to review the file?"

"I thought Jeff would bring it here. Or send a courier to Southport."

"I doubt that. If the material is classified, you'll probably need to review it in a secure location."

Sandy hadn't considered this. But it made sense.

"We've got a SCIF at BIW," assured Brian.

Sandy cocked her head.

"A sensitive compartmented information facility, SCIF," said Brian.

Sandy said, "You know, Brian, your IC world has so many acronyms and initials, I don't see how any other country could make heads or tails of it. Is that on purpose?"

Brian laughed. "You've uncovered America's national security strategy." And he held up his beer again.

Richard was not a shy young man, but he was shy around his mother. Vera, composed as always, viewed the world through the lens of a fifteen-hour flight and the resulting jet lag. She arrived at three o'clock local time in Seattle, checked into her hotel near SeaTac, then went to meet Richard at his favorite restaurant in Tacoma, ten miles south. MyungIn Dumplings wasn't really Richard's favorite. But his father had told him to be polite and pick a place where his mother might be comfortable. At sixteen and still growing, Richard preferred American cheeseburgers, two of them, with French fries.

He recognized his mother immediately. Should he bow? Like a real Korean? Hug her? He was at a loss. He stood.

Vera recognized him, as well.

Richard offered a respectful, "*Eomeoni*" and bowed.

Vera smiled, not expecting a formal Korean greeting.

Vera reciprocated with a slightly less plunging bow, and said, "*Nae adeul*." She smiled.

In the presence of this strapping young man, Vera warmed again with the pride of motherhood. This glowing bond had been dimmed in Russia and later nearly extinguished in Korea. Their years apart fostered a survival response, the walling of a safe quadrant that kept Vera's crippling guilt at bay somewhere beyond. Somewhere in the distance. Now, at the table with her tall and handsome son, there was no distance. Vera's realm unfractured and was whole again. She heard Sun-ja declare, *Cheon*.

Knifing through her jet lag, her weariness, her vulnerability, her bond with Richard filled her heart. Then she thought of Sun-ja. *Cheon*. Her mother would never share this moment, never meet her grandson. Love, longing, and regret surged, and the walls of Vera's will collapsed. Tears rushed to her eyes.

Richard saw this. In English, he asked, "Mother? Are you all right?"

Vera, fluent in English but unpracticed of late, said, "Ah . . . yes, my son. I am only very pleased to see you. I am very . . . happy."

Now Richard felt a tear dwell. But teenage boys don't cry, so he stifled the urge and looked away. When their eyes met again, Vera said, "Let us sit. We can talk. We have much to recount."

Richard's father had coached him, so he pulled a chair from the table and motioned for his mother to sit. Then he tried awkwardly to push the chair back into position under the table. Vera smiled at this. She could not remember a time when a man had helped her sit at a table. Vera sat erect, and it made Richard mind his posture. He foreswore the all-too-typical American teenage slouch.

MyungIn Dumplings was not a fancy place. It sat in a Korean strip mall between a billiards hall and a strength training gym. This informal, unpretentious setting suited Vera. In Busan, some of her coworkers, especially the younger ones, put on airs and made fun of mom-and-pop businesses. They frequented homey traditional hansikjib eateries posing in ironic videos. To Vera, this behavior was unbecoming, and disrespectful. Instead, these same people pretended to enjoy high-rent, trendy, must-be-seen venues, where they photographed themselves with servers and curated dishes. Then they bragged about expensive, paltry portions. She never understood this. She saw through these fake sophisticates like rice paper. The smell of frying pork and boiling dumplings made her hungry and homesick.

Her mind traveled back to Vladivostok and the Korean restaurants her mother would take her to. They didn't go out often, but when they did, Vera beamed. She and her mother dressed nicely, and she loved being seen in public with Sun-ja. She thought her mother a beautiful woman. That was before Chongjin and their return to Vladivostok. Sun-ja changed after their return. Her glow vanished, and her health began its slow decline. Both emotions raced through Vera, her happy time and the time she worried. She registered it all in an instant and held back the tears for Richard. But looking at him only made her more emotional. She mustered every ounce of discipline to stifle sobbing. A performative smile spread across her face as her thoughts churned.

Richard brought her back to equilibrium. "Mother, I received good news today. I got a letter from a prospect camp."

Vera cocked her head. "Richard, please tell me what that means."

"Remember, I told you about being scouted?"

Yes, she remembered. She nodded.

"The letter was a follow up. They want me to come to New England for two weeks this summer. It's an amazing opportunity. Scouts from the Red Sox, the Yankees, the Mets, the Bluejays, Philadelphia, the Os, the Nationals . . . they all attend. They want to watch me pitch."

A vague image formed in Vera's mind. Her son was . . . what? A prospect for these organizations? Baseball teams? He still had another year to complete high school.

She said, "My son, that is wonderful. Please tell me more about this camp."

"Well, I show up at camp. It's somewhere in Maine, and . . . play baseball. Coaches and professional scouts will look me over and judge me for my potential . . . to play professional baseball. That's a big deal in America. It's a big deal in South Korea, too. There are American players who play on Korean teams. The Dodgers and the Padres will play in Korea in a couple of weeks. It's part of their spring training. But American baseball is the best, that's where everybody wants to play."

Richard's energy and enthusiasm buoyed Vera. His happiness infected her.

Vera asked, "How will they judge you? Do they measure how fast you can throw the baseball?"

"Oh yeah. They measure speed . . . spin rate . . . all that. They use radar and digital analysis . . . video. But they judge on three things."

Richard held up his right index finger. "How well you understand the game. The fundamentals, and strategy, and cutoff positions, that sort of stuff."

He added another finger. "Am I a five tool player?"

Then he added a third finger. "And they'll check my workout, make sure I'm physically fit and smart enough to be coached."

"What is the meaning of . . . *five tool*?" asked Vera.

"An ideal baseball player can do five things really well: run, throw, defend, hit for average, and hit for power."

Vera nodded, considering this information. Then she asked, "Will you sleep in tents?"

"What? No?" Richard laughed. "They call it a camp . . . I don't know why. I'll stay in university housing. It's a Division I school. I'll stay on campus. Orono? I think that's the name of the town."

Vera nodded.

"So, maybe we can visit while I'm in Maine. I don't think we'll be that far apart. Those Eastern states are small. The camp starts in mid-June."

Vera smiled and offered her hands across the table to Richard. He clumsily took them in return. Vera said, "My son, we will certainly

be together then."
And with that promise, the mother in Vera lived once more.

The lights were dim, the chatter bright, and unseen speakers filled the penthouse with soft soul-jazz. Sandy pondered, George Benson? Servers passed through the assembled with trays of tooth-picked Thai chicken spears and fluffy crab balls. A champagne bar dispensed drinks from a corner opposite the fireplace. Sandy wore her hair up in a twisted low bun and drew eyes, especially of the men, most in their sixties or older, and not models of physical fitness. Women, too, looked her over. After a quick glance around the room, Sandy estimated she was in the presence of enough work to keep a plastic surgeon busy for a year.

When a server approach with appetizers, Sandy declined, and asked, "Do you know a Mr. Davidson?"

The server nodded to a walkout roof terrace where a propane patio heater warmed two guests in the evening air. The man swept his hand along the horizon, explaining intricacies of the landscape to Dr. Berg, who nodded along politely. Sandy said to no one, *In for a penny, in for a pound. Here goes nothing.*

She strode across the room to the bar, lifted a flute, and nodded to the attendant. Then she strode back across the room, through the doors, and onto the terrace where she presented herself as innocuously as possible. She had reached the same motivation point that she had with the interrogator. She didn't care what happened next. She wanted this test, whatever it was, to be over.

The conversation lulled. Sandy said, "Mr. Davidson? I'm Sandy Arsenault."

Davison, himself a flawless representation of the flawed males gathered, looked her up and down, smiled, and said, "Oh . . . Dr. Arsenault. Oh . . . so pleased to meet you. Ah . . . allow me to introduce Dr. Berg. I understand you and she have a lot in common."

Sandy realized it had been a mistake to get the champagne as she switched the glass to shake Vera's hand. A dribble sloshed onto Sandy's left hand. But she smiled anyway. Vera graciously acknowledged the introduction with a modest bow. She did not smile.

Davidson had his orders. He said, "Dr. Arsenault is also a scientist, an oceanographer. Bigelow Laboratories, is that right?"

Sandy nodded and smiled.

Davidson went on, "Bigelow is south of here in Boothbay. Dr. Arsenault grew up here, in Midcoast Maine, if I'm not mistaken. Is that right, Dr. Arsenault?"

Sandy smiled, "Yes. On Southport . . . in Boothbay."

The two women taken together were a striking pair. Both were fit, not overly made up, and exquisite in their understated attire. Vera's short, dark hair accentuated her Asian features. She wore a simple, long-sleeved, black dress that fell below her knees. No slits, no frills, no off-the-shoulder look-at-me declarations. She needed none. She, like Sandy, was an unadorned walking statement.

Sandy turned to Vera. She said, "I am very pleased to meet you. I've read much of your work, even some of your early papers from the Russian Academy of Sciences."

Vera perked, "Oh . . . which papers? I did not realize those works were available in English. I was but an undergraduate, hardly someone of status or importance. I'm surprised anyone bothered to translate them."

Sandy said, "You're being modest. I read them in French. I don't remember the title, but in one you analyzed tidal vortices in the Sea of Okhotsk. You described freshwater melts and discharge from the rivers through the Shantar Islands straits and how the rock outcrops, headland protuberances, capes, and small islands disrupted the laminar flow. You have a gift for the narrative. You make science readable.

"I cited your work in a chapter of my dissertation, in my research for Old Sow."

"Ah!" Vera's eyes brightened and her posture relaxed. "Old Sow! Yes, yes . . . I've read of this phenomenon. I hope to visit this anomaly during my time in the States. It is technically a whirlpool, is it not?"

Sandy nodded.

"It is the second largest in the world. Second only to the Maelstrom Whirlpool of Norway," said Berg.

Sandy said, "It is quite the sight. I will be happy to take you. It's about three hours from here in Eastport."

"Ah . . . yes. That would be splendid. We should plan a visit after I learn my schedule at the university."

Vera nodded to Mr. Davidson. Then she turned to Sandy with a coy smile.

Davidson said, "You can take that up with your department

head. I'm sure they can make accommodations."

Davison excused himself to talk to the other guests about fictitious matters. When he left, the two women were alone, the propane heater keeping the chill at bay.

Sandy walked to the iron railing and looked over the tree line to the Megunticook River, which formed Camden's waterfront. She said, "It's a lovely view from up here. Are you staying here, at the inn?"

"Ah . . . yes, it is most beautiful. I will stay here tonight and leave tomorrow. They have scheduled the conference adjournment for noon tomorrow."

"How will you get to the university?"

"I am supposed to ride with Mr. Davidson."

Sandy nodded.

Then Vera volunteered something out of character.

"Ah . . . Mr. Davidson is a cheerful man. But he is not a scientist. He owns automobile dealerships in Connecticut. He feels. . . ."

Vera trailed off and Sandy prodded with a cock of her head.

"He feels he must fill the conversation when there is nothing to be said."

Sandy laughed. She had no firm plans for Sunday. She offered, "I'll be happy to drive you. My car may not be as nice as his, but we can talk tides and science and get to know each other better. I'll need to call my daughter and tell her, but it's not a problem."

Vera smiled and nodded at the attractive offer. She said, "I would not want to offend Mr. Davidson. I understand he sponsored this event, this reception."

Sandy thought, *Davidson is here because of Kinnaird. He received instructions to introduce me to Vera. His work here is finished.* She said, "Mr. Davidson will not take offense. I will have a word with him. He will not lose face." Sandy understood the importance of face-saving in Asian cultures.

Vera was dreading her time with Davidson. Her trip to Camden, three hours in the car, had been tedious and not at all enlightening. Sandy, she could tell, would be much better company.

Vera asked, "Is your daughter old enough to take care of herself? Will your husband be able to watch her?"

Sandy smiled, "Yes. She is old enough, she's seventeen. And . . . I'm not married."

Sandy looked down at her diversionary wedding band. "The ring is, um . . . remembrance. My husband passed away many years ago."

Vera nodded knowingly and said, "Oh . . . I'm very sorry."

Sandy said, "No need. It was a long time ago."

Then Vera volunteered, "I, too, am a mother. My son is sixteen." Her words rode a wave of pride. With this spontaneous sharing came vulnerability, but also relief. She was unburdened. Sandy seemed a safe confessor.

Sandy acted surprised, a feigned reaction that made her uneasy. She asked, "Oh . . . is he in Korea?"

Vera answered, "No. He lives in Seattle with his father. I was with him before I came here. His father and I divorced many years ago."

Sandy didn't want to tread in deep water at the reception. She smiled and asked, "What is your son's name? My daughter is Caroline."

Vera answered, "Richard."

Sandy said, "Great. I can't wait to hear everything about him. Would you like another drink? I'm hungry. Let's go back inside and get some appetizers. We can talk more on our ride to the university. Okay?"

Vera warmed to Sandy's breezy openness and obvious intellect. She surrendered to an unusual sensation. She looked forward to spending time with this American woman.

The sun followed them south on a pleasant Sunday drive. Sandy arranged breakfast for herself, Vera, and Mr. Davidson before the conference wrap-up sessions. This allowed Mr. Davidson to save face and smoothed his ruffled feathers. Mr. Davidson's fill-in-the-blanks conversational etiquette was in full career during breakfast. Vera welcomed his exchange for Sandy.

Sandy was an excellent driver, and the traffic was light. She pointed out landmarks and places of interest along Route 1, and there were many. Maine hosted local oddities and peculiar haunts aplenty. Sandy commented on the oyster farms as they crossed the Damariscotta River. From the viaduct in Bath, she nodded toward the two Arleigh Burke destroyers undergoing refit and told Vera of her relationship with Brian. The destroyers piqued Vera, but she kept a poker face. Sandy made a point of driving through Bowdoin College in Brunswick because she wanted Vera to see their world-class library.

After Brunswick, they connected to Interstate 295. Farther south, just after Portland, I-295 merged into I-95. Sandy promised to give Vera a tour of Portland when they had more time. She sketched the lively restaurant scene and pointed out the heights of the Eastern Promenade as they passed. Sandy didn't mention her modeling at daybreak on the Promenade's Munjoy Hill, a teal-blue Casco Bay beyond. In the spring of her freshman year, she had posed shamelessly, the soft rays of the morning glow bathing her in a golden hue. One student, a man older than the rest, painted her as a materializing goddess, a study in light and form.

There was not a lot to point out from the Interstate, so over the next hour, conversation drifted to the personal. Sandy talked about Caroline. She spoke warmly and fondly. Caroline was a great kid, but sometimes their proximity denied Sandy the perspective of appreciating her daughter.

Vera was more a listener than a talker. Her sullenness damped the dialogue. Sandy worried that she had assumed the annoying role of Mr. Davidson. She said, "Please tell me if I talk too much." And she flashed Vera a big smile.

Vera said, "No. No. Your narrative is most welcome. I . . . I am . . . if I can be so personal . . . I am missing my son. Your description of Caroline, this I envy. You share a bond, you are a team with your daughter, no? I once felt this with my mother. Now, my son, Richard . . . we should have been a team. But it has been fourteen years since we were together. I am ashamed. He was two when I had to return to Russia in 2008. I didn't sleep well last night thinking of him."

Sandy wanted to pry. Why did Vera return to Russia? But she balked, worrying it might be a chapter too far for their emerging friendship. Vera could offer this in her own time.

Sandy remained upbeat. "Well, now that you're in the States, you can be with Richard more often, right?"

"Yes . . . of course. He will travel to Maine in June for a baseball camp. I will be with him then, but I hope to see him before."

Sandy nodded. Then she asked, "Where is the camp in Maine?"

"I believe Richard said the town is called Orion?"

"Is this camp at a college?"

Vera nodded.

"I bet it's Orono . . . the University of Maine. That's my alma mater and where Caroline will be going this fall," said Sandy.

Vera's mood lifted.

Then Sandy said, "Here," and she pointed toward the coast, "If you get off here at Exit 19, Wells, Maine, you can hike the Rachel Carson Wildlife Refuge. It's a salt marsh, with lots of wildlife. Does the name ring a bell?"

Vera cocked her head. "She is an author, no? She writes about nature."

"Yes. She wrote *Silent Spring*. It was a pivotal book. She was a marine biologist and spent summers writing where I live, on Southport Island in Boothbay. *Silent Spring* exposed the dangers of DDT to wildlife . . . all life, really. She labeled DDT a biocide. She published in 1962, and America banned DDT ten years later."

Vera said, "Yes. That is how I know her name. The Soviet Union banned DDT in 1970, although it continued to be used illegally. This I remember from undergraduate studies. We all took a required class in agricultural production as undergraduates."

Sandy nodded. "If you hike the refuge, you must visit the beaches in Wells, too. In season, you can watch the world's cutest birds, piping plovers. They'll arrive in April. They're down south right now. Plovers are a government protected species. They nest on the beach, and people guard them. They are lovely birds, very social. We're just a few miles from the university, so you can drive here should that please you."

The mention of birding stirred Vera. To Sandy's surprise, Vera perked up. "Sandy, that is most interesting. I love birds. Spotting birds with my mother. . . ."

Vera drifted off.

"Spotting birds with my mother was a special time in my childhood. We went many Sundays, like this one. I have seen pictures of plovers, but I have never seen them in nature. This I will look forward to."

Sandy blurted, "Oh, hey, speaking of birds! Boothbay had a visitor from your neck of the woods, the Sea of Okhotsk. She visited the winters of 2022 and 2023. She hasn't been spotted yet this year. She's a Steller's sea eagle."

Vera's head jerked to attention. She uttered, "What? You have a *morskoi orel*? An imposing bird, no? Bright yellow bill, yes?"

"Indeed. She is huge, and so is her beak. I say *she* . . . she's probably a she, right? The females are larger than the males, correct?"

Vera nodded, then noted wistfully, "My mother and I watched these birds in Vladivostok, on Golden Horn Bay. They return in December each year and make their nests in Kamchatka, Sakhalin, and the lower Amur River. They are grand. Their wingspans are two meters or more. They are so bold. I have seen them walk on the waterfront with no fear of people. They depart in March and return to their summer nesting. It is a sad time when they go. They brighten the winter.

"But what, Sandy, is an orel doing in Maine? Over ten thousand kilometers distant?"

Sandy sensed Vera's engagement and informality as she grew comfortable and energized.

"It beats me! Maybe she wanted a getaway? She may have gotten a taste for our lobsters and crabs. Nobody knows. She just showed up. And when she did, so did thousands of birders from as far away as California. She's quite the attraction. It was kind of crazy in Boothbay. We were as busy in January as during the summer. We were home base for sea eagle tourism."

Vera's mind raced. An orel omen? She recalled Sun-ja's reverence for birds as earthly citizens of heaven. Orel was preeminent among these hallowed creatures. Vera was a scientist. She wasn't superstitious. But she was a spiritualist. Her beliefs grew from her mother's, and these she coveted her entire life. Deep within her rose bliss, awe, the connection, the eagle, the reawakened sacred childhood memories. Without thought, she began the silent recitation of Chumun, the Chondogyo way of enlightenment:

> *May the creative power of the universe be within me in abundance. May heaven be with me, and every creation will be done. Never forgetting this truth, everything will be known.*

Vera returned to the moment and said, "There is much we do not know, much more than we know. But I believe the orel was a harbinger. It pleases me she visited you. You are anointed."

Sandy kept her eyes on the road, taken aback. She smiled and nodded and heard Caroline say, *Well, that's a twist.*

"We never really got around to talking science. She essentially wanted to unburden herself . . . of guilt, I guess. She regrets not being part of her son's life. She spoke warmly about her mother who died while Vera was in secondary school. I didn't get any details. That came up when we talked about me and Caroline . . . our team . . . our bond. I felt like an emotional provocateur. Is that weird? She seemed okay afterward. She said we should get together soon and continue 'our introduction to one another's lives.' She used that exact phrase. Pretty formal, right?"

Brian shrugged. "Probably just a Korean thing."

"Oh, and she's a birder, too. She knew all about the sea eagle."

"Really? That's interesting. The sea eagle is from Korea, right? Somewhere over there?" Brian asked.

"Actually, nearer to Russia, the Sea of Okhotsk."

Sandy stopped by Brian's house for dinner on her way back from the university. She had dropped Vera at her furnished, two-bedroom cottage just off campus. The university provided housing to select visiting professors. Sandy thought this a sweet deal. They even provided a car, a Subaru newer than Sandy's.

Vera invited Sandy into the house for tea and apologized in advance for the quick visit. Vera had another appointment. Sandy noted the lack of personal possessions. No photos, no certificates, no plaques. Perhaps Vera had yet to unpack them. Following Sandy's revelation of her relationship with Brian, she asked Vera if she had a significant other in her life. Vera waved this off with a chilly no. That seemed odd. A radiant woman, Vera was superbly fit and composed. She must attract men . . . or women . . . by the dozens. But Sandy, no student of Korean dating culture, wrote this off to unfamiliarity.

The two women talked about their schedules over tea, the only time they talked about science. Sandy told Vera about her work at Bigelow and her current team looking into the diversity and function of microbial eukaryotes. Sandy confided to Vera that while classifying protists as heterotrophs, then phagotrophic or somatotrophs might be necessary science, tidal anomalies and the structure of the sea floor fascinated her. Sandy even broached the topic of the 2008 Boothbay tide with Vera, who had never heard of it. Sandy promised to tell her more. Vera nodded thoughtfully and even used the word *collaboration.* After their tea, Sandy took her leave, and when she merged onto I-95 northbound, daydreaming about a paper coauthored with Berg, she smiled.

In an alley behind One Day Cleaners off Harvard Avenue in Boston's Allston neighborhood, a young woman got into a well used Toyota Corolla. Hers would be an hour and a half drive to Portsmouth. She would arrive after dark wearing ripped jeans, a hoodie, and a puffy vest. Vera's RGB handler in the States sported a nose ring, the Korean character for peace tattooed on her left wrist, and multicolored hair, mostly blue and purple. She presented as third generation Korean American. Vera would call her Janice.

Vera met Janice at Newick's Lobster House north of Portsmouth. It was their first meeting, and Vera did not like Janice. Her handler was young, entirely too young to have authority over Vera. Vera suspected Janice was the offspring of a prominent government official. The RGB had posted her to America, a coveted assignment, but not one she had earned by seniority. It was just as well they would not need to see each other often. Vera's work in America would be almost entirely PAI, publicly available information. American academicians didn't keep secrets. Everything was public, right there on the web, for anyone or any nationality to use. If Vera uncovered anything sensitive, anything that might illuminate potential military operations, Janice was to be her conduit.

Janice left behind an untraceable cell phone with instructions on how to get in touch. Vera listened carefully to these layered instructions, repeating back every word to the young officer.

Theirs was not an elaborate dinner. They shared a basket of fried clams, and each ordered a bowl of chowder. When they parted, Vera drove back to the university, drained. Her obligation and constant RGB oversight plagued her. How intrusive would RGB surveillance be in America? She assumed they would be cautious, more so than in Korea. But not knowing weighed like a leaden blanket on her spirit. That, of course, was RGB manipulation 101. Keep the asset guessing.

But America had buoyed her spirit on two fronts, and these she struggled to bring foremost to mind. Vera had reconnected with Richard. He was proximate, in her thoughts. That was positive. And Sandy, a personable scientist, a woman she liked. Vera thought she might become friends with Sandy. Friendship was a languished concept for Vera, but Sandy's freshness, openness, and intellect raised possibilities. She dutifully reported Sandy and many other contacts from the Camden Conference to Janice. The RGB would background these names to ferret out suspected agents. Vera's RGB instructions were to proceed normally with her science, not draw suspicion, and to avoid personal entanglements. She would honor all but the last.

Within the RGB, Vera's recruitment and activation fell to the Fifth Department, or Bureau 35. But within that department, sub-departments handled different theaters and countries. When Vera left South Korea, her oversight changed. She now fell under the deputy for intelligence within the United States. This deputy indeed had a daughter, a daughter who now handled Vera. And with Vera's move to a new sub-department, an operational orientation changed, as well. In South Korea, it was easy to manage and monitor Vera. The RGB had many operatives working in South Korea's large cities. Although they lost dozens every year to defection, there were hundreds more. In America, the RGB had fewer resources and operatives. To Janice, Vera was not an important assignment. She was a pretentious scientist who studied obscure phenomena on the sea floor. And Janice was not the most motivated RGB operative. She filled out all the forms, and she reported as ordered, but Janice, over the fourteen months of her US assignment, had grown to enjoy living in Boston. She fit in. She had friends and a boyfriend, and truth be told, she was not looking forward to her coming rotation back to the North. She had even mulled over defection, although she dared not talk to anyone about it.

Thirty-one thousand of her countrymen and women had defected to the South since the war. More had left for China. Nearly 80 percent of defectors were women. This was easy to fathom in the male-dominated, militaristic culture of the North. Also, women were shut out of typical men's employment, so they made do in the black market, a growing segment of the economy. There they met people who could facilitate their escapes. Most defectors routed their flights through China. There were many motivations, many reasons why North Koreans chanced this perilous path. Starvation, deprivation, and poverty, of course. But bootlegged DVDs and USBs of South Korean K-dramas egged many on. Keenly produced modern television shows, daringly acted by bold, assertive female protagonists, played like beacons against the drab, propaganda-sodden media of the North. The women in K-dramas dressed fashionably and moved with status in a modern world. North Koreans viewed episode after episode as snippets of what might be.

Janice's path to freedom would be simpler than that of her sisters in the North. Many of these women were first smuggled into China, at the mercy of criminals and brigands. They dodged sex traders and humiliating employment on both sides of the border before finding their way. From China, they sent money back to their family, and many eventually left for the South. Others stayed in China as arranged brides, in a country where men outnumbered women by thirty-three million.

Defections had risen over the last year as China dismantled stringent Covid restrictions. But the North built more guard towers, walls and fencing along the Yalu River, especially in the far north where cross-border smuggling was heavy. North Korean border police ordered that unauthorized people in the buffer zones between countries would be "unconditionally shot," and "shot without notice." These orders violated the United Nations basic principles on the use of force and firearms by law enforcement officials. But in North Korea, niceties like international law found little purchase.

Janice knew all this, and she thought she might still join their number. She would take the Orange Line metro from Allston to the US Department of State's office building in downtown Boston. It was less than an hour. She'd timed it. She would walk in, tell an official she was there to defect, and that would be that. All she would have to do from that day forward is dodge RGB retribution.

Vera didn't know this, but with nonchalant Janice in charge, she would be on a long leash in America.

"You've got three options. You can review the file at BIW in their SCIF. You can fly to DC on our dime and review it here. Or you can review it in Portsmouth at the Navy SCIF. Whatever you want to do, I'll need to reserve some time for you. They will all be busy," said Jeff.

"Jeff, how does this work? I'll need to take notes and jot down thoughts, outline responses to do my research," Sandy asked.

"All paperwork, electronic notes, and recordings will remain with the file. We will secure the file when you're not around. And you will generate your work product in a secured space and transmit it through a cleared contact. Most likely, me."

"So, I'm doing all my work in a library, of sorts?"

"More like a cross between a cloistered isolation chamber and a reefer trailer, but . . . yes. You will do all the work in a SCIF. Where that happens is your choice."

"What about accessing outside materials, other papers, studies, newspapers?"

"You may download from a secure terminal. It will have no send function. It's up-to-date stuff, mostly. We use PCs. I hope you're not an Apple fan."

Sandy pursed her lips. She said, "Jeff, I'm going to think about this and get back to you, okay?"

"Sure. Just tell me something by tomorrow so I can get your SCIF reserved. How much time will you need for initial intake?"

"How big is the file?"

"Big. It's a government file. So big would be a safe bet."

Sandy said, "Can we book at least three hours?"

Jeff said, "I'll see what I can do. You'll need a sequence of reservations. If you choose to come to DC, I'll book you over the weekend, when things are slow. The other two SCIFs will be busy twenty-four-seven, three-sixty-five. The military never sleeps."

Sandy said, "Oh . . . what about my file? I've collected a lot of information about the Boothbay tide and other anomalous tides. Can I bring that with me?"

Jeff asked, "Is it digital?"

"Well . . . I've scanned *most* of it."

"You'll need to digitize everything. If you need help, I can get someone assigned. Once its digital, we'll scrub it before we allow it into the SCIF."

"Scrub? Like look for viruses?"

"Yeah. Viruses, worms, trojans, ransomware, adware, spyware, rootkits, keyloggers, cryptojacking, and any other creepy crap. I can't keep up. That's what tech people are for."

"Jeff, do I get a badge or some sort of credential to show that I have clearance?"

"Nope. Your name is in a database. If you want access to classified material, someone will check the database. Just pull out your driver's license or passport and look into the camera."

"Facial recognition? But you never took my picture."

"Don't worry, we have your picture."

Jeff thought to himself, "And your prints and your iris and your DNA." The DNA was thanks to the Covid test. Jeff twinged imperceptibly with guilt.

He asked, "How did it go with Berg? I understand you drove her to UNH. That was a good move. Good thinking. Make sure to turn in mileage."

Mileage? What the heck was Jeff talking about? Sandy said, "Dr. Berg is happy to be in the States. She reconnected with her son, and she's proud of him. She mentioned something about Richard, that's his name, coming to a baseball camp in Maine this summer. Short of that, I found out she's a birder, and not much else."

Jeff made Sandy leery. She had a growing impression that Jeff was after something more than resolving the tide file. His fixation on Berg and Kinnaird's already hefty file on her sent up red flags. She didn't want to betray a budding confidence with a woman she respected. She kept her report short and sweet and didn't dive into psychological analysis or conjecture.

Jeff asked, "Birder? As in nature lover?"

"Yes."

"Did she say anything about her research?"

"Nope. I told her a little about what I'm doing, and we briefly talked about the Boothbay tide, but we didn't go into detail."

"Any sense of her mental state?"

"What? Jeff! I will not sit here and dish on someone I just met and hope to work with. What are you looking for, anyway? I don't get it. What is Berg to you? Give me an honest answer, please."

"Sandy, I'm just trying to develop an understanding of her. We, Kinnaird, profile people of interest, and Berg is a scientist of international renown and some celebrity."

"Are you profiling *me*?"

"Well . . . no. I mean . . . we *have* checked you out. You submitted the Standard Form 86. So . . . that's a profile of sorts. But that's not it, Sandy. We just like to know these things . . . who we're working with . . . what their motivation might be . . . that sort of stuff."

Sandy set down a marker. She wouldn't spy on Berg for Jeff.

"Jeff, thank you for arranging my meeting with Dr. Berg. If she turns out to be an axe murderer, you'll be the first I tell. Short of that, I'd prefer you and I stick to work on the tide file, and I'll talk to Dr. Berg at her discretion without compromising security."

Jeff didn't take the hint. "Did she seem friendly? Did you guys hit it off?"

"Jeff let's just leave it where it is. I'll get back to you about the file. Where and when. I'll call you tomorrow. I want to talk to Caroline and Brian."

"Yeah . . . okay. Let's do that." Jeff didn't want to push Sandy away any more than he had. But he needed a read on Sandy's bird-dogging. He asked, "Do you and Dr. Berg have any plans to get together?"

Sandy composed her ruffled feathers. She stated calmly, "No. But I expect we will."

"Great. Okay . . . we'll talk tomorrow." And with that half-order of nothing to go on, Jeff hung up the call.

Sandy queued at Gate 10 and boarded the American Airlines flight to DCA, a small plane and a quick trip. Portland Jetport hummed its mellow vibe on a Friday morning in the off-season. No crowds, no jostling, full flights, but zero madness. She had no one in front of her at TSA PreCheck. Sandy had been to Washington, DC, one other time years ago. She had come with a delegation from Bigelow to the National Science Foundation's Division of Ocean Science conference. But that had taken place somewhere in a nondescript Maryland suburb near the university, and on that trip, she had flown into Baltimore/Washington international airport, not Reagan National.

After she'd spent an hour seated next to a large lady more interested in her Danielle Steel novel than a conversation, the aircraft began its descent. Sandy sat at the port window and when the airplane made a sweeping left turn to line up for Potomac River Visual RWY 19 approach, Washington landmarks came into view. She spotted the National Cathedral, then the Washington Monument and the Capitol, the Lincoln Memorial, and the Jefferson Memorial and the Tidal Basin. The bridges over the Potomac looked like parking lots full of cars barely moving. DC was dense and busy. She hoped her decision to review the file here was not a mistake. But Brian was busy this weekend with local stewards' training, and Caroline wanted to work on her science project and, Sandy assumed, spend time with Jimmy as well. Jeff told her DC was the smart choice. SCIFs were plenty and weekends unused.

Kinnaird made all her travel reservations and even had a black car waiting for Sandy at DCA. She descended the escalator to the baggage claim area. A well-dressed Middle Eastern woman in a modest hijab held up an iPad proclaiming DR. ARSENAULT in bold block letters.

Sandy said, "Hi. I'm Sandy Arsenault."

"Yes, Doctor. Do you have any luggage?" The driver did not give her name, but she wore a plastic badge with AMEERAH.

Sandy said, "No. This roller is all I have."

Ameerah took the roller, leaving Sandy with her carry bag. "Follow me, please."

Sandy left the terminal through automatic sliding doors, and

Ameerah's gleaming Lincoln Town Car waited at the curb.

Sandy thought, *Am I in a movie?*

Ameerah put the roller in the trunk, and before Sandy could reach for the rear door handle, Ameerah opened it, and Sandy scooted inside.

They drove north on the George Washington Parkway onto Memorial Bridge. Ameerah asked, "Dr. Arsenault, have you been to Washington, DC, before?"

Sandy said, "No. Not to downtown Washington. I traveled once to the University of Maryland."

Ameerah said, "We are driving to the Mayflower Hotel where you have a room booked. If you like, I can point out a few landmarks along our drive. Otherwise, I will remain at your discretion."

Sandy said, "Oh . . . yes, please. I would appreciate your pointing out some sights. Thank you."

Ameerah nodded, "This is Memorial Bridge. We are crossing the Potomac River. The monument before us is the Lincoln Memorial. Behind us is Arlington Cemetery. To our left is the Kennedy Center."

Yep, Sandy thought, *this is a movie for sure.*

As they waited for the light at Constitution Avenue and 23rd Street, Ameerah said, "That is the Vietnam Veterans' Memorial on the right. Very popular."

Sandy scanned the memorial, then spotted the bronze statue of Albert Einstein across Constitution Avenue. She asked, "Is that the National Academy of Sciences?"

Ameerah nodded as she pulled through the intersection. "Here on the left is the Institute of Peace. And here on the right, the State Department."

Beyond the State Department north of Virginia Avenue, Ameerah said, "Now we're entering the George Washington University campus. Here, next to Foggy Bottom metro, is the renowned teaching hospital."

Past the hospital, 23rd Street teed into the chaotic Washington Circle. Ameerah navigated the impediment like a ninja and turned onto L Street NW. At Connecticut Avenue, she turned left and pointed to the two entrances for the Farragut North metro. She said, "Here are your nearest metro stops. Either will take you to the red line. And now here is your hotel. I will stay with the car and a bellman will help you with your bag. It has been my pleasure to drive for you today."

Sandy took a five-dollar bill from her purse and pushed it over the seat rest to Ameerah. Ameerah said, "Thank you, but that is unnecessary. I am well compensated. I belong to a union of drivers."

Ameerah was a member of Brian's union, the IAMAW.

Sandy said, "Oh . . . good, I'm happy to hear that. Thank you for the tour."

A tall African American attendant in a gray doorman's uniform and Pershing cap opened Sandy's door. He asked, "Will you be checking in, miss?"

Sandy nodded.

"Can I have your last name, please?"

Sandy said, "Arsenault."

"Please go to the front desk and check in, Ms. Arsenault. Your bag will join you in your room."

Sandy could get used to all this attention.

She checked in at reception, and when she turned to go to her room, Jeff stood behind her.

"Oh, hey . . . it's you. Are you early? I thought we said ten thirty?"

"I had to come downtown for another meeting that ended early. So . . . here I am. Should we go to your room, and I can tell you what's going on? Are you hungry?"

"No. I ate before leaving Brian's. I spent the night there."

"How is Brian?" asked Jeff.

"He's fine. He has a class of new union stewards this weekend. Someone from the international union came up, and they're doing training."

"Well, that'll keep him busy. Have you got a bag?"

"They said they would bring it to the room, so . . . Jeff, I might be more comfortable talking here in the lobby. Why don't you wait here, and I'll go to my room, get organized, and meet you back down here?"

Jeff grimaced, "The problem with that is . . . this is DC. There are a lot of eyes in this town. We should limit our time together . . . like right now."

Jeff sensed Sandy's unease. He suggested, "Okay, let's do this. I'll meet you at EXIM, in the lobby. Shouldn't be too many people around on Friday. We'll talk there. Okay?"

Sandy asked, "EXIM . . . you mean the Export-Import Bank, like we talked, right?"

Jeff nodded. "Can you find it?"

"Sure, so long as it's on Google."

"Check that," said Jeff. "I'll meet you at Fran O'Brien's in the Capitol Hilton, just around the corner. Wait . . . it's called Statler Lounge, now. That's a honcho sort of place. Less international traffic there."

Jeff seemed a little off his game today. Sandy asked, "Jeff, am I okay in slacks and a jacket? I'd don't need a dress, right?"

"Yeah, you'll be fine. Friday casual. Hell, every day's casual since Covid. Okay, I'll see you at the Hilton. No rush."

Jeff turned and walked down the block-long, ornate atrium to 17th Street.

Sandy's movie had taken a turn toward the mysterious.

Jeff sat at the far end of Statler Lounge on a high-back sofa, obviously placed there to provide privacy for patrons. Sandy could barely pick him out in the sparse, Friday mid-morning clientele. She sat at the opposite end of the sofa and said, "I thought this place might be busier."

Jeff said, "It will be. We're early for lunch. This place will be shoulder to shoulder in an hour. These days, this is mostly a business crowd . . . lobbyists, lawyers, some union guys, and the occasional principal. The international crowd hangs more at the Willard and Mayflower and other see-and-be-seen places."

Sandy understood Jeff to mean *politician* when he said *principal*. She didn't ask because she didn't want to be flagged as a rube.

Jeff continued, "I wasn't around then, but in the old days, the Soviet Embassy was a block up Sixteenth Street. This place was a hotbed of Cold War meet-and-greet, grip and grin. The Soviets built a new embassy atop a hill on Wisconsin Avenue in the 1990s. The place up the street is now the Russian ambassador's residence."

"Jeff, is what we are doing considered espionage?" asked Sandy.

"No. No. Heck, no. We're just reviewing classified material. Now, hypothetically, if you . . . or I . . . gave this material to a foreign interest, that would be espionage. The bad kind. And severely punishable. But no . . . we just need to be careful about . . . associations. DC has eyes everywhere, and people talk. Better to not be the subject of discussion, right?"

"But why in the heck would anybody care?"

"Sandy, I've been doing this for a while, and it's just better to be safe than sorry."

Sandy pondered what *this* might mean.

Jeff tried to lighten the conversation. "Okay, so you'll arrive at EXIM and go to the guard's station. Check that . . . *first* you'll pass through the magnetometer, *then* go to the guard's station. Tell them your name and tell them you have an appointment with the security chief on duty, and they'll take it from there. When you get to the SCIF, log in like we discussed and have at it. When you're finished, collect your bag from the security officer and welcome to Washington, DC, where there are plenty of things to keep you occupied. You have another appointment at eleven hundred hours on Saturday and one at nine hundred hours on Sunday. Your flight back to Portland leaves at fourteen hundred hours on Sunday. If you need anything from me, call or text. I'm headed back to Portsmouth tomorrow evening. Questions?"

"Jeff, why are we using the Export-Import Bank's SCIF?"

"One SCIFs as good as any other. I thought you'd get lost in the Pentagon. Hell . . . *I* still get lost in the Pentagon. Plus, the DoD, Department of Defense, doesn't call them SCIFs. They use the acronym SAPF, Special Access Program Facilities. The IC and most of the non-DoD agencies call them SCIFs. Confused yet?"

Sandy replayed Brian's comment about America's national security strategy.

Jeff continued, "EXIM is easy. It's close. Little activity over the weekend. And their SCIF is an actual room, not a reefer trailer. We just finished a project for these guys. They're satisfied customers. Plenty of goodwill."

Sandy nodded. It all seemed plausible, eerily plausible.

Sandy sprawled on the king-sized bed, staring at the ceiling of her hotel room. She squirmed on the plush, snowy-white spread, kicked off her boots, and heard them thud on the carpet. She still had on the khaki slacks, black turtleneck, and brown blazer she'd worn to EXIM. Her visit had gone much like Jeff said it would. Now, back in the hotel, she wondered what the heck she had gotten herself into.

The file was not what she expected. The executive summary read clearly enough. But it took three pages to conclude that there was no conclusion. The supporting documentation, the details and reports and pages upon pages of ship tonnage figures, tide tables, and weather summaries numbed her brain. Each report had its own peculiar format and layout. The one input on which she'd hoped to base her analysis, the opinion from the Woods Hole academician, read like an undergraduate geology term paper. No one had updated the file, regardless of Jeff's pronouncement. Sandy had more recent data in her own tide file. She smiled when she found her rebuttal from 2013 to the Vilibić, Horvath, and Mahović "Atmospheric Processes" paper.

Sandy didn't understand why the government classified the file until she came to a section referencing live-fire naval exercises in the North Atlantic. These reports detailed what ship fired, what type of ammunition, and to what effect, on what schedule. But target practice would have no impact on tidal anomalies.

The report from the Eastern Defense Sector of North American Aerospace Defense Command (NORAD) baffled her as well. NORAD reported no unusual activity over the North Atlantic for the timeframe requested. This summary they backstopped with many pages of radar range gate and velocity gate specifics that Sandy found unintelligible. Sandy wondered what airborne vector might raise concern in the NIS Special Investigative Body. Nothing came to mind that might cause a tide anomaly short of a nuclear blast.

Then she came to another section in the same folder, redacted and stamped "Restricted Top Secret." Sandy's clearance level was secret. The restricted data would have made no difference to her analysis. This portion of the file detailed the movement of America's boomers in the North Atlantic. Boomers are the nuclear-powered, nuclear-armed submarines America relies on to deter attacks. These vessels carry sensitive seismic monitors among other sensors for detecting explosions. A sentence following the redactions simply stated: "No evidence of energy events in the Atlantic Theater germane to the requested timeframe is material to this report." Following this declaration, Sandy squinted to make out the initials scrawled over "Commander, Submarine Force US Atlantic Fleet."

Another folder that got Sandy's attention contained listings of unusual tide and wave events on the Eastern Seaboard. There were seven over what appeared to be a five-year time frame. All happened near commercial ports and, from what she could tell from her quick review, none were as dynamic or as pronounced as the Boothbay tide of 2008. Most, she thought, were astronomical high tides or storm surge related events.

She paged through reams of scanned paper describing similar anomalies and verified tide and wave events. But nothing jumped out at her as relevant. Still, she would use her time in Washington to dig deep for the nuggets of knowledge that might add to her understanding of the Boothbay tide of 2008.

Jeff was right. The file was big. And since she had to read it all on a computer monitor in an unfamiliar workspace, making only digital notes, her time in the SCIF proved challenging and frustrating. Tonnages, production records, project reports on work deferred or denied. The Navy and BIW kept detailed records of shipbuilding, every nut and bolt. She assumed all these tedious pages belonged in the file to determine if a correlation existed between production delays and the anomalous tide. One report speculated that the tide might be a weaponized natural event, abbreviated as WNE. This theory held that if it was a WNE, perhaps it veered off course, missed BIW and hit Boothbay in error. Further speculation surmised that a possible misdirected WNE might have targeted the independent spent fuel storage installation (ISFSI) on Bailey Peninsula in the Sheepscot River just south of Wiscasset. This critical facility, within yards of the river, lies much closer to Boothbay than BIW. The ISFSI houses sixty-four twenty-foot tall, dry cask containers of toxic waste from the decommissioned Maine Yankee nuclear power plant. Each cask holds dozens of radioactive fuel assemblies. The plant shut down in 1997, and disassembly began soon after. But the waste is still there. If these containment vessels were breached and released their corrosive content into the air and water, the Midcoast would reenact Chernobyl.

The connective tissue was missing. The executive summary

attributed the Boothbay tide to a non-WNE of undetermined causation with 70 percent assuredness. But the through line, the narrative of the file, rang hollow. It was as if someone had created a picture salad of somewhat related but unconnected snapshots, mixed them all together, and randomly papered a wall with them. Sandy disappointedly gazed at that wall. But she was a Mainer and an Arsenault, and plugging away won the day. That was her final thought before she slipped into an afternoon nap.

Hers was a good nap. The kind where everything goes blank, you dream a pleasant dream, and you wake up not knowing if it's morning, afternoon, or night or where in the heck you are. It was early evening, seven o'clock. Her weird but non-threatening dream dispersed, and Sandy incrementally regained consciousness. Now she was hungry.

Jeff had briefed her on his favorite restaurants, but she had no reservations, and these she would need. She'd do that tomorrow night. Sandy was an adventurous eater and an accomplished cook. She looked forward to something unique while in DC. The Bombay Club attracted her and sounded exotic. Jeff had told her to dress nicely and that the Parsi cuisine offerings were his favorite—meat and vegetables, and not crazy spicy. Jeff had also mentioned Kellari Taverna and McCormick & Schmick's Seafood. These were on K Street. She could walk to both from the hotel. McCormick & Schmick's didn't appeal to Sandy because fresh seafood reigned supreme on the Midcoast for a fraction of the cost. Jeff told her that Kellari Taverna featured an upscale Greek-inspired menu with passable food but little authenticity. If she wanted authentic Greek food in a family-owned restaurant, Kellari didn't fit the bill. If that's what she wanted, she'd need to cab or Uber or, if she felt like an urban adventure, Metro to Alexandria and visit Taverna Cretekou. Jeff also mentioned the Iron Gate on N Street off Dupont Circle. He described it as a quintessential DC occasional place, a step above an everyday neighborhood spot. They served top-notch food, with a Mediterranean–Middle Eastern twist. It was off the street and featured the city's most inviting courtyard. He said it was romantic and a place she should take Brian. With the wisteria in bloom and the bees at work, they should order a bottle of Nykteri Assyrtiko from Santorini. Jeff had brought the fingers and thumb of his right hand together, raised them to his lips, kissed them lightly, then tossed them to the ether with a suggestive look.

Sandy went to the bathroom and splashed her face with cold

water. She sat on the bed and slipped into her boots. She had to fight the urge to pick up the phone and order room service. She thought, *This is the big city, it's Friday night, and I'm going out . . . somewhere*. She got as far as the hotel bar.

She was lucky to find a stool at the bar. The place was busy, but the shoulder-to-shoulder Friday after-work crowd had dispersed to homes or restaurants or families or liaisons. The bar was called Edgar's. The flirtatious barkeeper, Tony, told Sandy the bar was named after J. Edgar Hoover. He had eaten lunch at the Mayflower for twenty years with his "assistant" Clyde Tolson. Hoover ordered the same thing every day: cottage cheese, grapefruit, and iceberg lettuce, onto which he ladled salad dressing he brought from home. Before she finished her shrimp and crab risotto and her two espresso martinis, she had learned many newsworthy scandals at the Mayflower. Tony was a superb storyteller. He had all the details. But, the next morning, details were hard to recall.

She remembered something about Jeff Sessions, then the US attorney general, meeting with a Russian ambassador he denied ever having happened. She remembered the one about JFK keeping a room there for Judith Campbell Exner, his mistress. And the story about Marion Barry getting busted for cocaine there. Then something about President Clinton and Monica Lewinsky, a photograph, and a deposition. And Governor Eliot Spitzer meeting his escort from the Emperor's Club in a room there.

After the first martini, Sandy started flirting back with Tony. He was tall, good-looking and a safe foil. When she left the bar at ten o'clock, he told her to be sure to come back. She liked the attention, flipping her hair the more she drank. But she smiled and walked away as soberly as she could. Tomorrow was a workday.

Buried at the end of the anomalous tide file lurked a report from the Department of State (DOS). "US Extended Continental Shelf: Atlantic Region" had slipped past Sandy on her first review. But on her second visit, the prudent researcher began at the end of the file and worked forward.

The DOS chaired a task force, thus the eagle crest on the report's heading didn't grab Sandy's attention. She generalized that the DOS doesn't do science. No, they don't. But the United States Geological Survey (USGS) does. Sandy learned the interagency task force brought together many US government agencies, including the DOS, the USGS, and NOAA. Together, these agencies determined the geographic extent of the ECS deep-water maritime zone.

The continental shelf extends America's land territory under the sea. The Extended Continental Shelf (ECS) is the portion of the continental shelf beyond two hundred nautical miles from the coast. The USGS mapped the seafloor and determined sediment thickness. The US Department of State used these measurements to delineate the outer limits of the US ECS under the United Nations Convention on the Law of the Sea.

The ECS is geologically active. It is home to mountains, canyons, and treacherous landslides. Seamounts rise from the ocean floor to heights comparable to the earth's highest mountains. The Great Meteor Seamount on the Azores Plateau rises 14,800 feet. The Bear Seamount, just east of Georges Bank and south of the Gulf of Maine, rises to 6,600 feet. Bear Seamount is part of a chain called New England Seamounts, which is part of a larger chain called the Great Meteor hotspot. Anyway, seamount ranges are fascinating, and so are their corollaries, submarine landslides.

Sandy noted a reference to the Cape Fear Landslide east of Wilmington, North Carolina. During its survey, USGS had detected a mass transport complex (MTC) involving thousands of tons of sediment on the ocean basin sliding into an abyss. This kinetic energy can induce tidal and wave anomalies and, if large enough and focused, create a tsunami. It's happened before.

Sandy knew only the basics of submarine landslides. This geology occurred far from land. The one she was vaguely familiar with, the Munson-Nygren-Retriever landslide (MNR) between the Nygren and Powell canyons on the Georges Bank lower slope, rested 270 miles southeast of Boothbay.

A working hypothesis took shape in Sandy's mind. A quick search showed the MNR evacuation zone to be approximately 687 square miles, the same area as Tokyo, Japan. The MNR was a collection of landslides, often triggering one another. MNR headwalls, the precipices rising at the head of a canyon or landslide, are at a depth of approximately 5,900 feet. One mile underwater. Their evacuation extends for two-hundred-foot downslope to the top of the continental rise. Sandy thought, these dynamics involve enough mass and potential energy to affect a tide.

She knew submarine landslides were dilatory, spanning eons, until they weren't. MTCs of biblical proportion interrupted this gradualism. These convulsions changed the planet. Then the system returned to a torpid, boring seabed. Ocean basin volcanoes, earthquakes, tectonic events, or other landslides could trigger an MTC. The biggest MTCs changed coastlines with massive tsunamis. The geological record confirmed this on the frequency of an unperturbed planetary timescale. Could an MTC have generated the Boothbay tide of 2008?

That evening, before she left for dinner at the Bombay Club, Sandy texted Vera. It was a wide-open text. How are you doing? I hope you're getting situated. Are your classes manageable? Have you talked to Richard? And would you have time to get together? I would like to discuss submarine landslides with you.

The ECS report was public information, not classified. Jeff would call it PAI. Either way, it was fair game to discuss with Vera.

Vera happily received Sandy's text, almost like hearing from an old friend. But Sandy, as if triggering her own landslide, triggered in Vera a secondary emotion: suspicion.

Vera Berg, long a scientist of capability and concealment, did a double take when she read Sandy's subject of interest. Much of her work in Busan was to map the Ulleung Basin in the East Sea, which is what Koreans call the Sea of Japan. That basin contains landslides and faults that, if properly understood, mapped, and focused, could generate tidal waves to incapacitate the South Korean Navy 1st Fleet Command in Donghae. Or, if focused east, disrupt US Naval Forces Japan at Sasebo.

Did Sandy suspect Vera and want to draw her out? The RGB

had attached no caveats to Sandy. They'd checked her out, and she had come back clean, unattached. Vera heard nothing from Janice to make her cautious. Sandy was, after all, a scientist, an oceanographer. She was local, indigenous, and not a seeded plant. In fact, the RGB suggested Vera develop Sandy as an asset. This idea Vera let roll off her like water from a duck.

Sandy had mentioned the Boothbay tide. Yes, a landslide might be a credible line of inquiry. Perhaps, Vera thought, this open, inquisitive woman was what she seemed. Curious about a tidal anomaly and persistent in finding a solution.

Vera waited to reply to Sandy, and that evening, she texted she would look forward to their meeting and discussion. Yes, her portfolio included submarine landslides. She concluded with an uncharacteristic, "I will enjoy spending time together."

A baby step on Vera's path to friendship, an entry missing from her life and portfolio.

The dance of a stiletto. Her relaxed wave burst into a lightning strike, rendering an aperture in the air. Her first strike was fist vertical, like a boxer. The second horizontal, like a martial artist. A blur to the untrained eye. She dropped to the floor, writhing in a tight rotation, rose on her heels, and again flailed with intent. First the right fist, then the left. Kicks shot above her head, first the left, then the right, her feet and toes cemented in a ballerina's lethal point. She stood still, and her hands moved in an intricate dance before her face like the choreography in a Bollywood finale. She collapsed to the floor, squatting on her left leg. She extended her right leg a foot above the floor and cut like a syce, pivoting on invisible ball bearings. Again, she rose, bowed to no one, and this time dropped to the floor on her chest. She rose on her elbows and kicked both legs like a mule. She tucked her long limbs under her, rolled to a sitting position, and leveraged her rise without using her hands. She stood motionless, awaiting orders from the cosmos. She cuffed her right fist in her left palm, elbows extended, bowed, and exhaled.

Vera audited the University of New Hampshire Tae Kwon Do Club. Gjogsul had its origins in Tae Kwon Do, but the disciplines diverged. From bleachers in the university gym, she watched students, white belts to black, strike, kick, and fall on blue and red mats. She critiqued the instructors. She admired the club's commitment and energy, but it was not for her. With Gjogsul instruction unavailable in New Hampshire, Vera executed her katas in a denuded guest bedroom on a polished pine floor.

Vera was an exceptional woman, but also much like everyone else. When she moved into university housing, she sought to imprint new routines, patterns, and habits. Her disciplined life in Busan flowed predictably. There, she ran in a local park and walked to a Kyeok Sul Do studio where she practiced Gjogsul.

Kyeok Sul Do is the formal name for Gjogsul. This fighting discipline developed in the 1920s among Korean guerrillas resisting Japanese occupiers. Further refinement came when North Korean troops fought the larger, physically imposing American soldiers in the Korean War. North Korean communists exported this fighting technique to Soviet-aligned Warsaw Pact armies in the 1980s. Now, Gjogsul was to Vera much like yoga is to modern American women, except Vera's indulgence might disable or dispatch you.

The mental practice of Gjogsul returned as great a reward as physical fitness. With her katas finished, her mind clear and focused, she stood with her eyes closed and recited the Chondogyo Chumun.

May the creative power of the universe be within me in abundance. May heaven be with me, and every creation will be done. Never forgetting this truth, everything will be known.

And with that, her eyes opened to the awaiting universe. She went into the kitchen and flipped on the electric teakettle. A moment later, her tea steeping, she turned on her cell phone to retrieve messages. You could not reach Vera between ten and six because she turned off her cell. During these hours, she was dead to the wider world. The RGB, Richard, Busan Lab, anyone else—it didn't matter. The night was for sleeping, not distraction. Or rather, not for *external* distraction.

Vera dreamed like everyone else. The source and composition of her dreams was sometimes known and sometimes unknowable. She was a sexual woman, although ironclad in her rejection of male advances. Still, some of her dreams turned sexual, and these she recognized as normal. She remained self-contained on that front.

Other dreams arose from recent encounters, and still other dreams had their origins in recesses she never plumbed. Lately, she had dreams of Richard playing baseball. Quick dreams, fleeting, like viewing a snapshot through the window of a moving car. But her dream from the night before involved Sandy. She felt warm toward Sandy. And in that dream, they were on a beach with small white birds dancing at their feet. Sandy moved freely without crushing the frail fowl. Vera could not. The small creatures trapped her. Sandy prodded Vera to come her way. She waved her arms for Vera to move. But Vera froze, not wanting to harm the denizens of earthly heaven. That was all she remembered. Dreams were only that to Vera. Tricks of the mind. But they imparted actual feelings and induced emotions. Some good, some not. As she dabbed a teaspoon of honey into her tea, two feelings lingered: warmth toward Sandy, and regret she was not free.

Somewhere between dreaming and awareness, lasting only minutes while Vera lay in bed, she projected her day. These moments filled with the things she needed to accomplish, lectures, data retrieval, research, office hours. But these minutes also allowed Vera's thoughts to range into summations and judgments. Was she a worthy person? Why had she left Richard, a biological imperative, for a political commitment made under the most exacting pressures? Why, now, did she desire so much to become the mother she never had been? Richard was nearly a man. In a few years, he would be in the world with no need for attachment to her. He would go to college, marry, and have a family. Was her vacancy ever a repairable void? In these thoughts lay regret. Vera recognized this and labeled the guilt. But to look forward, to be creative . . . *every creation will be done.* This was worthy. Richard would always need a mother. Vera would honor Sun-ja and mother Richard's children, her grandchildren. She imagined walking on a shore, watching the birds and beasts. Vera would give these children the love that had shown her the way in her young life. This outcome she deemed welcome, creative, and worthy.

But how would she do this with the RGB controlling her life? She had no regrets about serving the communists. She didn't care if they were communists or imperialists or any stripe of politics. They had kept their share of the bargain. When she was low and alone, they had seen to her education and placed her in a respected institute. She would not be in America at this moment thinking these thoughts had it not been for the RGB. But she was not an ideologue. She was a scientist. And had she not given back to the RGB the years they had given her? Her education had taken ten years, and she had served eleven at the institute. That, in her mind, constituted parity. She would be a mother again, an identity deferred until now.

The soft voice in Vera's mind was Sun-ja . . . *Cheon.*

"Okay . . . here's an idea. We'll invite her over for lobsters. We'll keep it simple. Make her feel at home." Brian's contribution to brainstorming Vera's introduction to Sandy's life rang of simplicity and Maine.

Not a bad idea, thought Sandy.

He went on, "I'll fire the pit out back, and we can do it here. Then she can spend the night with you and Caroline, and you two can drive on to Old Sow on Sunday. She can drive or take the train back to the university on Monday. You said she doesn't teach class on Mondays, right? What time do you need to be in Eastport?"

Sandy said, "I don't know. I'll need to check the tide tables. We need to be there on an inbound tide."

"That way you can spend all day talking about . . . what is it? Submersible landfills?"

Sandy corrected him. "Submarine landslides."

Brian asked, "Why are you going to Eastport? Take her to Ovens Mouth. You've got a whirlpool ten minutes away. It'll save you six hours of driving."

"Yes, but it's not quite to the scale she's expecting. Old Sow is the second largest in the world. Ovens Mouth is way down on the list. Besides, the boat is in storage," said Sandy.

Brian continued, "So, the weather's supposed to be nice this weekend. They said temperatures might hit the sixties. You're free, I'm free. Caroline is welcome to come. She can bring . . . what's his name?"

Sandy nodded, "Jimmy."

Brian announced confidently, "Sounds like a plan. Let's boil some bugs!"

Unintended cataclysm lurked in the well-intentioned merrymakers' kindhearted, get-to-know-you proposition. First, Vera could learn Brian's last name, which was Agosti. With his last name, the RGB could connect Brian to his father, a known IC operative. Or the RGB might connect Brian to Jeff if they had a file on him. Or if Vera Googled "president of union at BIW," she could figure all this out. The second possibility was that Vera learned Brian's last name and didn't report it to the RGB. Or, a third possibility, the RGB,

Janice, didn't follow up because she was busy with her boyfriend. Otherwise, Brian and Sandy's afternoon lobster fest was harmless elbow rubbing with no more national security implications than a gull picking apart a crab. Nobody read in Jeff because Brian and Sandy didn't have the big picture, Project Brizo. So, with the best of intentions, a party took shape.

Vera took Amtrak's Downeaster from UNH to Brunswick. Sandy picked her up and drove her the eleven miles to Brian's house in Woolwich, where Brian was raking leaves away from his converted turkey fryer for the boil. At the far corner of his stone patio overlooking the Kennebec River, Brian worked his way around an attractive brick enclosure containing a propane tank and the boiler. With temperatures approaching the sixties, and the sun beaming, spirits soared. Maine's reintroduction to nice weather following a punishing winter unleashed an infective spirit akin to nirvana. Birds sang and chirped in the late morning, crows cawed, while eagles and ospreys feasted on the river's bounty. A flotilla of small ducks swam upriver in a V-formation.

Vera took in the view as she and Sandy walked onto the patio through Brian's sliding glass doors. Brian looked up from the boiling station. "Hey, you're here. I guess Amtrak was on time."

Then he walked to Vera with his hand extended. He said, "Hi, I'm Brian. Good to meet you."

Brian, much like Sandy, had an easy, engaging personality, and Vera, by her standards, responded warmly. She said, "I too, am pleased to meet you. And please, I have brought you something."

She handed Brian a bottle of Allen's Coffee Flavored Brandy. It was in a brown bag with the price tag still attached, $15.97.

Brian said, "Wow! Okay, let's get this party started. Thank you." And he made a polite bow, which Vera reciprocated.

Vera said, "A colleague at the university told me this drink is typical for the people of Maine."

Someone had spoofed Vera. Yes, Allen's had a place in Maine. It was the number one selling spirit. Fishermen splashed it in their morning coffee. Brian and Sandy thought of it as a stereotypical swipe at Mainers by someone from New Hampshire. As if New Hampshire had anything to brag about.

Brian smiled. "Let's save the brandy for later, okay? Would you like a beer or some wine?"

Sandy said, "I'll have some wine, but I'll get it. Vera, what would you like?”

“Perhaps some wine. I’ll have whatever you drink.”

Sandy said, “I’m having a pinot grigio. It’s dry if that suits you?”

Vera nodded with a hint of a smile.

Sandy said, “Come with me, and we’ll let Brian get set up.”

Vera reluctantly followed Sandy into the house. She wanted to stay outdoors with the birds. Sandy registered her reticence. She said, “Let’s open the wine; then we can sit outside and watch Brian and the birds.”

Vera smiled.

The women stood at Brian’s kitchen island while Sandy wielded the rabbit ears bottle opener. Vera said, “Brian’s house is tidy, nicely organized.”

“Yes. He’s made a lot of improvements and did most of it himself.”

“You are fortunate. He is a man with valuable skills, good employment, no? And he is handsome.”

Sandy blushed.

“Do you plan to marry him?”

Sandy spit a sip of her wine back into her glass. She wiped her lips with the back of her hand.”

She said, “Ah . . . we haven’t talked about that.”

Vera said, “Oh . . . I am sorry for presuming your intention. In Korea, women discuss this matter casually. I am sorry if I have offended.”

Sandy assured, “No offense taken. We just haven’t discussed that . . . yet. Let’s sit outside and admire the birds. What do you say?”

Vera nodded.

In Adirondack chairs facing the Kennebec, they watched birds swoop and spiral from limbs awaiting the buds of spring. Nosy crows warned the wary aviary when eagles passed.

Sandy asked, “How was your train ride?”

“Most comfortable. And convenient. I walked to the station on the university campus. Thank you for picking me up and driving me this weekend. I look forward to our examination of Old Sow.”

“Yep, we picked a great weekend. Nice weather forecast all the way through. And no summer tourist traffic.”

Brian walked over, wiping his hands on a kitchen towel. He smiled and asked, “Caroline’s coming, right?”

Sandy nodded. "Yep, she and Jimmy are bringing the lobsters. They're going to stop at Pinkham's. They should be here around three."

Brian said, "Good. I look forward to meeting Jimmy."

Brian could not help his intonation, which guardedly implied he would scrutinize Jimmy and divine his intentions. Brian had grown protective of Caroline.

Brian asked, "So, Vera, how do you like the University of New Hampshire?"

"It is fine. Well funded and most welcoming. I am well cared for. The students are smart and motivated. Theirs is a hard discipline and one that I do not seek to make easy for them."

She looked at Sandy.

"In our field, since we cannot directly observe much of our subject, we must infer and examine the science through repeated experimentation and theoretical adjustments. The students are young and impulsive. They often leap to obvious but incorrect conclusions. This caution one must learn with experience. The ocean is a busy place and not our world to live in. One must have an active scientific outlook and imagination."

This was more of an answer than Brian sought, but he nodded and looked at Sandy, who smiled.

"Well . . . you've got your wine, so just whistle if you need anything else, and we'll wait for the lobsters and guests to arrive." Then he looked over at Sandy. "I'm going inside to peel potatoes and onions. I couldn't find any corn on the cob this time of year, so I had to go frozen." Brian's phone rang as he walked away.

The two women sipped their wine and watched nature unfold before them. Vera spotted a large woodpecker with a robust red tuft on his head and white stripes down his beak and chest. He worked his way among the leafless oaks near the river. She pointed him out to Sandy.

Sandy said, "They are beautiful birds. But many people don't like them. They peck into wooden siding and gutter eaves. They are sort of like porcupines. They will damage anything wooden."

Vera considered this. "Yes, I can see they might be destructive. Porcupines, I know little of. But a woodpecker is a marvel of nature, no? Imagine if we hammered our heads into wood a dozen times a second. We would damage our brains, no? Concussions would kill us or leave us immobile. How did they evolve this mechanism?

Wondrous, no?"

Sandy shrugged. She said, "I imagine nature offered a source of food . . . boring bugs and insects . . . then evolved a creature to take advantage of that energy source. Birds are ancient. Paleontologists have traced them all the way back to dinosaurs. So they've had a lot of time to evolve."

"But Sandy, do you believe this force . . . nature . . . do you believe this to be divine? Does nature have a purpose and a direction? Or is it perhaps random and unknowable?"

The philosophical twist surprised Sandy. She said, "Ah . . . I'm pretty sure nature has a direction, but I'm not sure we can know what it is."

Vera considered this. Chondogyo taught that the universe and nature are divinity. God, if you will. The universe, and to Sandy, nature, is a pantheistic deity. All-encompassing, expanding, changing, for all time, as it has since the beginning. Chondogyo venerated the sky. Thus Sun-ja's notion that birds, nature's dwellers in that sacred space, were of a high order and due immanent respect. Chondogyo preached unity, peace, and righteousness in the world. Afterlife, reward, or punishment had no place in Chondogyo.

Vera warmed to Sandy's spiritual presumption. Vera shied from the strict Western religions with their impenetrable canons of sin and hell and heaven as a reward. These, to Vera, were mutable constructs, ancient superstitions. To Vera, heaven was all around her. It was neither reward nor perfection, only the infinite act of being. Vera's approving appraisal of Sandy grew. Sandy had opened her thoughts beyond self-imposed religious limitations. And Vera opened to Sandy.

Sandy asked, "Have you talked with Richard?"

"Ah . . . yes. We spoke last weekend. He was going skiing with friends. He said they were driving to Stevens Pass. Do you know the area?"

Sandy shook her head.

"Richard told me that this is probably the last weekend they will ski. The snow has not been good this year.

"Sandy, is it unusual that I am concerned about who Richard is traveling with? He said they will drive in two cars. I am concerned that he and his friends may travel with young women. When I inquired, he laughed but didn't provide an answer."

Sandy chuckled, "Welcome to teenage mothering!" The wine

animated Sandy's response.

Sandy went on, "He's a smart boy. He'll be fine. From what you've told me, he makes good decisions. His grades are good. He's motivated by baseball. If he's going to a prospect camp, it shows that he takes that seriously. He'll be fine."

Vera flashed on the decisions she faced at Richard's age. Sunja had died a lingering death. Vera had to navigate between the KGB and the RGB, finish secondary school, and find her way to college. The universe had turned on her. She was alone and at its mercy. She held back telling Sandy this story. But she wanted to. Her mind fought with her emotions. Unburdening, indulging, sharing her story, she struggled to douse these urges. She kept silent. What did she want from Sandy? Sympathy? She sensed Sandy to be an empathetic soul. But what good was sympathy? Weakness, nothing more. She was strong. Why would she burden Sandy with a sad story? Besides, she couldn't tell Sandy the complete story. She'd have to leave out the KGB and RGB. How would she explain her education? Such interaction was pointless, but her compulsion was strong. She wrestled these thoughts in a corner of her mind when Caroline opened the sliding glass door to the patio with a shy Jimmy in tow.

Sandy said, "We were just talking about teenagers, and here you are."

Caroline looked puzzled.

Sandy said, "Caroline, I'd like you to meet Dr. Vera Berg. Vera, this is my daughter Caroline and her friend Jimmy."

Vera rose from the Adirondack and bowed.

Caroline performed an awkward imitation of the bow, as did Jimmy. Jimmy held a large paper bag in his left hand. He held it up and asked, "Where should I put these?"

Sandy said, "Ask Brian. He should be inside."

Caroline said, "We didn't see him when we came through the kitchen."

Sandy said, "I'll find him. Set the lobsters over there in the shade. They'll be fine for now." She pointed to a covered spot near the patio entrance.

Sandy got up from her chair and walked into the house, leaving Caroline and Jimmy with Vera. Vera was the first to speak.

"Caroline, you look much like your mother. This must please you."

Caroline gaped, eye rolled, then remembered she was to be

respectful. She nodded and said, "Thank you?"

Vera smiled. She said, "Your mother told me you are working on a science project. May I ask your subject?"

Caroline and Jimmy sat backward on the picnic table, facing Vera. Vera sat in her chair.

Caroline said, "We have two possibilities. One involves seaweed and seeing how it responds to higher water temperatures, since the Gulf of Maine is warming. And the second is more statistical and nerdier. We had a couple of big storms in January that wiped out dozens of lobster landings and waterfront structures. They must rebuild all of them. So, we might come up with an app for builders to estimate the height of these structures so that they are not as vulnerable to storms and rising seas."

Vera said, "Oh . . . the second project sounds practical. Do you have someone to design such an application?"

Caroline nodded toward Jimmy.

Vera nodded her approval.

Sandy returned to the patio, distracted, carrying a well used lobster pot with six inches of salty water sloshing in the bottom. She found Brian in the bedroom on the phone with Jeff. Brian broke off the call, and Sandy asked, "What's up?"

"Jeff acting strange. He called to talk about Mom's birthday coming up next month, and I told him about having Vera over for lobsters. Then he got weird. He made me promise not to mention him or talk about Dad's IC connection. Like I would . . . or like Vera would even care. I think he suffers from job induced paranoia. He asked how Vera was acting, and I told him she seemed pleased to be here. No big deal. What's Taylor say . . . 'Shake it off'?

"I heard Caroline come in. I guess the lobsters are here."

Sandy nodded.

"I still need to peel the onions and potatoes. If you don't mind, you can start the boiler and put on some water. Make it salty, like the ocean." He leaned in and kissed her on the cheek. Sandy smiled and replayed Vera's question about marriage.

The sea swirled in gyres. Old Sow boiled and roiled, making sucking sounds and spawning smaller piglet whirlpools. A maelstrom the size of a football field grew angrier with the running tide. Funnels in the ocean, twelve feet deep and fifty feet across, beckoned like black holes to lap in anything nearby. From the deck of the tour boat, Vera had to raise her voice so Sandy could hear.

"Sandy, how high does the tide run?"

Sandy held up two fingers, then an O with her thumb and forefinger. She yelled, "Twenty feet, today! The captain said it can run to twenty-nine!"

The diesel's thumping and Old Sow slurping made conversation difficult. Sandy noticed that Vera showed as much interest in the eagles as she did the whirlpool. She tracked the commanding birds as they surveyed the turbidity, scattering gulls diving into the foam for disoriented quarry. Vera smiled at the lazy seals, basking on exposed ledges, barking their wishes and warnings, awaiting slack and their breakfast swim. A pod of frisky porpoises and a pair of determined whales swam in the fog just beyond. Vera smiled for a long time. The longest Sandy had seen. Old Sow was a navigational hazard, marked clearly on charts. But her upswell brought bounty from the depth, nutrients, creatures, and fish, all to the delight of surface and submarine hunters. Old Sow teamed with wildlife.

Vera smiled, not only at the spectacle, but at the arithmetic. Everywhere she looked, creatures paired or grouped. Even the eagles flew abreast. The social symbolism landed for Vera as deftly as the fog.

Back ashore in Eastport, the two women sat across from one another in a booth at the WaCo Diner. A sign in the window proclaimed it the OLDEST DINER IN MAINE, EST. 1924. They had left Southport at five in the morning for low tide at 8:31 in Eastport. Now, late morning, the diner was not busy. Business would pick up after local churches let out.

A woman in her fifties approached their table with an order pad. She wore a ponytail with a pencil behind her ear, a gray T-shirt with a black apron, and tight jeans. She had a sturdy build. The front of her shirt declared WACO DINER, EASTPORT, AMERICA and a faded

American flag waved on the back.

She said, "Morning, ladies. I'm Heather. Can I get you some coffee to start you off? Are you here to see the Sow? Was she rooting heavy this morning?"

Sandy said, "She looked heavy to me."

Heather said, "It's the wind. When it's out of the northwest, it pushes against the tide. Makes her fierce. We had a northerly this morning. It blew all night."

Sandy smiled. "I'll have some coffee, please."

Sandy looked over at Vera. Vera said, "I would like some tea, please."

Heather asked, "Is Lipton okay, hon?"

The informality surprised Vera, but she nodded her approval.

Heather smiled and said, "I'll get your drinks and be right back. The fisherman's omelet is my choice."

When Heather left, Vera said, "Are the people of Maine typically this informal?"

"You mean Heather?"

Vera nodded.

Sandy said, "She's being friendly. This is a working community. She probably knows everybody and their brother in this town. Small towns like this put little stock in formality. No reason for it."

Heather was back with their drinks in short order. She asked, "Do either of you need any cream?"

Sandy and Vera shook their heads.

"Are you ladies ready to order?"

Sandy had looked over the menu, and while the fisherman's omelet was inviting, it would be too much for her. She asked Vera, "Would you like to split the omelet?"

Vera looked up at Heather. "May we?"

Heather said, "Sure, hon. Anything you like. We can do that. Would you like a double order of toast?"

Sandy nodded.

Heather asked, "Are your drinks, okay?"

Sandy nodded again. Then she asked, "Heather, are you from here?"

Heather said, "Born and raised, married and divorced."

Sandy said, "Oh . . . sorry about that."

Heather said, "Don't be. He was a waste of time. Let's leave it at that. He was a better friend than a husband."

"Heather, what can you tell us about Old Sow? We know the tide collides with currents from the St. Croix River, then underwater structures mix it up. But what's it like living with her? Do people talk about her? Do they talk about accidents? Boats going down? Have you ever seen that? And how did she get her name?"

"Oh, hon . . . she's taken many. And she got her name from a Scottish word, S-O-U-G-H, sough. It means a sucking sound. Americans liked S-O-W better.

"In the old days, before diesels, sailors would cut 'er too close and get sucked in. Without power, they couldn't pull out. Old-timers say you shouldn't fight the Sow. All you can do is right your vessel and she'll spit you out in her own good time.

"In 1835, a two-masted schooner from Deer Island . . . the boat's name was *Laggard* . . . it got pulled in and sunk with two brothers aboard. Deer Island is only half a mile from Dog Island, but that half mile is where the Sow lives. She straddles the border. Sometimes Canada, sometimes America. But up here, people don't pay a lot of attention to the border, not on the water. Anyway, the boy's mother on shore watched it happen. They never found the bodies. No one ever saw 'em again. Now those two souls haunt the passage between Canada and America. Some people say at night on a full moon, the Sow lets them speak ,and you can hear their screams and cries.

"Then, there was a sardine hauler headed to St. Andrews, New Brunswick, in the forties. She got too close, and people onshore watched her bow sink into the whirl and her propeller rise out of the water. Old Sow spun her around like a twig. It took her ten minutes to escape. Her propeller finally dipped back into the water, and she motored out. Her crew was lucky.

"And it's not just the funnels. The troughs and trenches will get you, too. Kayakers, canoes, rowboats, windsurfers, paddle boards— don't tempt her. She'll fool you every time. These days, Canadians, and Americans both have powerful rescue boats that can navigate her. They had to rescue a couple of recreational divers. They dove off Deer Island and got swept into the Sow. In the old days, they'd be goners.

"Listen, ladies, I could go on and on about Old Sow. But let me get your order in and I'll be back. The best thing about Old Sow is that she used to be something to avoid. The fishermen wouldn't go near her. Then the sardine industry died off. Things changed, and now she's a tourist attraction. Funny, ain't it?

"I'll be right back."

When Heather left their booth, she was hailed by a salty, gray-haired fisherman seated on a stool at the counter. His was a big friendly, I've-known-you-a-longtime hail.

Vera and Sandy talked about Old Sow on their drive to Eastport. Vera was well-versed, and Sandy had described the phenomenon in her dissertation. When the tide rises in Eastport, forty billion cubic feet of water floods Passamaquoddy Bay from the Bay of Fundy. There, the tide meets countercurrents from the St. Croix River north of the bay. A 400-foot-deep trench southwest of New Brunswick's Deer Island Point becomes a 327-foot trench to the northwest. Bisecting that trench is a 281-foot seamount. The tide flooding into the bay must make a right-angle turn to get around Deer Island Point, where it slams into the seamount. Add heavy winds pushing against the tide and the turbulence is called Old Sow.

To Sandy and Vera, the bathymetry was absorbing and of prime intellectual interest. But the color and detail and rooted perspective of Heather painted a vivid picture. Vera asked, "Sandy, do you think Heather has many friends?"

Sandy had learned to expect the unexpected from Vera. She answered, "I assume she has many friends . . . around here. She grew up here. Got married here. So, she probably has a bunch of friends, and maybe family, too. Why do you ask?"

Vera said, "I ask only because I wonder if proximity and locality make friendship more likely than travels and experience?"

Sandy said, "I think people have to want to make friends . . . no matter where they are."

Vera sipped her tea, put down the cup, and looked at Sandy. She said, "I have only had two friends. First was my mother, Sun-ja. She was a mother and a friend. When I married, I was in love and young. Thomas was a friend, too, but much more."

It took all of Sandy's willpower not to pry about Thomas. Sandy asked, "Don't you have friends in Busan?"

"No. Not really friends, just work associates."

"Are you lonely?"

Vera hesitated. "I'm uncertain. I've always been this way."

Vera wanted to tell Sandy about Chondogyo and Cheon, but that bridge had yet to be built. A bridge even further would be a discussion about how the RGB discouraged any friendship fearing counterespionage infiltration.

Vera said, "It's just that . . . this subject . . . friendship . . . it has occupied my thoughts of late."

Sandy said, "Well, that's natural. Everyone needs friends. Some more than others. I know people who can go to the grocery, meet a stranger, and before they checkout, they're friends. Others, it takes a long time."

Then Sandy barged ahead, caution to the wind. She had reached that same point she had with the interrogator and at the Camden reception. "Vera, do you want to be friends?"

The formality that was Vera's armor chinked with Sandy's openness. Sandy already knew much about Vera, her love of birds and nature, her commitment to Richard. These were personal matters to Vera. Sandy's query was open and honest, her empathy abounding. America offered opportunity, a new start. Sandy was, to Vera, a steppingstone into a new world, a world where *Cheon* called. A righteous and worthy world. But how would she rid herself of the obligation, the one that made all her efforts at a new life, a life with Richard and friends, meaningless?

Vera answered with a level look at Sandy, a look nearly as potent as her kata stare. She said, "Yes . . . this I would like."

"Mom, why are you watching videos on your phone at eight o'clock in the morning?"

"It's not a video, it's a lecture. I couldn't get Skype to work on my laptop."

"What lecture? And why don't you cast it to the TV?"

"Dr. Berg is lecturing on a subject of interest, and I don't know how to cast."

"Here, let me show you."

Caroline held out her hand for her mother's phone. Sandy gave it to her, and they moved from the kitchen table into the family room. Caroline turned on the TV and two swipes later, Sandy had a full screen view of the University of New Hampshire logo. A minute later, Dr. Vera Berg appeared at a lectern with a wall of whiteboards behind her.

Sandy said, "Thank you for your help. Am I the only one who can't cast?"

Caroline said, "Pretty much."

Caroline inspected Vera for a minute. She said, "She's an attractive woman. Do you think she tries for unapproachable?"

"I don't think she's unapproachable. She told me she wants to be friends."

"Really? She just came out and said she wants to be your friend?"

"Well . . . more or less. She's from a different culture. She's Russian and Korean. You must allow for that."

"But . . . she's wearing that gray jacket and gray slacks and what's with the turtleneck? She just looks . . . unapproachable. Good-looking . . . but unapproachable. In fact, with the right look, she could be downright hot. Maybe even hotter than you!"

Sandy shook her head. She had yet to show Caroline the selfie of her and Dr. Berg taken on the balcony at the Camden Conference.

Vera began her presentation. A flat-screen monitor to her left announced SUBMARINE LANDSLIDES.

"This morning, we begin our examination of submarine landslides. This is a departure from the published course syllabus. I have adjusted the order to accommodate a friend and colleague from

Bigelow Laboratories. Before we delve into technical dimensions, I will present three events. Starting in the distance, closing in the present. Please keep in mind, these events occur on a planetary timescale, so if they seem to you far apart, you have the wrong perspective. Submarine landslides precipitated all these events."

Vera fingered the remote to bring up her first graphic with a map of Norway's Atlantic Coast labeled STOREGGA SLIDES AND ASSOCIATED TSUNAMIS.

"Before we review these events, what are submarine landslides?

"The United States Geological Survey tells us that landslides happen on inclined areas of the seafloor. Triggers typically involve strong environmental stresses like earthquakes, large storm waves, and high internal pore pressures. These affect weak geologic materials. Gravity is the force acting on a landslide. A landslide occurs when the downslope component of stress exceeds the resisting stress.

"Submarine landslides can involve unimaginable amounts of material and can move great distances, as with the events we will review. Researchers have reported landslide volumes as large as twenty thousand cubic kilometers and runout distances over a hundred forty kilometers.

"Landslides can originate near shore and retrogress back across the shoreline. These landslides are conspicuous by their impact on human life and activities. But most landslides happen far from land.

"We analyze submarine landslides using the same mathematical and mechanical principles we use on land. But loading mechanisms for submarine landslides can be unique: storm waves, other landslides, earthquakes, and tectonic movement, for example.

"After our review, this morning's lecture will discuss recent advances in submarine landslide in-situ investigations. Then, how limited-deformation landslides transform into sediment flows. There will be four lectures over the next two weeks.

"But first, how do submarine landslides cause tsunamis? The nontechnical answer is simple, and we'll leave it there, for now. When the earth recedes under the ocean, the evacuation leaves a hole in the water column, creating a wave on the surface or perhaps a tidal anomaly. If the energy associated with this evacuation is great enough, a tsunami forms."

Caroline commented, "Wow. She talks like a walking Wikipedia."

Sandy replied, "She may have written the entry."

Caroline said, "I've got to get ready for *real school*. I'll leave you to your correspondence course."

Sandy said, "Thanks for the cast. You'll have to show me the trick sometime."

Caroline said, "Check YouTube."

Vera continued, "Several large prehistoric submarine landslides, the Storegga Slides, occurred in the Norwegian Sea. The first landslide occurred thirty to fifty thousand years before resent. The second happened six thousand to eight thousand BP, and the most recent occurred about six thousand BP. In aggregate, these three landslides moved fifty-five hundred eighty cubic kilometers of sediment and had runout distances of as much as eight hundred fifty kilometers. Researchers have found tsunami deposits associated with these landslides in eastern Greenland, eastern Iceland, Norway, and northern Scotland.

"Ruptures producing these landslides occurred at the continental shelf break one hundred kilometers off the Norwegian shore. The second landslide estimated around eighty-two hundred BP had an area of ninety-five thousand square kilometers. It extended eight hundred and ten kilometers with a thickness of four hundred thirty meters. The volume of this landslide was twenty-four hundred to thirty-two hundred cubic kilometers and was so severe that it cut into the continental shelf at its top. The triggering mechanism was probably an earthquake.

"The Storegga Slides created massive tsunamis. Estimates of the tsunami run-up heights on the Norwegian coast are ten to fifteen meters for the first landslide and five meters for the second. Please see your handouts for details."

Vera advanced her presentation. The new graphic read: LISBON EARTHQUAKE AND TSUNAMI (1755). She began, "Before we continue, the citations for dates and estimates in this presentation are provided in your handouts."

"Now, moving ahead on the timescale into the modern era, a large earthquake struck Lisbon, Portugal, at nine forty a.m. local time on All Saint's Day in 1755. The earthquake and associated tsunami destroyed much of the city, killing thirty to forty thousand people of the city's two hundred thousand inhabitants. The direct cost of the earthquake and tsunami was between thirty-two and forty-eight percent of the Portuguese gross domestic product. The Bay of Cadiz in

Spain and the coast of Morocco also experienced the tsunami.

"The earthquake's most likely cause was a thrust fault at the margins of the African and Eurasian plates to the west of the Strait of Gibraltar. Such a fault lies on the seafloor about two hundred kilometers southwest of Cape St. Vincent, on the southwestern point of Portugal. The northwest–southeast fault is approximately fifty kilometers long. Seafloor topography played a large role in determining the tsunami's propagation to the west.

"Although the tsunami reached Newfoundland, the nearby Gorringe Bank, Josephine Seamount, the Mid-Atlantic Ridge, the Azores prevented the tsunami from reaching the broad East Coast of the United States. It did, however, reach southern Florida. Please note that a potential tsunami source to the south near the Bay of Cadiz might present a larger hazard to the East Coast of the United States. This source can generate a significant tsunami, but none has occurred . . . yet."

Vera advanced her presentation. Her new graphic read: GRAND BANKS TSUNAMI (1929).

"Moving right along to yesterday on the geologic timescale. This event is close to home, is it not? If my measurement is correct, only 1,100 kilometers away. Around the corner, so to speak.

"The most recent large Atlantic Ocean Basin tsunami occurred on November eighteenth, 1929, on the southern edge of the Grand Banks, two hundred eighty kilometers south of Newfoundland. A magnitude seven point two earthquake triggered a submarine landslide, causing the tsunami. The earthquake occurred offshore from Newfoundland. The coordinates are in your notes. New York and Montreal reported tremors.

"The submarine landslide had a thickness of several hundred meters and flowed for at least four hours at speeds of sixty to one hundred kilometers per hour. It had a runout distance of over five hundred kilometers and transported about two hundred cubic kilometers of sediment. The landslide's turbidity cut twelve telegraph cables on the continental slope and in the ocean basin. The exact time of cables being cut was used to estimate landslide propagation speeds.

"The tsunami killed twenty-eight people in Newfoundland. It was recorded on the Atlantic coasts of Canada and the United States, as well as in the Azores, Bermuda, and Portugal. In Newfoundland, tsunami run-up heights reached thirteen meters. You can Google the event and review the photographic record and contemporary news accounts.

"This concludes our introduction. I hope we are now in agreement that submarine landslides and their associated tsunamis are alive and well and a part of our planetary existence. Now, on to the details."

Vera advanced her presentation to a screen that read: RECENT ADVANCES IN SUBMARINE LANDSLIDE IN-SITU INVESTIGATIONS. Listed below the title were nine bullets.

Sandy sipped her lukewarm coffee and thought, *I guess I'm going back to school.*

Kenny worked as an engineering draftsman at America's oldest boatbuilder, Lowell's Boat Shop in Amesbury, Massachusetts. Korean American, thirty-one years old, and a US Army veteran, Kenny had served two tours in Iraq as a first lieutenant, then as a captain in a ground support unit. Part of this was true. Kenny had been in the Army. But he, like Jeff, had served in special forces as an Army Ranger, tabbed and scrolled. He'd seen serious, in-your-face combat with the 75th Ranger Regiment in northern Syria. In Army shorthand . . . he'd been in the shit.

Five years ago, the Defense Counterintelligence and Security Agency, DCSA, had recruited Kenny. Over the past three years, Kenny worked in the DCSA Counterintelligence and Insider Threat Unit. For the past nine months, Kenny had posed as Janice's boyfriend. And, no, he didn't work as a marine draftsman, but Amesbury was an hour from Boston, and Janice never found out. She was over the moon for Kenny.

DCSA knew about One Day Cleaners in Allston. North Korea practiced commendable operational security, but DCSA was better. They tracked Janice to her rendezvous with Vera, using the tire pressure monitors on her Corolla. Yep, that's a thing.

Anyway, at his boss's "suggestion," Kenny sat in a comfortable office chair at an impressive wooden conference table in a room next to Joan Samuels's office. He stood up when Jeff and Joan entered. Joan carried a thick file in an accordion folder. Jeff rounded the table to shake Kenny's hand, and Joan simply sat at the table's head.

She started by saying, "Mr. Kim, we are pleased that you could make the trip to Ashburn, and we apologize for keeping you waiting." Our delay was unavoidable. So, now that we're all here, let's get down to business.

"Your director informed me that your assignment may have crossed over into one of our ongoing projects. What can you tell us about that?"

Kenny, like all undercover operatives, hesitated to tell strangers anything. But his orders had been to "fully brief Kinnaird representatives on your current assignment. Kinnaird is engaged in a private sector project authorized by the Deputy Secretary, DoD. This project is of parallel priority to your own assignment."

The reason Jeff and Joan had shown up late for the meeting was because Jeff wanted to hear the latest from Sandy. Sandy didn't appreciate him calling before work on a weekday. Jeff called using the excuse that if Sandy needed more SCIF time, he would need to book it soon. She was circumspect. But Jeff gleaned that she and Berg were on casual terms, working together on an aspect of the anomalous tide, and, for lack of a better term, bonding.

"Let me begin by saying that no one has briefed me on the counterespionage significance of Dr. Vera Berg. I know her only as a contact for my principal. My principal is a North Korean female, age twenty-seven, daughter of the director of RGB Bureau thirty-five. That's their North American bureau. She's been in America for fourteen months. She runs four contacts besides Berg, and all other contacts are in the medical implements and technology sector . . . industrial spies. She is based in the Allston neighborhood of Boston, and we believe she will rotate back to DPRK in twelve to fifteen months. Our behavioral people gauge her lethality potential as unlikely.

"I am currently in a romantic relationship with the principal. Her disposition is uneven, with occasional hints of defection. Right now, I'd put that possibility at no greater than fifty-fifty. She has . . . usually after drinking . . . manifested grievance and ideation. Using our protocols, that is the first stage of recruitment. She has yet to display the subsequent phase, preparation. So, per our protocols and profile, she has five more phases to manifest before recruitment or escape. And again, per our protocols, escape means defection, and recruitment means betrayal. In our experience, these advanced stages can happen quickly or take much longer. No way to know.

"Other than an initial face-to-face in March, Berg and my principal have not met. We have three signet intercepts which seem to be the extent of their communication. We assume these are reports of contacts. All have been coded brief texts. The lack of continuous contact indicates the low priority my principal places on this assignment."

Jeff asked, "Where are you in the apprehension cycle?"
Kenny said, "Status quo, wait and see, watch and follow."
Jeff asked, "When do you see that changing?"
"Above my pay grade, sir."

Joan asked, "Mr. Kim, you mentioned that your principal is the daughter of a highly placed RGB official."

Kenny nodded.

"Let me ask your opinion of using your principal as leverage for hostage retrieval or other sensitive matters that may come before our organizations."

"Again, ma'am, that's above my pay grade. But if you're asking if she's Daddy's pet . . . that she is.

"Her legend is that she is from the South and her family owns dry cleaners in the town of Paju-si. She's well backstopped and plays off her North Korean accent to the town's proximity to the DMZ. She claims to have no brothers or sisters, and only her father survives. She's educated, intelligent, and integrated into the Korean community in Boston. She swims like a fish in familiar water."

Joan asked, "Is your principal link one?"

Kenny nodded. "She reports to the deputy under her father. She has no more senior commanding officer in the States or Canada."

Joan looked at Jeff. They both thought the same thing. Vera Berg would prove of little value as a *turn*. Vera was at the end of the chain. Other than describing RGB methods and means, of which the US IC was well-versed, she could not point to any superior officer other than her contact, Janice. Vera's true value would be in revealing the scientific and technical capabilities of the North. Playing Vera back against the RGB was out.

Jeff asked, "What name does your principal go by in the States?"

"Susan Lee. Her real name is Park Yeonmi. We're not sure what name she used with Berg. We didn't have audio of their meeting, just photos."

The dialogue cooled for a moment; then Kenny asked, "What can you tell me about Berg?"

Joan looked at Jeff. Jeff began, "Berg is a notable scientist, an oceanographer. She is prominent in her field, well published. She is ethnically Korean but a Russian citizen. She was born on Sakhalin Island, but her mother's family is from Chongjin in the North. She's worked at the Busan Institute of Ocean Science and Technology for the past eleven years. She's in the States at the University of New Hampshire for a six-month visiting professorship. But you probably have that."

Kenny nodded.

Jeff looked at Joan, and she nodded her head for him to go on. "She's a source of scientific and technical expertise for an RGB special project on weather and climate modification. The success of that project is undetermined."

Kenny asked, "What are your plans for her?"

Joan inserted, "We are developing that side of the equation. For now, we will monitor and report. Our arrangement with DoD has options."

Kenny relaxed and said, "The RGB is a ruthless organization . . . especially in Korea . . . and especially in the North. They've gone off the reservation a few times, mostly in Asia. The most recent took place at the Kuala Lumpur International Airport in 2017. Two female operators used VX nerve agent to kill Kim Jong-nam, the older half-brother of Supreme Leader Kim Jong Un. The scuttlebutt is that Jong-nam was a CIA source."

Jeff asked, "Did we respond?"

Kenny said, "That's classified, sir. In-house and eyes only."

Jeff nodded.

Kenny went on, "They ran the op in broad daylight, in the middle of a crowd. It turns out the two vectors were Vietnamese and Indonesian, and the diplomatic situation got FUBAR real fast. It was a clumsy, clumsy hit. We're ninety percent certain RGB ran it.

"Otherwise, the RGB plays by the rules . . . at least, here in the States. We don't kill them, and they don't kill us. If we snatch a big fish, they go after one of ours, then we trade in the dark out of public view, typically in Switzerland. We tend to get a lot of defectors, and fewer hardcore types. Most defectors ask to be relocated to the South . . . Korea."

Joan said, "Thank you for coming, Mr. Kim. We'll stay in touch with pertinent developments. If we can be of any help from our side, just let us know. Good luck with your assignment."

Kenny nodded and rose from the table. Jeff said, "I'll walk you out, Kenny."

The two men left the conference room, and when they reached the parking lot, Kenny thanked Jeff for the brief, then said, "Watch yourself out there. We Feds play by the rules. You private guys are fair game."

Jeff shook Kenny's hand and said, "If you ever want to play without a safety net, just get in touch."

Jeff walked back inside Kinnaird HQ and straight to Joan's

office. She ushered him in and said, "He's an impressive young man. What was your take?"

Jeff said, "We've been warned. DCSA wants us to play by the rules."

Joan considered this. Then she said, "Berg is of little value as a turn. We already know the chain. That leaves defection and associated interrogation, or. . . ."

Jeff said, "Yeah, but . . . we've been warned. There's daylight between the DoD arrangement and DCSA. So, what's the play?"

Joan said, "Our arrangement is with DoD."

Jeff asked, "Should we clarify?"

Joan said, "Proceed per the original arrangement with DoD and I'll see to the clarification."

Jeff nodded and fought the urge to snap a quick salute.

As he rose from his chair, Joan asked, "Jeff, is your 'best friend approach' still viable?"

"Um . . . yes. The two women are bonding and working together. From what I hear, Berg is warming toward Arsenault. As a bonus, Arsenault has found a line of inquiry for the anomalous tide file. She might just solve the damn thing. That would ice the cake."

Joan said, "A positive disposal of Brizo is our primary objective."

Jeff nodded, "Yes, ma'am."

The Tide of Deception
Chapter 38

"The problem is, Sandy, no correlation exists between seismic scale or seismicity rate, and landslides. So even if you had a full set of data for the North Atlantic from October 2008, it would not be dispositive. A seismic wave of less than one local magnitude can ripple across an ocean and trigger a slide. The ocean floor and impediments are as important a factor as the scale of the triggering disruption. Water conducts energy, and a small triggering event can cross vast distances and retain much potential.

"You might review seismic data for the timeframe. This would be prudent. But unless a significant event or MTC generated a measurable tsunami, we cannot prove cause and effect. Not based on what you've described to me. It appears that the anomalous tide of Boothbay, while interesting, was of local scope only. To me, that implies if a landslide caused this incident, it was likely in proximity, set off by an unmeasurable tremor or a cascading series of landslides. The anomaly would be focused by the seafloor and associated impediments. Thus, bathymetry is a better avenue for investigation than seismology. You know the seismic data for the period, correct?"

Sandy listened to Vera's critique and nodded. "Yes. The data did not show activity proximate to the event."

"Then map the seafloor in the direction from which the tide appeared. Are there measurements or estimations of the directionality?"

"Estimates . . . perhaps. I assume the tide propagated north, originating south of Boothbay. I'll need to check my file again."

"I am sorry to disappoint you, but some natural events are unknowable. The earth and its oceans are indeed a mystery, one that we are only privileged to observe and learn from. You said this yourself, did you not? Nature has a direction, but one we may never know."

A stillness passed between the women. Sandy drove to the UNH campus and met Vera at her cottage. The women sipped coffee and tea in the small living room and discussed submarine landslides. Vera had done little to decorate the place, and Sandy noted that the guest bedroom was cleared of furniture. They planned to discuss Sandy's anomalous tide, pack lunch, then drive to Wells to check on the plovers, which had reportedly winged in over the past week.

Vera sensed Sandy's disappointment. She sought to change the mood as empathy flowered and a new sensitivity arose in Vera. She asked, "Is Brian disappointed you are not spending Saturday with him?"

"No. He and a buddy drove up to the Georges River for some early fly-fishing. I'll see him tonight and spend the night at his place."

Vera said, "He is a nice man. He was a gracious host cooking lobsters. I enjoyed that afternoon very much. Thank you, again, for inviting me."

Sandy said, "Yes . . . he's a keeper."

Her words surprised her. It was the first time she said that out loud. The thought had often flashed in her mind, but she'd never said it to anybody. This openness to Vera . . . it's possible theirs truly was a budding friendship.

"Sandy, may I ask you another question? This has nothing to do with landslides, but it is important to your quest."

"Sure, Vera, ask me anything."

"Well . . . I applaud your focus and determination to find a cause for the anomalous tide. It is science worth pursuit. But you told me that Bigelow Laboratory wants you to focus on organic projects."

Sandy nodded.

"So . . . in this pursuit, are you without an institutional portfolio?"

Sandy said, "Ah . . . yes. Bigelow granted me the time off and reimbursed me to attend the Camden Conference. But the lab has no interest in the Boothbay tide. No team assigned."

"Then . . . if I may ask . . . why is this so important to you? Is there a personal connection? It happened where you live. Is that part of your motivation?"

Sandy nodded, "Maybe."

"Still, in terms of publication, should you find a cause, the professional reward might prove negligible in the scientific community."

Vera found the nub. It was the question Sandy had dodged with Dr. Lines. Vera's question was innocent, like a child asking for the first time why the sky is blue. Sandy couldn't answer, but she didn't want to shut Vera out.

Sandy said, "I may associate the tide with another event. But I don't know why that is."

Vera cocked her head and employed the same telepathy that Sandy used to keep Caroline talking.

"This is hard. But . . . there is a connection between my husband's death and the tide. At least in my mind. They intertwine. I've never said that before . . . to anyone."

Vera had struck a nerve, and Sandy's declaration was more than she expected. This was unfamiliar territory, the intimacy of friendship, and Vera's skills were not yet honed. She said, "Sandy, our minds are capable of much mystery. I am not qualified to diagnose what you just told me. I'm uncertain it even requires diagnosis. Perhaps your motivation is pure. You want to solve a puzzle. A mystery of nature. One that happened very near you. Might that be?"

Sandy exhaled deeply. "Maybe."

"Your husband's death may arise as an association. One embedded subconsciously. Our minds do this. I practice a martial discipline called Gjogsul. It teaches that the mind is two things at once. It is a source of resolve and discipline for practice and routine, but should you engage in physical defense, your mind is not your friend. Then, your instincts must command your body.

"Yours is a disciplined mind, Sandy. But thoughts and thinking have limits. What is good for publication and professional accomplishment may not be good for seeing the universe. Or for being in the universe.

"Your husband's death will always be with you. Much as Sun-ja's death is with me. I think of her every day. She taught me many things. She taught me love and a way of seeing the world. It is normal that you remember your husband. His name was Noah, right?"

Sandy nodded.

"There is a void in your life, no? To fill the void, you search for something . . . an answer to your tide?"

Sandy snapped out of her deep well. She asked, "Where did you learn Gjogsul? And where did you earn your PhD in psychology?"

Vera jerked her head at the questions. Then they landed as the joke Sandy intended. Vera faked an offended pose and pronounced, "I do not consider psychology a science!"

Sandy laughed loudly, and Vera joined a second later.

The bond between the two women was not like a delicate rose unfurling its dewy petals under the warm touch of morning light. That simile might tell the tale of unburdened characters in a fanciful novel where romance and lyricism rule. No, both women were scientists, saddled with personal matters and work, and inching forward in their new relationship. Both women visualized their budding friendship as a trend-line on a standard two-axis graph. Y, the vertical axis measured the intensity of their sharing, and X the frequency, talks per week (TWP) if you will. The gradual slope over the past few weeks now showed the start of an exponential rise. The data point happened on the beach at Wells while the women enjoyed the first wave of returning piping plovers in the early days of establishing their colony.

Vera loved the small, frisky, social, undeterred birds. They skittered about the sandy beach with straw, twigs, and seaweed in their beaks, building what, for them, would be a summer home. Yes, plovers summered in Maine arriving from as far away as the Bahamas. And so did local volunteers who guarded the plover world from free-range dogs, cats, too-curious humans, and any order of plover pilferers. Authorities posted signs on the beach that read: RESTRICTED AREA, MAINE AND FEDERAL LAW PROTECT THESE RARE BIRDS, THEIR NESTS, AND EGGS.

Of course, airborne threats were harder to discourage. Eagles, crows, hawks, gulls . . . the skyborne predators had little difficulty penetrating human and natural defenses. And the nighttime raiders played havoc—the coyotes, raccoons, foxes, and owls—but that was nature doing its thing. Plovers could out-reproduce natural predation but perish at the hand of selfish humans.

Sandy had seen a change come over Vera when they were in a natural environment. She'd seen this at Old Sow, earlier on Brian's deck, and the same transformation was underway now on Wells Beach. Vera smiled. A lightness entered her personality. She made small jokes and attempted wittiness, though in a scientific vein. She smiled and said to Sandy, "Do you think cat owners are welcome here?"

Sandy replied, "The owners, but not the cats."

Vera kept smiling.

A voice from behind the women said, "I love cats, but they are enemy number one on this beach."

The women spun around, and a tall man stood behind them holding a long pole net. He wore Army fatigues pants, Army boots, a blue T-shirt with a stylized plover stenciled on the front, and a gray floppy Panama Jack, boonies-style fishing hat. He was in his fifties, with kind eyes. His trim build and army attire gave him a military aura.

He said, "Hi. I'm Sam. Is this your first time on the beach?"

Sandy looked at Vera and raised her eyebrow.

Sandy looked back at Sam and said, "I've been here before, many years ago, but this is the first time for my friend. My name is Sandy, and this is Vera."

Sam shook both women's hands, to Vera's surprise. His grip was firm but not threatening.

Sam, smiling all the while, ventured, "You're a Mainer and your friend is not. Am I right?"

Sandy said, "Good guess."

"So . . . would you like the two-minute rundown on these little strangers? I volunteer to patrol the beach, and I've learned a little about them. Are you familiar with them?"

Sandy stated, "They are protected and they are cute as heck."

Vera still hadn't spoken. But Sandy registered Sam's eyes directed more toward Vera than her.

Sam smiled and said, "Well . . . first, you see how well camouflaged they are. Can you find the nest?"

He pointed with the long end of his net to a shallow indentation in the sand, lined with grass and twigs. Sparse dune grass surrounded the small nest. The women had to strain to see the four eggs whose speckling rendered them indistinguishable from the sand."

"They're off the nest for now. But one will be back in just a minute. They share incubation duty. It takes about twenty-five days.

"The chicks fledge in about a month. The females leave after two or three weeks, but the males stick with them until they can fly."

Sam looked to the shoreline where the water had made the sand firm. He said, "Look over there. Watch that little guy. See how he stomps his foot? He sprints ahead, then stomps his foot, sometimes the right, sometimes the left. Do you know what he's doing?"

Vera's answer was dry, and her academic distance set a chilly tone. She said, "This animal is a male. He is stomping his feet to flush sand worms."

Sam, now the unintended schoolmaster, said, "Yep . . . you are right. That's how they scare up dinner. Are you a birder?"

Vera said, "I have an interest in birds, but I am only a hobbyist."

Sam nodded his approval.

Sandy asked, "So . . . Sam, do you live around here?"

"Not far away. I'm at UNH."

"How often do you volunteer at Wells?"

"Depends, but I'm here ten to twenty hours a week."

"Are you retired?"

"Ah . . . sort of . . . semi-retired."

"Why plovers?"

"Have you seen 'em? They're so intent yet so vulnerable. And their biggest threat is humans. Real estate and waterfront development. ATVs on the beach. These poor guys have no place to go. They can't nest in trees. This is their life, and we're destroying it so people can live on the beach, show off their homes, rent their condos . . . I don't think it's a fair trade. These little guys belong here, and they don't ask for much. A few sand worms, dead grass, and a little solitude. I think we owe them that. What do you think?"

Sam looked at Vera.

Vera said, "It is worthy that you protect them. I approve."

Then Sandy noticed something. Vera finished her sentence by sweeping her hair behind her right ear. Was she flirting? Yep, that's it. Sam was attractive, attached to the university in some capacity, and not wearing a ring. Plus, he was a birder. That's what it was. Vera was flirting in her own, stiff, academic, out-of-practice fashion, but flirting. Sandy felt intrigued.

Sandy, seeking to advance this dynamic, asked, "So . . . Sam, what do you do at the university?"

Sam, smiling his perpetual smile, said, "I teach and write, mostly write."

Sandy deployed her telepathy to keep Sam talking. Sam went on, "I'm a biologist, an ornithologist."

Sandy tilted her head toward Vera and raised her eyebrow. She was prompting Vera to engage in this get-to-know-you moment. Vera caught on. She said, "I too work at the University of New Hampshire. In earth science. I study the oceans."

Sam uttered, "Really? I haven't seen you around campus or at any meetings, and I've been there for fifteen years."

Vera said, "I just arrived in February. I'm here for a six-month visiting professorship."

Sam repeated, "Really? Well, we'll have to get together. I can show you the ropes. What's your last name?"

Vera again touched her hair and said, "Berg. Vera Berg."

"Good, I'll find you in the staff directory, and we can set a date. How's that sound?"

Vera nodded and said, "That would be welcome. And what is your last name?"

"Lawrence. Sam Lawrence."

Vera wanted this information so she could report the contact to the RGB.

The women talked with Sam for ten minutes; then he excused himself to continue his patrol. He'd spotted a young couple with an unleashed kid on the beach and feared the child would disturb a nest. He said, "It's been nice talking."

Then he looked at Vera. "Enjoy the plovers. We'll get together on campus."

Back at the parking area, Sandy asked, "So . . . are you interested in seeing Sam again? He seemed nice. He works at the university, and he wasn't wearing a ring."

Vera thought for a moment, then offered a studied reply. "Yes, he seemed nice. He would be well-versed in birds, and that, to me, is of interest."

Sandy prompted, "Yes . . . but did you feel a spark? You know . . . something more than birds? He's an attractive man."

"Sandy, I do not have the time for a romantic relationship."

"Yeah, but you liked him. I could tell."

"Perhaps, but it will never work."

"Why?"

"Sandy, I have a serious obligation that I cannot discuss."

"You mean Richard?"

"No. Richard is not the reason."

"Then what is it?"

Vera wanted to tell Sandy about the RGB. She wanted to leave the RGB behind and live her life as she saw fit. She valued her new friendship with Sandy and knew that a refusal to discuss her limits would pour cold water on it.

She said, "I have an obligation to the funders of my education."

Sandy gave Vera a puzzled look.

"What? Like a loan?"

"No. More permanent than a loan."

Sandy again looked puzzled.

Vera said, "Thank you for the visit. I enjoyed seeing the plovers. I must return to the university now. Have a safe drive home and please say hello to Brian."

With that, Vera got into her Subaru parked next to Sandy's, started the car, and backed out of her parking space. She offered a small wave to Sandy, who watched her leave dumbfounded.

Back at her UNH cottage, Vera began an unscheduled Gjogsul session. Sweat poured from her intense brow as her kicks and thrusts burst the afternoon calm.

On May 13, the FBI arrested Park Yeonmi, aka Susan Lee, aka Janice. This came as a surprise to the Defense Counterintelligence and Security Agency, the Counterintelligence and Insider Threat Unit, and Kenny. And everybody else. Including Kinnaird. The FBI had turned one of Janice's industrial spies, a South Korean metallurgical engineer working on a H-1B visa for Tecomet. After less than a day in custody, the engineer blew the whistle on Janice as part of a get-out-of-jail deal. He folded like an overboiled rice noodle. The Feds swooped in and arrested Janice without communicating up the chain to the Director of National Intelligence, DNI. More accurately, the Boston Field Office reported up the chain, but only on the Department of Justice side. The FBI is supposed to report intelligence findings to the DNI, as well as the DoJ. Anyway, DCSA's development of Janice got FUBAR real fast.

A week after her arrest, The United States informed North Korea through the Swedish Embassy in Pyongyang they had detained a North Korean national under the Espionage Act of 1917. Three days before that, DCSA found out, and Kinnaird entered the loop soon thereafter. Discussions with the FBI, DCSA, and Kinnaird as a contractor for the Deputy Secretary of Defense devolved into incivility, registering just above a cage match. How could the FBI barge into an ongoing counterespionage investigation without notifying the DNI? Why had they rushed the arrest cycle? Did they background Janice before the arrest? Did they know of her father's position in the RGB? Did they target Kenny as a known associate? Kenny, what about Kenny?

The DCSA and Kinnaird wanted to leave Kenny in place as a romantic foil, hoping to prompt Janice to spill all the beans. The FBI said they alone would interrogate the suspect and had no need for "outside" prompting or help. An undercover lover would only complicate the scenario.

But what was the scenario? Did the FBI see Janice as a turn? If so, did they plan to run her against her father and the RGB? That seemed farfetched. Did they plan to use her as a pawn in a spy swap? All Feds agreed to gloss over the swap scenario and concurred that only their agency directors could make such a decision. No, the FBI

seemed focused on busting up Janice's network and calling that a win.
DCSA and Kinnaird saw that approach as shortsighted. What if the
FBI released Janice, allowed her to reunite with Kenny, then allowed
Kenny to persuade her to defect, or, as a long shot, turn on the RGB?
And what about Janice's chain, the contacts she oversaw in the States?
One was already on the hook and had cut a deal with the FBI for
blowing the whistle on Janice. He was going back to South Korea for
the National Intelligence Service to deal with him. He had promised to
expose the RGB in exchange for asylum.

But what about Vera? And who even knew about Vera? The
FBI didn't mention her. DCSA and Kinnaird kept their mouths shut.
Kenny said nothing, and Joan Samuels remained stoic. As a contractor,
Kinnaird was on the back bench for negotiations. But to add heft to
their delegation, the Deputy Secretary of Defense sent a high-profile
staffer to take notes. One might sum up the agendas like this. The FBI
wanted to make arrests. Like shooting ducks in a pond, they wanted
bag numbers. The DCSA wanted penetration into the RGB and
ongoing surveillance of known links in Janice's chain. Kinnaird would
only receive payment if Vera flipped, defected, or became indisposed.

The DNI Deputy Director of the National Counterintelligence
and Security Center allowed robust bantering but drew the line at
name-calling. She had worked as a strategic analyst for the FBI, but
she wasn't a loyalist. She'd seen firsthand the agency's insularity and
uncooperativeness. They were an eight-hundred-pound gorilla in a
kid's bouncy palace. And their director was not above going to the
White House to lobby a runaround of any decision she rendered.

It was a half hour drive from the National Counterterrorism
Center in McLean, Virginia, to Kinnaird HQ in Ashburn. Joan had
foresworn her usual driver and black Suburban for Jeff and his, per her
instructions, randomly rented Toyota Sequoia. She wanted to talk over
Project Brizo, and that would have been impossible with her assigned
driver.

Joan asked, "What do you make of our situation relative to
Brizo?"

Jeff said, "Do you want it in military slang or polite
conversation?"

Joan nodded. "We need to approach Berg sooner rather than
later. I'm uncertain the FBI is laying all the cards on the table. In fact,
I'm certain they are *not* laying all the cards on the table. But they
didn't mention Berg, so . . . either they are planning a surprise for her,

or they are in the dark. They said their interrogation of Lee, or whatever name she's using, is preliminary, and she has yet to admit any connection to the RGB. She claims to be from a family who owns dry cleaning businesses in the South. She has a visa, and she travels on a South Korean passport. She claims no connection to the informer.

"My read is that the FBI only partially knows what it has. They jumped the gun, rolled up Lee, and looked ahead only so far as their annual tally of arrests. Congress has the FBI under the gun, and they need every feather in their cap to prove their worth. I believe it is unlikely that the FBI knows anything about Berg's connection to the RGB climate modification project.

"Jeff, is your friendly approach ready to transition? We need to make contact."

Jeff swallowed, cleared his throat, and said, "Probably not. The women are bonding, but I doubt they are at a level where Arsenault could facilitate outreach. I'll have to be involved."

"Then let's set something in motion. You'll need a supportive setting, a clear read on Berg's emotional state, and a carrot and a stick. I'll need to see something early next week. Are we clear?"

"Yes, ma'am. Five-by-five, Lima Charlie."

Sam was no slouch. He met Vera at Wells Beach on Saturday, and he emailed her Monday morning. He proposed they meet at Breaking New Grounds, a coffee shop near campus. He looked up Vera's schedule and found that she lectured on Wednesdays, and she kept office hours until noon. So, he proposed Wednesday at one o'clock.

Vera used the encrypted iPhone Janice had given her at their first meeting. She texted Sam's name on the Signal app for backgrounding. She did that Sunday evening and heard nothing in response from Janice. This was not unusual. Janice was not the most responsive RGB handler. Slow seemed to be her norm. The standard protocol for RGB meetings with uncleared contacts went like this. A) Could the contact advance RGB interests, and B) Did the contact present an immediate threat to RGB mission goals? In lay language, this meant: A) Could RGB turn or exploit the contact for information, and B) Was the contact a known or suspected law enforcement agent? If A was true and B was not, the RGB allowed subsequent meetings, but did not encourage them, in lieu of RGB backgrounding.

Vera didn't care about the RGB protocol. She divined Janice not a stickler for RGB rules and regulations. She emailed Sam back and said she looked forward to seeing him on Wednesday. He sent his cell number in the email, and she sent hers in her reply.

Janice and her encrypted iPhone now resided with the FBI. The FBI had rolled up Janice and all her identifiable property a week before. Now the FBI was working to unburden Janice of all North Korean security secrets and unlock her electronic devices. Janice had been sitting in the Boston holding cell for over a week. She felt conflicted. Interrogation had started on day two, and she'd sat through two hour-long sessions each day since. Her training would have her remain silent, and, if tortured, dribble outdated information at a pace designed to placate her captors and bide her time, waiting for diplomatic intervention. Of course, the FBI didn't torture. Their interrogators used sophisticated approaches based on their psychological profile of the detainee and exigent matters. In Janice's case, there were no exigent matters known to the FBI. The FBI assumed Janice ran industrial spies in the Boston area; six was their guess. To the FBI, they had arrested a suspect, a communications conduit to the North, of no exceptional importance. They did not suspect Janice of operational capacity or involvement in active measures against the United States or any ally. Janice was a small fish, but one that would grow into a whopper when reported to the oversight committees of Congress.

Janice repeated her legend. She was the daughter of a South Korean dry cleaner who owned stores in the South and had sent Janice to America to open a store here. Other than the FBI's incessantly repeating questions, they had yet to confront her with any documentation or other evidence to blow her cover. All they had was a deposition from a man who stated that Janice was his RGB contact who transferred information from his worksite to someone in the RGB. Janice claimed she had never met the man. But Janice, as she sat in her cell and considered her options, thought long and hard about offering herself for defection. That had been her unconscious goal since falling in love with Kenny. She asked to see Kenny and talk to him on the phone. But the FBI said she had only the right to a lawyer and, given her detainment under the Espionage Act, they would limit her external contacts. A lawyer came to speak with Janice on day three, but she didn't trust him and told him little. On day four, the FBI provided a young female lawyer, one of similar age to Janice, but Janice saw through the manipulation and told this lawyer even less.

By day five, Janice became convinced that she needed to negotiate a deal, defect, and relocate in America in exchange for an in-depth account of the RGB. She would not turn. Hers would be a onetime revelation of information and contacts. Her father, whom she loved, was her major impediment. She did not want to disappoint him or put him in jeopardy, but he would be fine. He was well positioned in the North, lived a comfortable life, and enjoyed the political support of the regime. The Americans, she was certain, already knew of her father's position in the RGB, but they did not know he was her father. She registered no concern for the fates of her active contacts, especially not for the pretentious Russian scientist who studied the ocean.

Vera noticed the student auditing her fourth lecture on submarine landslides. She wore the baggy, loose-fitting jeans and jacket that many students preferred, and she obscured her eyes with oversized glasses and a long-billed baseball cap. She sat in the last row of the auditorium, just inside the entrance and pretended to take notes on her laptop. Students often audited classes. But they asked permission from the professor. She had not. Vera continued the lecture, and when she had finished, she looked around for the young woman. She was gone.

Jeff was preparing to confront Vera, target Brizo. The Kinnaird surveillance team mobilized. The mystery student was a lookout. While Vera taught, Kinnaird had wired her cottage for sound and video. The two-man team dressed as university maintenance staff and drove a UNH panel truck. The installation had taken less than ten minutes.

Vera had not been subject to standard surveillance before now because Jeff thought it too risky; it could blow Sandy's friendly approach. RGB might sweep for electronic devices. If Vera found something, she would go defensive. Now he had no choice. With her handler in custody, Vera's technical support had vanished.

Jeff had a big problem, and it wasn't just devising an approach to Vera that played both persuasive and threatening. His problem was Sandy, and, by extension, Brian. Both were in the dark. The safest thing to do, the smart thing to do, the hard thing to do, was to bring them into the picture before he confronted Vera. This would be tricky. If they heard about Project Brizo after Jeff's contact with Vera, they would never trust Jeff again. Nor should they. He'd been leading them on. There was no way around that. Still, they had to know. The ramifications of not telling them in advance would outweigh the hit to his personal credibility. If things went well, he might even get some pointers on calibrating his approach. He would only mention the positive outcomes for Vera. First, she might defect, become an American citizen, have Richard in her life, work in her chosen profession, and live out her days. That would cost her all her secrets up front. A complete debrief of North Korea's environmental warfare capabilities. Second, she might turn on the RGB, play the role of a double, an informer. This seemed unlikely. Vera had never, to Jeff's knowledge, exhibited the resentment or greed necessary to motivate a traitor. And she wasn't a hub in a chain or link one. Merciless captors would torture and kill her if she were blown. The third outcome Jeff would not talk about. The first outcome provided the least profit for Kinnaird. The second and third each paid better. He knew which outcome Brian and Sandy would support.

In shorthand, Jeff needed to come clean . . . mostly. And it all needed to happen quickly, before the eight-hundred-pound gorilla bounced in uninvited.

The Tide of Deception
Chapter 43

Sam looked different now in his sport coat, white shirt, and dress slacks. His gray hair trimmed, and stubble beard shaved, he looked almost refined, scholastic. Vera wore her least off-putting cream blouse and dark slacks. She left two buttons undone at the top and tried to relax her image for this, their first date. Sure, it was only coffee, but to Vera, this was a date, a first step in a romantic process she was uncertain she wanted to embark upon. Sam might be the real deal. He was a birding expert, good-looking, employed, and, as far as she knew, unattached. The RGB had yet to nix the contact, so she proceeded with a newfound sense of independence. She liked the freedom.

Sam arrived first and sat at a sidewalk table outside the coffeehouse. He stood up when she approached and said, "Well, I'm pleased you could make it. I'm glad to see you."

Vera answered stiffly, "Ah . . . yes. I too am pleased to see you."

And that was it. No cute comment, no inviting smile, no hair flip . . . nothing.

Sam, undeterred, asked, "How did your class go this morning?"

"Yes. It is funny, you might ask. You have been at the university for years, correct?"

Sam nodded, "Fifteen."

"Is there a rule governing who can audit a lecture or class?"

"No. Not that I'm aware of. A student will usually talk to the professor and ask permission. Did you have a problem?"

"Not a problem. I had a student audit my lecture without asking permission."

"Were they disruptive?"

"No. I found it unusual, and she left before I could talk to her."

Sam shrugged, "It's college . . . who knows? Want some coffee? We'll need to order inside."

Vera, trained to detect the out of place and suspect the unusual, filed away the mystery student and walked inside with Sam to order her tea.

Sam got Vera to talk. She recounted a skeleton version of her childhood in Russia and omitted her two years in the North. She offered a curriculum vitae but sidestepped her marriage in the States and her son, Richard.

Sam was a Midwesterner who had grown up in a small town in Wisconsin. He had always been interested in wildlife. He had excelled in biology in high school, earned his undergraduate degrees at Purdue University, then studied ornithology at Cornell and earned his PhD. He talked about birds and Vera found this . . . exciting? A warmth arose inside her. A stirring.

Sam apologized for talking too much and urged Vera to tell him more about her studies. Studies were a safe topic for a first date, and Vera spoke about her field. They talked for an hour and a half, back and forth, fluidity increasing with each anecdote. When they parted, Sam asked Vera if she would like to go to dinner.

Vera smiled, maybe stiffly, but a smile. She said she would check her calendar and text Sam. Vera didn't have a calendar, save Sandy and her classes. But she put her toe in, and the water felt warm.

"Damnit, Jeff! I *knew* you were lying to us! I knew it, and I should have called you out back in January! God damn it! How could you do that?"

Jeff nodded and took the heat. Brian was right. But Jeff was only a cog in the machine. He didn't call the shots. Project Brizo would have come along either with or without Jeff. With or without Sandy. That part wasn't his fault.

Sandy, Jeff, and Brian sat in Brian's living room with a mesmerizing view of the Kennebec, but nobody found it enchanting today.

Sandy asked, "Jeff, are you telling us the truth now?"

Jeff nodded, "Yes. I am telling you all that I can. I can't get into operational details or any of that. And . . . please . . . anything I've said or tell you now is confidential, a matter of national security."

"Damn it, Jeff! You can't hide behind national security, not when you put people at risk and play them like puppets. Your own family, damn it!"

"Brian . . . honestly . . . I thought this might work to Sandy's benefit too. I mean, Sandy and Berg might come up with another angle on the Boothbay tide. I . . . I wanted them to get close, work together, and give me a leg up on Berg's state of mind. Honest."

Sandy said, "So . . . you put me in touch with Vera and pumped me for information so you could set her up for . . . what?"

"I need to talk to her. I need to layout her options."

"What are they?" Sandy asked.

"Well, like I said . . . she's an asset of the RGB of the DPRK, North Korea. She feeds into their secret environmental warfare bureau. She is a principal scientific asset. In short, I need to confront her and give her some options."

"Like what?" asked Brian.

"Well . . . the two main options are that she defects and tells us everything she knows about the environmental bureau and RGB. Or she works for us as a double agent, what we call a turn. She would go back to Busan when her UNH professorship is over and report to us, the CIA, or the South Korean National Intelligence Service. Or . . . she gets arrested, prosecuted, and imprisoned here in the States.

"This is going to sound pathetic . . . but I need your help."

Brian uttered, "Man . . . you've got balls."

"No . . . listen, Brian. Berg is smart, complex, and emotionally charged. We've monitored calls between her and her son in Washington state. We've done voice analysis and detected stress in their communications. She's agitated. And Sandy has borne this out . . . reluctantly."

Jeff shifted his gaze to Sandy. "But Sandy . . . I need to understand how important her son is to her. I need your sense of this. It matters because we need her motivation. Can I ask you a couple of questions? Please?"

Sandy didn't answer and stared through Jeff like he wasn't there.

"Would you say that Berg shows ideological commitment?" Has she ever presented as a committed communist?"

"Jeff . . . the answer is no. Vera is a scientist."

The room fell silent for a spell. Then Sandy added, "She . . . she mentioned once, the last time we were together, that she owed a *permanent* debt for her education. I asked if she meant Richard, her son, and she said no."

"So, she's never raised a critique of the West, of capitalism, any kind of spontaneous criticism?"

Sandy shook her head.

Jeff continued, "Does she have money problems?"

"Jeff . . . no . . . I mean . . . who knows? She's never mentioned money.

"If you're looking for motivation . . . ah, why am I telling you this? She wants to be part of her son's life. She hopes to be near as he matures, gets married, has kids, so she can impart her love of nature all the while. The only reason I'm telling you this is because . . . if what you've told us is true . . . a big if . . . I want her to defect and live here in America. This spy-verses-spy crap that you're selling sounds dangerous, and I want her to be happy. I'd like to keep her as a friend. Okay, there it is. I like her. She's from a different world, but I like her. She has a good soul. Put that in your pipe and smoke it."

"And how did she get hooked up with this reconnaissance bureau in the first place? Tell me that."

"We're not sure. That will be part of her debrief, should she defect or turn. Her initial contact could be connected to her mother's death. Did she tell you she spent two years in North Korea as a child?"

Sandy shook her head.

"Apparently, her mother worked for the Russian security services in North Korea in ninety-three and ninety-four, and somehow, the RGB ended up with Berg as an asset. It's all murky."

"How'd you find that out?" asked Brian.

"Well . . . this is open source . . . PAI. Have you ever heard of the Mitrokhin files?"

Brian shook his head.

"Mitrokhin was a KGB archivist. He made public a trove of files and notes. They are available at the Churchill Archives Centre of the University of Cambridge in the UK. There's a lot of material, and we're pretty sure we found a link."

Brian raised an eyebrow.

Jeff said, "Look . . . she's a smart woman. We have an emotional window to approach her. Let me ask you, where should this happen? Where would she be most at ease?"

"Wait . . . you're going to walk up to her and tell her you know she's a spy? Then . . . what? Lay out her options? She'll run away like a deer from a dog." Sandy shook her head.

"What are you suggesting, Sandy?"

"Jeff . . . if what you're telling us is true . . . again . . . a big *if* . . . you're going to spook her. She'll run, and she's smart enough to get away, unless you intend to arrest her on the spot?"

"Ah . . . no. That's not the plan."

Jeff didn't mention that he and Kinnaird had no arrest powers in America or any other country. Unofficial detention, aka kidnapping, but not arrest."

"Okay, Sandy, what I hear you saying is that Berg may need an introductory third party."

"Stop! Jeff! I don't like where this is going," inserted Brian. "You're angling to have Sandy introduce you. That puts Sandy at risk, and I'm opposed to that. Hard and fast."

"Brian, honestly, I don't think Sandy is in danger. I haven't told you because it wasn't relevant until now, but they arrested Berg's handler . . . her contact in America . . . a week ago. Now, without spilling all the details, the FBI is involved. And believe this if you believe nothing else, once those guys get involved, the only option Berg will have is prison. We've got the support of a ranking official in the Department of Defense. We can make these other options happen, but we need the right approach. We just need to talk."

Sandy absorbed the avalanche of contradiction and severity. Spies? North Korea? Taken by surprise, without a clue, Jeff's brief washed over her like the news of Noah's death. She couldn't believe it. In as calm a voice as she could muster, she asked, "Jeff. Are you certain of your information? Are you certain that Vera is . . . what do you call her? An agent? Of North Korea? It's too much."

Jeff said, "Sandy, without going into methods and means, we are one hundred percent certain that Dr. Vera Berg is an asset of the North Korea RGB."

He paused, "Why she is doing it? Unknown. What is North Korea doing with her information and research? Unknown.

"If she wants to work for the good guys . . . we can arrange that. If she wants to work for the bad guys, she's going to prison. And if we, Kinnaird, don't get to her first, the FBI will see to it she chooses door number two."

Jeff didn't mention the still-on-the-table, lucrative door number three.

Brian, still steaming at his brother's duplicity, came to Sandy's side. He walked across the living room and put his hands on Sandy's shoulders where she sat on the sofa. Sandy wanted Vera in America and safe. So did Brian. He had watched Vera transform the afternoon of the lobster bake and agreed that a natural setting would be best for "the talk." He was not so surprised by his brother's confession as was Sandy. Jeff was a known quantity to Brian. Now he kicked himself for not ferreting out his brother's manipulation sooner. He should have known.

Brian said, "You want to confront her in a natural setting, right?"

Jeff nodded, "Yep . . . that's how this is breaking down."

Jeff paused, nodded, then asked, "Sandy, is your boat in the water?"

Memorial Day weekend broke clear and warm, the weather forecast fair, and the plan in motion. Jeff kissed his sleeping wife on the forehead and, using his thumbprint, opened his biometric gun safe disguised as an oversized LED clock atop his bedstand. Of the two pistols stored there, he picked the Beretta 950 Jetfire, a .25 caliber, easily concealable backup. Ejecting the clip, Jeff checked it held eight rounds and reinserted it. Then he picked up a single bullet from the padded safe, popped open the tip-up barrel, and slid the round in. He lowered the barrel, checked the safety, and put the gun in his right pants pocket. He left his larger Beretta M9 in the safe and closed the drawer. Before leaving for Southport, he went to the kitchen, opened the refrigerator, and grabbed a bag of sandwiches Georgia had made the night before. He walked to the garage and got a twelve-pack of Peroni Nastro Azzurro from his stash. Just a pleasant day on the water. A little sightseeing, a few seals, ospreys, and eagles, then a conversation that would change lives, or . . . end one.

Sandy and Brian, of course, knew nothing about the gun or the door number three option. They had agreed to set the day afloat for Vera, who immediately said she would come. This way, she didn't have to decide about Sam's dinner invitation. This was Maine at its best. Nice weather, a nice boat, and immense, rugged beauty. The biggest problem, beyond the confrontation brewing, was that when the tide started running on the Sheepscot, lobster trawls and aids to navigation could disappear, pulled under by the swift current. But neither Sandy nor Brian were rookies. Their local knowledge told them, if all else failed, follow the lobster pot buoys because they were set in deep water. And, if you couldn't see the buoys, slow down and follow the chart.

The first time Sandy and Brian had taken the boat out, Sandy experienced transient PTSD. The twenty-nine-foot Dyer, named *Dolphin*, had been Noah's pride and joy. He loved the boat, and to Sandy, the association was inexorable. Brian at the helm worried her. The *Dolphin* curse? The temptation of fate? Hubristic folly? This was stupid. Noah had died years ago. She'd seldom used the boat in the interim. She'd considered selling it, and during the height of Covid, she might have gotten a premium price. But she couldn't do it.

Dolphin equaled Noah. Brian boated to Southport in his Whaler. But his sixteen-foot center console, open to the elements, was neither big enough nor plush enough for four people to enjoy an afternoon on the water. Brian's boat best fit two guys who wanted to fish. And it smelled like it.

It wasn't fair to say Vera had a suspicious mind. Hers was an analytical mind, trained, honed, and equally applicable to science and spying. She processed the sequence of unusual recent occurrences in her life. Her meeting with Sam. The mysterious student auditing her lecture. The paint fleck missing from her cottage doorjamb. The note from UNH maintenance that they had been in her house to check for a gas leak. And now the invitation from Sandy to take a boat ride, see Ovens Mouth, and meet Brian's brother. Sandy had never mentioned Jeff before. Sandy told Vera the brothers wanted to shakedown the boat and make sure it ran right after machining the prop shaft.

Sandy hated lying. It drained her soul. She felt swept into this charade like Noah being swept by the tide. How in the hell did she get herself into this shit show? Like her cousins would say, this is a shit show with no good outcome. Regardless of how Vera reacted, Sandy's credibility would suffer . . . forever. Vera would be right to distance herself from Sandy, and never again trust what she said. Sandy saw no way out. Damn Jeff!

Vera didn't question Sandy. She had no reason. But she questioned the compilation of unusual occurrences of recent days. The RGB had coached Vera on an escape scenario before she left Busan. Janice had never mentioned escape and offered no support or details. The RGB had told Vera, "Should you be exposed, you are to make your way to Washington. Once there, locate the Cuban Embassy on Sixteenth Street, Northwest, and present yourself for protection and repatriation to the DPRK."

But Vera didn't want to run. She didn't want to live in the North. She wanted to stay. Richard was in America. She had grown fond of Sandy. And UNH, in the past week, had offered her a full professorship with expedited tenure. She even considered Sam. She entertained romantic thoughts, thoughts long left behind in another world and another time. But she was an agent of the RGB, and an indispensable cog in their environmental warfare effort. She seldom confronted herself with the notion. She saw her research, her writing, and her lecturing as neutral science. Knowledge for its own sake. But that wasn't true. The RGB wanted a weapon, and her contributions helped them in that effort. She knew that, but she sidestepped thinking about it. The RGB, with their oversight of her life, was second nature, something that she lived with and lived around when she could. Now, in America, in proximity to Richard, her emotional anchor, she wanted freedom. She wanted to be in his life and the lives of his children. She knew now her purpose. The essence that Sun-ja had imparted to her must be passed to the coming generation. This would honor Sun-ja. It was worthy . . . *Cheon*. But, like it or not, she was an enemy of the United States. She had no clue how to extricate herself. She had never investigated defection, asylum, or any method of disappearance and reconstitution. She didn't think that way. But on her drive to Southport, she began to do so.

"What the hell are you doing with that?" demanded Brian.

Jeff wore a pair of khaki tactical pants whose deep pocket bulged in a familiar outline. The two men met at the Boothbay Harbor Yacht Club, where *Dolphin* lulled on a mooring in the mid-morning breeze. The steward had just delivered the brothers to the boat when Brian saw the gun. Now he was kicking himself for not noticing it sooner.

"You can't bring that on this boat, Jeff. And what the hell are you doing with it, anyway?"

"I always carry this thing," answered Jeff. "Prudence . . . right?"

Jeff left unsaid. *Prudence called for when engaging a known agent of the RGB. One that might require elimination.*

Jeff had no plans to eliminate Vera on this outing. Should that become necessary, her demise would be a verifiable accident. Kinnaird had specialists to draw that up.

"Take the gun ashore and leave it in the car." Brian handed Jeff the keys to Sandy's Subaru.

"Come on, brother. I'm skilled. Chill. We're already late and it'll cost us another fifteen minutes to go back to the club."

Brian shook his head. They wanted to reach Oven's Mouth on an inbound tide, and the clock didn't lie.

Brian said, "All right. Give it to me and I'll keep it in the cabinet. You don't need to have it on you. And hell, if I can spot it, a trained RGB agent can spot it. You'll have a hell of a rapport if she thinks you're gunning for her."

Brian was right. He handed the Beretta to his brother butt first. Brian released the tip-up barrel, removed the round, handed the shell back to Jeff, shaking his head at his brother. He put the gun in the cabinet inside the sleeping berth.

Brian went to the helm, tuned the VHF, and engaged the electronics. Before he turned over the engine, he said, "Pack your sandwiches and beer in the refrigerator and then make ready to leave the mooring."

Jeff, an observant US Navy SO, knew there could be but one captain of the boat and did as his brother ordered.

The engine fired. The diesel issued the black smoke of ignition, then resolved into mellow thumping. Brian signaled Jeff to unleash the mooring pendant. Once free, the *Dolphin* took a southern heading, rounding the tip of Southport on its way to Cozy Harbor, a short walk from Sandy's house. Sandy and Vera would meet the brothers there. Sandy's float and dock were still on the disabled list from the January storms. While the structure was stout enough to handle Brian's Whaler, *Dolphin* would be too much. At Cozy Harbor, Brian pulled alongside the public dock and Jeff lashed them to a cleat. The women came aboard. Sandy carried her binoculars, and Vera handed Jeff a thermos of tea. This was Jeff's first exposure to Vera in the flesh. Even in baggy jeans and a rough jacket, she was a beautiful woman. Striking. She wore no makeup and greeted Jeff correctly when she stepped aboard. Her eyes penetrated, chilly beams of no nonsense. Warmth she reserved for Sandy and, by extension, Brian. Jeff received none of the reflected sociability.

Jeff stood next to Brian at the helm, and Sandy and Vera sat in the cockpit. The river churned with light chop as they cruised north at a pleasant eight knots. The tide had started to run, and *Dolphin* surfed the inbound current effortlessly. The Sheepscot, always a chilly river, had everyone zipping up their jackets. Jeff grabbed a wool blanket from the berth and carried it to Sandy and Vera, sitting together at the transom. He smiled as he handed it to Sandy, who thanked him with no reciprocation from target Brizo.

Less than a thousand meters from Cozy Harbor, *Dolphin* passed Hendricks Head Lighthouse and Hendricks Head Beach to starboard. This was where Noah had washed ashore. Sandy was the only one onboard aware of this detail, and her mind skipped a beat. She fell silent. It was noisy in the cockpit, and not great for conversation. But Sandy's reticence was reverence and reflection. An emotional tug pulled at her, and she fell into a flood of memories and a rush of guilt. It seemed wrong to have Brian at the helm of what would always be Noah's boat. But she whisked away that thought. A boat was a thing, and people used things, tools, and devices. *Dolphin* was only that. What she couldn't rout or sidestep was a premise. What would Noah think if he were alive today?

Sandy lapsed further as she imagined the cold Noah must have felt as he drowned. The dark spell lifted a mile north. Vera spotted a colony of fat seals lounging and yacking on Bull Ledge. She said, "Oh . . . over there, Sandy. It's seals."

Vera grew excited. She smiled, and Sandy welcomed the transformation. Sandy joked, "They're telling each other where the fish are."

At that very moment, a few of the gray blobs slipped into the river, causing not a ripple, disappeared beneath the surface, and vanished from view.

Sandy said, "Somebody must have shared a hot tip."

Vera smiled.

Three miles north, they spotted more seals on Stoven Ledge. This time, Jeff was the first to point them out as he walked to the cockpit with a pair of Steiner binoculars from the helm station. He handed the optics to Vera and smiled. She said thank you. Jeff nodded and returned to the helm.

Vera scanned the twenty fat, boisterous, submarine killers; then, two hundred feet above them, over the Barters Island shoreline, she spotted an eagle. Now she engaged. When she noticed the second bird, she said, "Oh . . . Sandy, look! They are hunting together. I wonder if they are paired?"

Sandy brought her glasses up and spotted the birds. She asked Vera, "Is it unusual for them to hunt together?"

Vera said, "When they hunt together . . . it is called tandem . . . they can take larger prey. On this river, they might take goose or a heron, perhaps a plump duck. Although they can take ducks without a partner. When they hunt together, it is often a breeding pair.

"They also raid other bird's nests in tandem. One will distract the nest guardian and the other will snatch a chick or steal a catch. They are not above robbery."

Sandy said, "Nature has a lax criminal code."

Vera didn't respond. She rotated on the seat cushion and kept her eyes on the birds.

As *Dolphin* motored north, the birds fell away to continue their sorties.

When Vera returned her gaze forward, she said, "Sandy, I have been thinking about our conversation in the parking lot after watching the plovers."

"Really? What about it?"

Vera had to raise her voice in the cockpit. This made her uncomfortable. She wanted this conversation to be between her and Sandy. She scooted closer to Sandy on the bench seat.

Vera said, "I have something important I want to tell you . . .

but you must promise not to tell anyone."

Sandy's thoughts raced. She had already betrayed Vera to Jeff in a situation that seemed unresolvable. If Vera was who Jeff claimed she was, then Sandy could not keep her confidence. If Jeff was wrong, Sandy could keep her promise. It was just that . . . she didn't feel Vera was manipulating her. Vera seemed honest. And Sandy had a sixth sense for manipulation. She had a teenage daughter.

Sandy hated lying. Her soul emptied. She dodged, "Vera . . . we're friends. I wouldn't do anything to hurt you."

Vera whispered, her face close to Sandy's, "I need to make a change. I have decided what I want, but because of constraints, it will be difficult to attain."

Sandy asked, "What do you want?"

Vera said, "I want to be in Richard's life and the lives of his children. This is important to me. It is what I want, and it is a way to honor my mother."

Sandy said, "Well, I'm sure you can find work in America. I'm sure you can get a visa . . . and apply for citizenship."

"Yes, the university has offered me a position. But it is more complicated than that."

"Is this about the *obligation* you mentioned at the beach?"

"Yes . . . it is."

"What is it? What's stopping you?"

"Sandy, I have not been truthful with you. But now, I've decided what I want. You are a smart woman, and you may help . . . help me . . . disconnect . . . from my obligation."

Was Jeff's plan working? Vera wanted to come clean about something sensitive and threatening. It was her tone, the worry in her eyes, her shaken confidence. Sandy wanted to bail and hand this conversation off to Jeff. But how? How would she do that without being abrupt, or jarring? She'd spook Vera. Shit! Now Sandy was doing the manipulating, and she hated it. Shit! She had about reached the point she had with the interrogator, and at the Camden reception. Sandy wanted to throw her hands in the air and let the chips fall where they may.

Sandy said, "Vera, we've only known each other a few months, right?"

Vera gave a thoughtful nod.

"Well, in that short time, I've grown to like you. I count you as a friend. I want the best for you," Sandy assured. "If I can help you, I will. But we have a lot of personal history we have yet to share. We're both in our forties, and we've lived lives full of consequence and happenstance. Nobody can know everything about another person, but we can share the important parts.

"When I met you in Camden, I knew you were an important scientist. I hoped we might work together on solving the Boothbay tide anomaly. That was my motive. Since then, I've grown to like and respect you. I can tell that you are struggling with something in your past that is preventing you from attaining . . . happiness. Fulfilling your passion. I can tell."

Vera nodded.

"But Vera, I just found out more about you. And . . . I didn't know this until a couple of days ago."

Vera came to attention with questioning eyes.

"Jeff," and Sandy nodded toward the helm, "Jeff works for an employer who deals in confidential government information. He told me some things that were hard to believe. As a friend, whatever the truth, I want you to be happy. We can fix your problems, if they are what Jeff says."

Sandy's handoff was, if not jarring, less than a full endorsement of Jeff. But she couldn't go further; she wasn't certain that Jeff was telling the truth.

Sandy continued, "Jeff is in touch with people in the government who can help you. I think when we get to Ovens Mouth and drop anchor, you and Jeff should talk."

Vera looked down at the cockpit floor and shook her head. When she raised up, she said, "Sandy, I do not know Jeff. It is hard for me to trust anyone. What I have to say is . . . dangerous. What I want is . . . prohibitive."

"Vera, Jeff knows who you work for."

A bolt of lightning flashed in Vera's eyes. She looked to Sandy like a wild foal fighting off a training halter. Fight or flight. Sandy saw Vera's forearms tense as the veins in her neck strained.

"Vera, it's going to be okay. Just talk to Jeff. He's well-connected. He can make it happen. You want to stay in the States, right?"

Vera wasn't tracking; her mind had shifted to instinct. Gjogsul had kicked in. She sat with her hands on her knees, staring without recognition.

Sandy put her hands on Vera's hands, and Vera pulled them

away. She looked to Sandy like she might jump into the Sheepscot and make an escape. Vera weighed the option.

Sandy said, "Vera . . . Vera . . . look at me!"

Vera stared ahead with a quick glance Sandy's way. Her mind swam in a mix of warning signs and reality. The student auditing her class. The maintenance men in her cottage. Sam. Jeff. She replayed thoughts from her drive to Sandy's house. Could she be a fugitive? Could she run from authorities? How? Where would she go? How could she make a living? She didn't want to live in the North. Where would she go? She would abandon Richard . . . again.

"Vera! Vera! We must be creative," Sandy insisted.

Chumun! Vera began a recitation, triggered by Sandy's urging creativity.

May the creative power of the universe be within me in abundance.

She struggled to recall the remainder. Her mind a bumble. Focus.

May heaven be with me, and every creation will be done. Never forgetting this truth, everything will be known.

At that moment, Brian turned *Dolphin* to starboard, passing to port a large red-and-green can buoy marking the junction of the Sheepscot and Cross Rivers. On top of the buoy, an osprey nest the size of a bushel basket chirped and fluttered. The nest guardian had his or her hands, or wings, full of chicks mouthing and demanding breakfast. Sandy saw it first. She said, "Vera . . . pay attention . . . see the ospreys." And she pointed to the buoy.

Vera's head jerked in the direction.

Sandy yelled at Brian, "Slow down, Brian! We want to check out the ospreys!"

Brian cut the throttle back to idle.

Vera focused, and Sandy watched the transformation. Vera went from caged animal to student of nature in less than a minute. She brought the Steiners to her eyes and counted the chicks. The exercise grounded her. She returned to a cognitive state. Her facial muscles relaxed, and she was once again communicative.

Vera said, "I see four nestlings. They appear healthy . . . and hungry. Their guardian has a fish, and it looks like they are trying to decide which one to feed first."

Sandy said, "The chicks. Their mother will feed them and teach them all they will need to know . . . how to survive. They will fledge, begin hunting on their own, grow to adulthood, and pair. Then they will be off to find a buoy of their own and raise their own chicks. It is the way nature wants it to be. It is the way *you* want things to be. This is good. We can make it happen, Vera."

Vera said, "They will live with their parents until the fall. That is when they will find their way."

Sandy said, "That nest is going to get crowded."

Sandy saw the hint of a smile come to Vera's lips.

"Vera . . . we must treat each other as friends. This may be new to you . . . you told me you have few friends. But friends help each other when they are in tight situations.

"I'm sorry I sprang this news on you but when you talk to Jeff, he'll tell you why your situation is urgent. I'm sorry."

Vera didn't speak. Her mind was still with the ospreys, but she circled her circumstance like the second osprey she spotted circling the buoy.

Vera lowered the binoculars, faced Sandy, and asked, "Is Jeff going to arrest me?"

Sandy shook her head.

Vera looked down to the cockpit deck, then back up to Sandy, then to the ospreys.

"She's at the University of New Hampshire. She's an oceanographer. Her name is Vera Berg. I've communicated with her via encoded text, and we've had one face-to-face. She's in America on a six-month professorship. She's scheduled to return to Busan sometime this fall, August, I think. She works at an oceanographic lab in Busan, and she's been there for years. I've checked out her contacts, but she hasn't requested that I transmit any data for her.

"I do not know what she studies, no idea of her importance. She's just a scientist, and stuck-up, at that. And she's Russian. She's a half-breed. She looks Korean, but she's Russian. She was born there, and she's a Russian citizen. That's all I can tell you."

While Vera transited through a fog of self-doubt and uncertainty aboard *Dolphin*, Janice spilled her guts to the FBI. She'd decided to defect in exchange for a total debrief and confession of her spying sins. She heard in her deal what she wanted to. The FBI made only the promise that she could request asylum. They made no promises about Kenny, or where Janice might live, or how long her interrogation would last. Janice had in writing only that she would not face arrest in exchange for "cooperation on matters of national security." Meanwhile, she would stay in custody, in a nicer cell, with no visitors save her attorney, one call a week to Kenny, and no computer.

Her first call to Kenny, after ten days' absence, was a mishmash of forlorn regret, confession, profession of love, chiding, more professions of love. She encouraged Kenny to "hang on. We'll get through this, babe."

Kenny played along . . . the confused lover willing to do anything to help. She was the love of his life. He would be her unbendable support during this impossible mistake. Was it a mistake? He couldn't believe it. Had the FBI mistreated her? A spy? What should he call her? He was confused. He would visit her. He would come today if she wanted. Did she need a lawyer? Where was she being held?

Sad days ahead loomed for Park Yeonmi, aka Susan Lee, aka Janice.

The tide ran full when Brian reached Ovens Mouth. As he entered the passage, he increased *Dolphin's* speed to nine knots. The water below him moving into the estuary flowed at six knots. So, through the tight, tricky passage, Brian added three knots to keep command of his vessel. Luckily, he saw no other craft in the channel, so he could use its entire narrow width for error correction.

This morning's tide wasn't astronomical, but it was heavy. At the eastern end of the passage, where the tide emptied into the broad estuary, the current slowed, and Brian reduced *Dolphin's* speed. And right there, at the end of the fast water, a whirlpool churned, not as massive as Old Sow, but a good thirty feet in diameter. The bathymetry of Ovens Mouth, unlike Old Sow, was elementary. A pit in the riverbed caused this whirlpool. For some geological reason, the depth of the water, right at the end of the passage, increased from twenty feet to seventy feet. This "hole" caused the running tide to circulate in a clockwise direction, stirring debris and bait and attracting stripers and blues to feed on its bounty. The screen on *Dolphin's* fish-finder filled with two-dimensional graphics swarming in and around the food source. Brian motioned Vera to the helm.

He said, "Look, Vera, see the fish? The whirlpool draws the bait, and the bait draws the stripers and other fish, along with seals and ,sometimes, porpoises."

Vera steadied herself on the back of the helm seat, looking over Brian's shoulder. She asked, "Brian, are the fish represented by their size?"

"Roughly. This sounder uses three icons, so it's an approximation."

"There are some big fish, no?"

"Oh, yeah. They are most active on a going tide. But when the tide comes in, they still feed, and the whirlpool still draws the bait."

Vera's mind swirled like the whirlpool. Jeff stood next to her and didn't say a word. Vera turned to Jeff and said, "Sandy says we should discuss important matters. She said you may help."

Jeff nodded. "I can help. Let's wait until we anchor, and we can talk up here in the cabin berth."

Less than a mile from the whirlpool, motoring farther south in the estuary, Dolphin dropped anchor near a rocky outcrop. Beyond this point, the estuary became shallow. At high tide, it was navigable. But it wasn't high tide. Brian thought it best to anchor. The outcrop drew stripers, and if he got bored, he might cast a lure and maybe hook a schoolie. The outcrop also drew cormorants and gulls. Brian thought familiar sightings, friendly encounters might keep Vera calm and help keep "the discussion" on track. He was guessing, but it felt right. So as *Dolphin* settled on her anchor in the southerly breeze, Brian cut the engine, and conversation in a normal tone resumed.

Jeff and Brian joined Sandy and Vera in the cockpit. Sandy asked, "Is anybody hungry?"

It seemed like a silly question. "The discussion" was the first thing on everyone's mind.

Jeff said, "I could eat a sandwich, but coffee's good for now. Vera, would you like some tea?" Jeff reached for the thermos on the bench seat.

Vera protected her thermos. She said, "I can pour my tea . . . thank you."

Jeff lost round one in his charm offensive.

Sandy wished they had towed the dinghy on a painter so she and Brian could jump ship and leave Jeff and Vera on their own.

Brian said, "So if you two want to talk, I'm going to rig a rod and cast toward the rocks. Let me get that from the cabin, then it's all yours. Sandy, do you want to fish?"

Sandy registered Brian's obvious ploy. She shook her head. She said, "I'll watch you and grab the net if you get lucky. I can hold off for lunch."

Jeff rose from his seat on the engine cover and poured a cup of coffee from Brian's thermos. Brian said, "You can leave five bucks on the galley."

Jeff shook his head. "Always the joker." Then he looked at Vera and said, "Let's sit together in the cabin. More privacy in there."

Vera said, "Privacy is unnecessary. Anything I say, Sandy and Brian can hear, as well."

This left Jeff aghast. If Vera wasn't worried about sharing secrets, he was. He said, "If you don't mind, I think keeping the discussion between us, for now, might be best."

Vera said, "We can go to the cabin, but the door will remain open, and there we will talk. Brian and Sandy will not overhear."

She was negotiating with Jeff right out of the gate. He

respected this. She would not be easy to rattle. She had her wits about her.

"Okay, let's do that," Jeff agreed.

The two climbed down the steps into *Dolphin's* cabin and sleeping berth. It wasn't a large space, but there was enough room that each sat on a cushion to port and starboard with three feet between them. Jeff held his coffee in a steel mug. Vera's hands were free.

Jeff began, "Dr. Berg, I work for a government contractor at the discretion of the deputy director, United States Department of Defense. Our intelligence tells us you are a . . ." Jeff shied away from the provocative term *agent*. ". . . a contact working with the North Korea RGB."

He looked at Vera for recognition. She gave none.

"You provide research and analysis for an environmental warfare bureau within the RGB. We've verified this with the South Korea NIS. They've watched you for many years."

Again, Jeff saw no recognition from target Brizo. Her cold beams bored through him as if he were not present.

"Dr. Berg, the United States government would like to hear what you know. And we would like to hear more about the DPRK's intelligence apparatus, the RGB, and your special project. That information is what we want.

"Now, before we go any further, I need you to acknowledge what I have said."

Vera straightened on the cushion and pronounced, "You said I am a spy for North Korea, and you offer no proof."

"Your case officer . . . you called her *Janice* . . . is in custody, in Boston, and she has offered testimony against you. You met her at least once, soon after you arrived at the university. We have photos."

Jeff pulled an iPhone from his inside jacket pocket and swiped a series of photos of Janice and Vera at the restaurant. Then he played an audio recording of Janice's confession describing her asset, Vera. Including the part about Vera being stuck-up. Then Jeff said, "Besides this evidence, we are decrypting your text messages with your handler."

"Your case officer . . . her real name is Park Yeonmi . . . is being held by the Federal Bureau of Investigation. The FBI recorded this yesterday, so we need to discuss your situation. We don't have a lot of time for negotiations.

"You won't understand this, but the FBI plays by a different set of rules than we do. They want you in prison. Period. They will not offer what we can offer. We can make our offers because the Department of Defense endorses them, and we can overrule the FBI. But this must happen quickly.

"Dr. Berg, Sandy is your friend, so I want you to understand she had nothing to do with the two of you meeting and becoming friends. She did not know who you worked for. She wanted to work with you to solve the Boothbay tide. I set up the meeting at the conference to get her close to you to provide feedback on you. She wouldn't. She only told me you were from a different culture but she liked you. She considered you a friend. And . . . she told me about Richard.

"Richard came up in your backgrounding. Dr. Berg, I have twin boys, age ten. I understand the bond between parent and child. I would do anything for my kids. And . . . I think you would do anything for Richard. Richard's older, but I believe you want to be in his life . . . here in America. He seems like a proper young man. He has baseball potential, and his school grades are first rate. He's never been in trouble with the law, and from what we can tell, he's a proper young man."

At this mention of Richard, white light flashed in Vera's frontal cortex and her stomach turned. Her adrenal glands primed her system, and a chill stiffened her spine. The United States government had invaded her life and Richard's life. She spit out the words, and soon regretted them. "You must never mention my son again. Stay away from him. Stay out of his life!"

"Dr. Berg . . . we can't do that. We have no desire to harm Richard. In fact, we think we can help Richard. We can help him by putting you back into his life."

Jeff's pledge of *no harm* showed only one side of the coin. The other side was just as true. The thought landed like a knife through Vera's heart. Jeff had planned it that way.

"You returned to Russia after your divorce. We suspect this was your activation by the RGB. Is that correct?"

Overwhelmed, Vera's eyes drifted up the cabin way. She considered running. It showed. Jeff saw the stone wall ahead. He said, "Okay . . . let's leave that until later.

"Dr. Berg . . . there are two ways for you to turn your predicament into a positive. But you must agree and sign a contract. Otherwise, the FBI will arrest you under the 1917 Espionage Act, the

Department of Justice will prosecute you, and you will go to prison.
The Department of Defense can't hold that off for very long. You
don't have to sign today, but we need to agree on a plan this afternoon.
I need to inform people you have agreed to an option before us. Then
we can work out the details.

"Dr Berg . . . we can offer you two scenarios. The first will pay
you handsomely and involve some risk on your part. In this scenario,
you will continue with your service to the RGB and report to us
everything you learn about them. You will return to Busan at the end
of your professorship and reestablish your relationship with the RGB."

Vera regained a measure of composure. "You want me to spy
on the RGB? And for this I will be paid? Ha!"

Jeff nodded. "We understand this is risky, but your
compensation will be handsome and . . . in due course . . . you could
apply for asylum in America, and be with Richard."

"And how many years would this require?" she asked.

"That is hard to say. I imagine . . . five, ten . . . I don't know."

"You realize the RGB will kill me if they even suspect such a
ploy? And, if I am in Korea, North or South, I will be an easy target.
Why would I go to Korea, if . . . like you say . . . I want to be part of
my son's life?"

Jeff said, "The next option is that you agree to a complete and
total debrief. For this, you will stay here in the States, receive no
compensation except expedited asylum and citizenship consideration,
and detach yourself from the RGB. We will help you find employment
in your field, and your former association with the RGB will remain
secret."

"So . . . in this scenario, I would live in America, work here,
and be with my son. Is this correct?"

"Yes."

"Then please tell me why the RGB will not come for me,
kidnap me, take me to the North, torture me, and then kill me. Can you
protect me from that?"

"We don't believe that will happen."

"Oh . . . what is that *belief* based on?"

"Dr. Berg, you are not the first RGB asset to face this
predicament. We have never lost an asylum seeker turned American
citizen in the States, and there have been many. The RGB does not kill
people in America and we, for our part, do not kill their people in
Korea, North or South. You have an added advantage, too. You are a

Russian citizen. Russia and the North have entered into a friendship agreement and are making nice with each other. The RGB murdering a Russian citizen, anywhere, would be a setback in their affairs."

Vera's analytical mind weighed the options. She had most definitely been blown. They had the tapes and the photos and would soon have her texts. She could not run to Washington, find the Cuban Embassy, and ask for protection. From this moment forward, they would watch her every move. She knew that. Besides, she did not want to live in the North, and she had burned her Russian bridge all those years ago when she throat-punched the KGB officer. She didn't need the money. She had never needed money. It was not a motivator in her life. She needed an education, which the RGB had provided. But money didn't worry Vera. The royalties on her publications were enough to get her by.

Jeff didn't want to kill Vera, or . . . more correctly . . . arrange for her accidental death. He was getting soft. There was something enticing about this woman, and not just sexual. It was her mind, her sharpness, her determination. He admired her correctness, unalloyed by ideology or corrupted by cultish mind control. She'd yet to bring up anything about communism versus capitalism, about centralism versus democracy. Sandy was right. Berg was a scientist. He remembered the initial brief from Joan Samuels where she had described Vera as devout Chondogyo. He wished now that he had studied that angle more. She had an underpinning, not communistic but disciplined. An underpinning, an anchor that formed a base for her thoughts and actions. Damn! He should have read up on this . . . what was it? A religion? Eastern mysticism? Buddhism? Animism? Shit.

At that moment, Brian's rod bent double, and he struggled to steady the reel and slacken the drag. He had a big one. It might be a slotter. He yelled, "Sandy, get the net!"

Sandy, who had been watching herons on the eastern shore through her binoculars, dropped them to the bench seat and rushed to the cabin entrance. She said, "I'm sorry! I need the net! Brian's hooked a fish." The net rested in spring steel gripper clamps attached to the port hull of the sleeping berth.

Jeff wheeled around and pulled the net from its clamps. Then he lay back on the bunk so he could pass the net to Sandy. Sandy lifted it carefully up and through the cabin way.

Brian's battle with the striper had preempted "the discussion." Jeff looked at Vera. "Do you want to watch?"

Vera nodded, rose from her berth, and climbed the cabin steps. Jeff followed. They both stood at the helm and smiled as Brian tugged and reeled to keep the fish away from *Dolphin's* prop. It was a big one. It surfaced thirty yards away, and everyone onboard got a glimpse. Jeff estimated thirty-six inches, at least.

Brian was under-equipped for a fish this size. He fished with light spinning tackle and eight-pound test line. That should have been plenty of tackle for the typical twenty-inch schoolies that fed near these rocks. But he'd gotten lucky, and now he needed skill.

The fish made a run, and Brian's reel spun off twenty yards of line. Brian kept the line taunt, rod tip up, and let the fish exhaust itself. The key was not to over task the line, and fingers crossed, not to over task the knot he had tied the lure with. The reel hummed as it played out the monofilament.

At the end of the run, Brian began pumping the rod and retrieving line, coaxing the fish back toward the boat. He'd regained maybe five yards, when the fish took off again, but only made a run of ten yards this time. Sandy stood at Brian's side, peering over his shoulder with her net at the ready. Brian said, "If I can bring him alongside, get the net into the water before he gets close to the boat. I don't want to spook him."

Sandy nodded and wondered why Brian assumed the fish was a *he*. The big ones were usually females known as cows. But this was not the time for niggling details.

Vera watched the battle and equated it to her quandary. She was the fish that Jeff hoped to land. She had already decided. She would not spy on the RGB. That was a death sentence in a land far from Richard. Nor would she run. That option begged two questions . . . how and where? No, she would debrief, disclose her secrets, apply for asylum, and stay in the States to be with Richard. Her mind probed for options beyond this. The way of Chondogyo. She must be creative. But try as she might, the conclusion stared her in the face. Each flight of fancy, each run from reality ended with her exhausted return.

Caroline wore white like her twenty classmates, all proper young women soon to be graduates of Boothbay Region High School. A like number of young men wore white, too. White jackets, black trousers, and black bowties. The young women, of course, were much more stylish. Slits and off-the-shoulder numbers flowed and clung. Hemlines stretched to heels which were white and high. Caroline stood out. She was tall, poised, and every bit as good-looking as her mother. In fact, she might double for her mother all those years before. Her blond hair fell to her shoulders and bounced with the buoyancy of a meticulously applied curling iron and a basket of rollers. She looked good, very good. She looked so adult, so capable. She brought her mother to tears. Sandy sat on a folding chair arranged on the basketball court in front of the bleachers, primo seats reserved for parents and grandparents, and their guests. Proud alumni and well-wishers occupied the bleachers. As the procession began, Sandy cried. Vera sat to her right and Brian to her left. Brian offered a handkerchief, and Sandy dabbed and sniffled.

Brian said, "What a spectacle. I've never seen anything like it. It's a cross between prom and graduation . . . only . . . better organized. What pageantry. Boy, they put some work into this event."

Sandy whispered, "It's the Grand March. They've done this since 1911. The first one was at the Knights of Pythias' auditorium in the Opera House. It's a Boothbay tradition. I've been told we're the only school in the country that does this. How about that? Little old Boothbay."

Sandy smiled through her tears. "I've watched them . . . these kids. They start out as freshmen and sophomores declaring they will never take part in such a menacing event as the Grand March. The boys don't want to dress up and the girls don't want to embarrass themselves marching. They don't want to flub or disappoint. They worry about their style. Then, by the time they're seniors, they change their tune. Everybody's in. We fundraise so all the students can afford the tux rentals and gowns. The Alumni Association holds a cookout and an alumni banquet. Balloons and flowers are donated. So, it's a community effort. It doesn't come out of the school budget. It brings the region together.

"Don't they look good?"

Brian nodded. "Yep . . . they're a handsome lot. Caroline is stunning. And she's taller than Jimmy. You've had the talk, right?"

Sandy stared back at Brian. Her eyes conveyed, *Did you have to ask?*

The graduates began on opposite sides of the auditorium, boys on one side, girls on the other. They came together in a practiced cadence, joining arm in arm in front of the musicians on the raised stage. As they met, they turned toward center court and began an intricate march around the gym, then through interposing lines. Jimmy and Caroline paired, and Caroline looked like she'd done this every day of her life. Jimmy, stiffly at her side, played a B-list supporting role.

Vera said, "Sandy . . . you must be such a proud mother. Caroline is . . . so poised. You have raised her well. She will go far."

Sandy said, "My dear friend, you will experience this for yourself next spring when Richard graduates."

"Yes. But Richard's ceremony will not be so lavish. It will not include such . . . what did Brian call it?"

Brian answered, "Pageantry."

"Yes . . . pageantry. This parade, I find evocative, no?"

Sandy teared up again. She couldn't help but think of Noah. Not that Caroline looked like Noah, no, she favored her mother. But Noah was there. Was it Caroline's style sensitivity? Was it associational? Small gestures? Sandy checked her slide into the pit of remembrance as Caroline and Jimmy passed right in front of the threesome. The graduates had been coached to march with their eyes straight ahead. But when Caroline passed, she smiled a bit smugly at her mother. There it was. Sandy laughed.

The drill lasted twenty minutes. Formations of all varieties were performed with intensity and admirable seriousness. At the end, the Grand March had been accomplished for another year. The graduates changed out of their stylish clothing, reverted to the casual everyday dress of high schoolers, and motored off to parties of a less formal bent. Tomorrow, they would once again be costumed, this time in robes for their formal graduation.

Sandy, Brian, and Vera returned to Sandy's house on Southport. Sandy opened a bottle of prosecco, poured three flutes, and the adults toasted the day. They sat on Sandy's porch overlooking the water. It was late afternoon, breezy, and the bugs had yet to muster. It was a lovely day but unsaid, the anniversary of Noah's death. Sandy told no one.

The three Adirondacks formed a semicircle. The mood was light, and Sandy did her best to play along. Right out of the bag, Brian asked Vera, "How's it going with Jeff?"

Brian knew Vera couldn't discuss details. Still, Vera's agreement to a full debrief was common knowledge.

"It is a tedious occupation. I do not see Jeff often. Most of the dialogue is with subject matter experts from different government offices. I thought the DPRK was bureaucratic, but the Americans . . . from what I can tell . . . equal the number of departments and divisions. I cannot talk about specifics."

Both Sandy and Brian nodded.

"I can only say that the dialogue is civil and often repetitive. Initially, they administered a polygraph. This they have yet to repeat so . . . perhaps they believe me. It matters not. I will do as promised and, so far, they have honored their bargain."

Brian asked, "Where do you meet?"

"We meet at the Portsmouth Naval Shipyard and discuss matters in a room they call a SCIF. It's an impenetrable structure to assure confidentiality. It's all manageable."

"How long will the debrief take?" asked Brian.

"Probably weeks . . . months. They want details . . . and they go over answers many times. I believe this is how they test for consistency. I understand. Taken all together, it is a small price to pay for my reward. I applied for asylum, and I will apply for citizenship soon. And so far, they have been helpful."

"And do you plan to stay on at UNH this fall?" asked Sandy.

"Oh yes. They made a most attractive offer. I will need to find my own housing, but my responsibilities will be unchanged. They encouraged me to write a book about the seabed, a summary of my studies. This I will begin in the fall. Sandy, we may need to collaborate for a section on anomalous tides."

Sandy smiled. Then she probed, "So . . . what about Sam?"

"I have seen him twice since my defection. Two dinners. He knows nothing about my debrief or my involvement with the government. I will strive to keep it that way. He is happy that I will continue to teach at the university."

"He seems like a nice man," added Sandy.

This garnered a dispassionate, "Yes . . . he is."

Brian smiled. Then he asked, "Will you be meeting us in Portland on Sunday?"

"Yes . . . I hope to. And thank you for arranging the purchase for Richard."

"No problem. My pleasure. We'll pick it up before we meet."

"I do not understand the sport of baseball. I plan to study it more so I can be conversant with my son. I had no idea about the gift you suggested. But I'm certain Richard will love it."

Brian smiled. "It wasn't hard to figure out, once you told me Max Scherzer was Richard's favorite pitcher. Rawlings offers a Max Scherzer Custom Glove. So that was easy."

Sandy asked, "And are we still planning to drive to UMaine when Richard goes to camp?"

"Yes. That will be in two weeks."

"So . . . you can drive to Southport, and the three of us will drive to Orono."

Brian asked, "Three?" He thought he had been included without discussion.

"Yep . . . three. Vera and I will take Caroline along for her freshman orientation."

"Oh . . . good move. Plus . . . she'll get to meet Richard," Brian offered with a sly smile.

"Okay mister matchmaker. Cool your jets."

"Well . . . I'm just sayin' . . . Jimmy's not going to UMaine, right?"

Sandy said, "University of New England. He got a partial scholarship, and he's going to study math."

"Good for him. He's a smart kid. But he's out of the picture. Plus, he's not tall enough."

"All right . . . enough of this romantic engineering," Sandy scoffed.

Brian laughed.

"He pulled me into the rack. I had no choice," Brian pleaded.

Sandy and Brian were on their way back north after a hugely pleasant visit to Portland. They had eaten a wonderful lunch at the Porthole in the Old Port. They'd shown Vera Munjoy Hill and the Eastern Promenade, and toured the Portland Museum of Art. They'd even found a vendor to gift wrap Richard's baseball glove. After Vera left for UNH, Brian and Sandy stopped in George Anderson's contemporary art gallery on their way back to the car park. George had been painting for a long time. His bold representations of sails, sailing, fishermen, and all things nautical were his crowd pleasers. These were prominently on display. George had a sharp eye.

Sandy and Brian entered his gallery, dinging the bell over the entrance. George did a double take. After friendly introductions, Sandy began paging through the countless oils stacked standing on the wooden floor. That was when George motioned for Brian to come near. George, with his wizen white beard and laser blue eyes, summoned Brian. "Brian, step over here with me, behind this rack."

Brian thought this unusual, but harmless.

Behind a rack of supplies, George leafed through a set of 11x17 oils. About a third of the way in, he lifted one out and turned it to Brian. George asked, "Does this remind you of anyone?"

Brian balked, speechless. It was Sandy nude in the morning light of Munjoy Hill. Tastefully struck and slightly representational, but it was Sandy . . . in the nude. Mist rose around her legs, a cloud of deification.

George said, "I painted her as a goddess."

Brian, still dumbfounded, nodded his head.

George asked, "Are you two . . . close?"

Brian said, "Yeah . . . we just got engaged."

"Then it's yours, son. A wedding present!"

Brian said, "Ah . . . thanks. You are too kind."

At that moment, Sandy rounded the rack to check on Brian. She saw the painting. She exclaimed, "Oh . . . my God."

George smiled.

She said, "Brian . . . do not buy that thing!"

Brian said, "I can't. He gave it to me. A wedding present."

It had been a long drive and a long day at UMaine. Sandy and Caroline met Richard and remarked on his resemblance to his mother. Caroline nonchalantly concurred, and more than once, pushed loose strands over her ears. She wished now she had done more with her hair than a ponytail. Vera and Sandy noted Caroline's interest.

The four of them ate lunch at Woodman's Bar and Grill, and Richard showed them the baseball camp dorms and Mahaney Diamond next to the practice fields. Sandy showed Caroline the classroom buildings and the commons, and they visited the black bear mascot statue, Bananas, on the mall. Sandy, of course, emphasized the library and told Caroline she would spend most of her time there. Caroline offered a perfunctory nod.

Richard was over the moon with his Scherzer glove. He kept pounding his fist into its pocket to limber it up.

Vera planned to stay in Orono for three days. She would take the bus back to UNH. Richard warned her that she might not be allowed to sit in on the strength testing, but she could watch the playing and elemental skills tryouts. She assured Richard she wanted to be with him for support. Whatever he needed.

On the two-hour drive back to Boothbay, Caroline napped. Sandy looked over at her daughter, and a flood of emotion washed over her. It was time for Caroline to be gone. Sandy wasn't sure how that would play. But by this time next spring, Brian would be a permanent fixture. Still, she'd miss Caroline, the banter and the obstinance. About halfway south, Caroline woke, and with no introduction or explanation, said, "I'm going to study oceanography. Don't act smug."

Sandy was now wide awake. This was exceptional news, and her spirit soared. But, of course, she remained contained. She said, "Oh . . . that's great!"

Caroline feigned a dramatic sigh, then announced, "Since you've had no luck, I guess it falls to me to solve the Boothbay tide."